ZIP SIX

ZIP SIX

A Novel

JACK GANTOS

Bridge Works Publishing Co.
Bridgehampton, New York

The author wishes to thank the Massachusetts Council for the Arts for its generous support.

Library of Congress Cataloging-in-Publication Data

Gantos, Jack.
Zip six : a novel / Jack Gantos. — 1st. ed.
p.   cm.
ISBN 1-882593-15-4 (hard cover : alk. paper)
I. Title.
PS3657.A5197Z36   1996
813'.54—dc20   96-7436
CIP

2   4   6   8   10   9   7   5   3   1

Book and jacket design by Eva Auchincloss
Jacket Illustration by David Gothard

Printed in the United States of America

First Edition

For West Street

Part One

THE SHADOW
OF
ELVIS PRESLEY'S
HIPS

AFTER THE FLUORESCENT LIGHTS WERE turned off, the blue night lights were switched on. Above us, they glowed in two rows down the corridor ceiling like an airport runway. But we weren't going anywhere. From my cell I continued to watch the men on the other side of the corridor. They sat open-legged on the edges of their bunks and picked at their crabs. The guard's desk lamp cast enough light to silhouette their faces and fingers as they stalked methodically through their crotches.

The men were tight-lipped as they pressed their nails together, and when the crabs were crushed, the small noise, click-click, sounded good and clean and was followed by a satisfying grunt of relief. If any of them looked up, they'd see me doing the same thing, and they might hear my hiss and sigh, might watch my face soften and my back slump down for a moment before it stiffened and I continued the hunt.

The prison was thick with crabs. They had been carried in from the outside on one man, and now the entire population was infested. Night and day we worked at crushing them. All clothing and bedding had to be disinfected daily and washed in hot water. Each of us new inmates in the orientation wing, and the ones kept here for their own protection, were given a plastic tube of parasite killer to wash with. It looked like tar and made us, the shower room, and the corridor smell of licorice. It didn't work, and every morning when I woke up my crotch was covered with a lace of shifting parasites.

Still, there was nothing to do but fight back. One day I was on the outside. The next I was in prison. And the next I was infested with crabs. I had to draw the line somewhere. I sat and culled through my hairs with a tiny fine-toothed comb that had come with the parasiticide. It was painful. The hairs I pulled out I burned in a tin ashtray along with the crabs I dropped one by one into the fire. Their small bodies sizzled, grew plump, then popped. I smiled. It was incredibly satisfying to kill them, and I went right back to work tracking them down, levering them out of their burrows with the tip of a razor blade, and sentencing them to death by fire.

"The judge has spoken," I pronounced and torched another. I'd give a little scream, "Eieeiii," as it fried up into a black speck.

I chain-smoked all day while I battled to keep myself clean. I lit one cigarette off the other and continued to exhume the buried crabs until the quilted flesh around my cock swelled up and became too tender to touch.

I slept with my legs spread wide open, but woke in the night scratching myself. The sores grew like bloody buds aching to open, and the crabs continued to burrow deeper as they sowed their tiny eggs. They were winning the battle. The area was hot and red, and I lifted the scabs with the razor when I could bear the pain.

When the lunch cart came around I stopped picking at myself and washed my hands. The food was more texture than taste, but it split the hours. It was warm and served in a pool of water on a tin pie plate. There was coarse corn bread and white bread and yellow cake and a piece of steak so thin and hard and chipped along the edges it resembled wood-grain Formica. But I was hungry, and I ate it all. I wanted more but I had nothing to trade for seconds, and the food cart worker, Ebbers, charged cigarettes for every favor. When I finished eating, I slipped into a depressed stupor until gradually the thrill of catching and killing another crab brought me around. Then I searched for a less abscessed area to work, like a junkie looking for a good vein.

ONCE A DAY I WAS ALLOWED TO SHOWER BY myself for five minutes. The cell house guard, Mr. Vespi, would unlock my gate and escort me down the corridor to the shower room. He seemed neither mean nor sympathetic but more like someone paid to walk a dog. I obliged and did my business. I turned the hot water on until it was so painful on my feet I danced on my toes, and then I thrust my hips forward and let it scald my crotch. I bent backwards, doing the limbo, my arms waving over my head for balance. I moaned and quivered. I gritted my teeth and endured the pain. I imagined the crabs steaming up like tiny grains of rice, then dropping to the floor. It was good to kill something inside myself, almost as good as plunging into the pure cotton of drugs.

It was Vespi who explained to me what my sentence meant. "Zip six," is what he called my six years for smuggling a ton of hashish. "You can do anywhere from zero days to six years. It's a roll o' the dice." So far, he said, he hadn't met anyone with the same sentence who did less than two years. "Bad dice."

I had thought I'd do two weeks, or two months, but two years, until 1981, seemed impossible. I didn't believe him.

I HAD NEVER BEEN IN PRISON BEFORE, BUT I knew that having my own cell was better than sharing. I felt almost safe with the gate closed and locked. Ebbers, the leering inmate who delivered the food, gave me a Zane Grey novel and the autobiography of Christine Jorgenson. I read the cowboy story and passed it to the guy in the next cell but kept the autobiography hidden in my mattress. I didn't want to be seen reading about a transsexual, so after I read a page, I'd rip it up and flush it down the toilet. I immediately distrusted Ebbers for giving it to me. Did he think I might be interested in a sex change? Did he think of me as a woman? I was terrified of being raped. After my sentencing at the federal courthouse in Foley Square I was sent to West Street. It was a warehouse holding pen for men who had just been sentenced and would be transferred elsewhere, and a

[6]

place for those who couldn't make bail and had to stay in the city before sentencing. The first night I entered, the orientation guard ordered me to strip down for full body photographs. He walked around me, circled the long scar on my knee with a red marker, and took a Polaroid photograph and slipped it into my file. "You're gonna need a chastity belt or population is gonna bend you over like a shotgun," he said, all in good nature. I figured the line was practiced, but it got to me anyway.

"Any tattoos?" he inquired.

"Nope."

"You better get some," he suggested. "You need to make yourself ugly."

Later that first night I woke up and felt those insects creeping up my legs, crawling over my hair, and drilling into my crotch. I felt as though I were dead, already decomposing inside my coffin and tunneled through with clever insect designs. Their hunger was unrelenting. The man across the aisle, Feeney, a bank robber, was awake. He lit match after match. I watched carefully because I knew he was trying to rid himself of the crabs and I wanted to copy his method. Just after he blew out each wooden match he'd press the tip of the stick against his flesh and hiss like a cat.

"Hey," I whispered. "Does that work?"

"You bet," he replied. "Just wish I had some lighter fluid and I'd have a weenie roast."

I lit a match, blew it out, and jabbed the tip into an open tunnel. The pain bent me over double and I flicked the match across the cell. I couldn't do it that way. I just wasn't tough enough.

I HAD RUN OUT OF CIGARETTES, AND started to pick through the butts I'd saved to find one to relight. The prison gave us free tobacco and papers, but the tobacco was bad and tasted like rotten apples. It wouldn't stay lit, and it sputtered and stank when it went out, which was after every puff. I couldn't find any leftover butts. After I had crushed them out, they all looked like bullets that had been shot into walls.

Because I didn't have the guts to burn the crabs out, I removed the razor from my locker and began to shave off all my pubic hair. I felt as though I was losing my mind, but it was a good feeling, the sensation that I was cleaning myself. I wanted to be left pink and smooth as a sheared lamb. I started with my ankles and worked up. I kept splashing water on my legs, rubbing them with soap, and shaving as fast as I could. It was dark and blue. I couldn't see very well but felt when the razor went too deep. I reached my crotch and grabbed the hair with one hand and hacked at it with the razor. The blade was dull and the hair pulled away from the skin. I shaved my arms up to my elbows, then chopped at my armpits. I caught myself thinking that I must look like a woman. I was afraid someone else might think so and I began to hurry. I didn't want Ebbers to pass by and see me. I plucked out most of my eyelashes and shaved my head as best I could. I wanted to feel clean. Instead, I felt blood dripping from my sliced eyebrows down into my eyes and an uneven stubble over my grated skin which sizzled and burned when the sweat got into the cuts. After I couldn't cut any more hair, I gathered up all the cigarette butts from the floor, pinched out the tobacco, and rerolled it in new papers. I sat on the edge of my bunk and smoked. The tobacco tasted like cold dirt.

When the morning lights came on I looked into the polished metal mirror over the sink. My face looked thick and yellow, asymmetrical like a gourd. I turned away. I thought, I haven't changed. I'm still here. My hair will grow back and I'll soon look the same as before. I wanted a permanent change. A new face and a new future. But even the lousy mirror let me know it was still me. Brown hair. Hazel eyes. Straight nose. In trouble.

When Ebbers brought the food cart around I asked him for a real cigarette and extra coffee. "You look pitiful," he said, shaking his squarish head. "Pitiful." He squatted down and slid the plastic tray under my gate. His sleeve was rolled up and across his wide forearm was a freshly healed tattoo of a large musical note. In the circle of the note was a crude portrait of Elvis Presley, and beneath the note was written in a child's uneven script, "Rest In Peace."

He caught me staring at the tattoo.

"You dig it?"

He held it close to the bars, but not so close that I

could grab his arm, pull it between the bars and snap it sideways at the elbow. In orientation we had been repeatedly warned *never* to stick our arms out through the bars or into anyone's cell.

The tattoo looked like it had been hand stitched with an upholstery needle. "You must be an Elvis fan," I ventured, trying to be friendly. I wanted a second cup of coffee.

"He's my man," Ebbers replied, and looked down at his forearm which was cradled like a baby across his yeasty stomach. "I love him and now we'll be together for life."

"Looks like it could use some detail work," I ventured.

"Hey," he shot back and surprised me. "You could use some work yourself. You're uglier looking than DuBoise."

"No way," I said. "I can't be that ugly."

DuBoise was a man who had worked in the kitchen with Ebbers but last week had been locked up in protective custody. He had a mouthful of decayed teeth. His skin looked like blue cheese. He had tried to kill himself by standing on a wet towel and sticking a dinner fork into an electrical outlet. The jolt had knocked him unconscious, burned the tips of his fingers, and splintered his fingernails. He showed them to me when I passed his cell on my way to the shower room. "Hey! Listen to this," he hooted. He put his finger tips in his mouth and blew on them like a clarinet. A sound like a quack came out.

"That's pretty good," I remarked. His eyes were

like shiny little gyroscopes spinning at a million miles an hour. He grinned, then blew a few bars of "Dixie." He had gone around the bend.

I didn't want to talk to Ebbers anymore. I picked up the food tray and set it on my bed. I scratched my arms and legs as roughly as I could without lifting the scabs. Still, just from bending over, I began to crack and ooze from a dozen tiny cuts.

"Lordy," he testified, shaking his head back and forth. "You should see the doctor."

I stared at a chain of migrating lice in his sideburns. They didn't seem to bother him.

"You got any real cigarettes?" I asked.

He removed a flattened half pack of Kools from his back pocket and flipped them at me. "You owe me a full pack next week," he said. "Or just give me a blow job." He pushed his bunchy crotch against the bars and reached for his zipper.

I jumped back.

"You're cute," he said. "I'll catch up to you later." Then he rolled the food cart down to the next cell. When he completed his rounds he must have said something to Vespi, because the guard marched down to my cell and looked me over.

"Aw, Jesus!" he groaned, stepping back. I was wearing only undershorts. They were stained dark gray from hand washing them in parasiticide. I was standing in the center of the cell with my legs and arms spread apart, so that I looked like a large X smoking a cigarette and wearing a filthy diaper. It was the only position in which I felt a slight relief.

"Shaving your head's against regulations," he said. "I'll have to write you up."

Ebbers stood behind him, grinning, with his hands resting on the bloated clamp of fat above his high hips. I could read his lips. "Ugly," he mouthed, "Ugly, ugly, ugly." Then he rubbed his tattoo over his crotch, formed a lewd circle with his mouth, and rolled his eyes in a silent swoon.

I looked away. I hadn't known shaving my head was against regulations. I just wanted some relief from the crabs.

"You're not allowed to change your appearance," explained Vespi, in a tired, matter-of-fact way. "What's your name?" He removed a small notepad and pencil from his pocket and flipped to a clean page.

"Ray Jakes," I said. "And I need to see a doctor."

He wrote down my registration number and walked up the corridor.

"What about the doctor?" I called behind him.

"I'll let him know when he shows," he said without breaking stride.

I lit a cigarette. I lay down on my back and blew smoke rings, large perfect O's that drifted up like lassos toward the naked light bulb. Then from the corner of my eye I saw a mouse laboring across my cell. It was covered with crabs, as though it had been carefully decorated with sequins. I sat up and looked into its small face, pink and wrinkled. It was young but looked old. Most of the blood had been sucked from its body. I leaned forward with my plastic cup and covered it.

Ebbers strolled past my cell. "Hey, ugly booty bitch," he said. When I turned toward him he rubbed his crotch. "Caught ya lookin'," he sang, winked and kept going. I didn't eat my cake. Instead I carefully lifted off the glazed layer of icing and put it to one side. I hollowed out a small grave in the center of the cake. I removed the mouse from under my cup and held its neck between my thumb and forefinger. "Sorry little mouse," I whispered. "It's better this way." I squeezed its neck until it's back legs stopped kicking, then carefully tucked it in. It looked so peaceful inside the yellow cake, like a tiny corpse in a coffin. Then I replaced the shiny layer of icing so that the cake appeared untouched. "Rest in peace," I said, and made the sign of the cross.

When Ebbers picked up the food trays, he put the desserts to one side. He continued up the cell house corridor collecting the untouched leftovers. When he finished he sat down at Vespi's desk and chatted while he ate. I listened hard. The desk was tucked into an alcove out of sight. It was a football weekend. They were going over the betting card. And faintly, I could hear the Stones singing "Shattered" from Vespi's radio.

Suddenly Ebbers yelped and banged his fists on the table. He pushed his chair back hard and spit. "Fuck," he shouted and gagged.

"Oh, Jesus H. Christ," groaned Vespi. "Did you swallow any of that?"

Ebbers passed my cell as he ran down the corridor toward the shower room. His fat body shivered and his horsey brown eyes rolled as though he were having a seizure. When he reached the shower he filled his mouth with water and continued to spit. "Oh nasty . . . nasty." he wailed. I heard him choke, then vomit.

"It's a mouse," Vespi said, joining Ebbers in the shower room. "They baked a mouse in the cake."

"I'll kill whoever did this," Ebbers said. "I'll fucking kill 'em."

I slumped back onto my bunk and looked up at the ceiling. I shouldn't have done that, I thought. I should have just kept my hands to myself and minded my own business. But I had always been this way. Kinda sneaky. Doing dumb shit, and lucky enough to get away with it. Until the Moroccan hash. And maybe that meant I wasn't going to get away with any more shit, either. I had run out of luck.

THERE WAS A TIME WHEN I DIDN'T DO drugs. I worked. I had a job after school at a grocery store. I was staying away from the wrong people, I was saving a little money, I was thinking about college but something was wrong. I kind of fell into a no-family no-friends depression. I felt like I was just drifting along and that whatever I did didn't matter. Not to anyone, at first, and later not to me. And when nobody seemed to be there to help me along, I just started to drink. My Dad drank a lot, and I did too. That's about what we had in common. And when I started I couldn't stop. I went over the edge sucking on a bottle of vodka.

In high school I kept a quart of cheap Cossack in my car. On the morning drive across Fort Lauderdale I'd pop a Dylan tape into my deck, reach under my seat for the bottle, unscrew the plastic cap, and take a couple long pulls. I remember the warm vodka exploding in my mouth like gasoline. It gave me a buzz and got me through homeroom while I propped my head on my hands and breathed so deeply I coaxed the perfume from Sandra Soto's copper neck.

After the bell rang I'd drift back to the car and take a couple more pulls. That got me through to lunch, when I'd go to Burger King and order an orange soda to fix a mixed drink. By the end of the day I'd feel better, even more distant from my surroundings and sunk into a kind of plush vodka pillow.

Even drunk I had good enough test scores to be accepted to the University of Florida in Gainesville. I wanted to get a degree in forest management and live out among the trees. I figured trees didn't talk back, didn't move around behind my back, and wouldn't kick my ass if I screwed up. Toward the end of my senior year in high school, I drove up there in my green '64 Olds and cruised the campus. Everyone wore shorts and carried cold beers next to their exposed bellies. It looked good. But when I had my admissions interview, it all went bad. I would have to live in a dorm on campus, with roommates, for the first two years, and wouldn't be allowed to keep my car. I turned them down. I wanted to go to school, but I didn't want to live like a student. I figured if I wanted to be around trees I could just go live among them. It was a lot more direct than studying bark and leaves and bugs while being treated like a kid.

After high school graduation, I stayed in Fort Lauderdale, rented a tiny apartment from Davey Crockett's great-great-granddaughter, and enrolled in Broward Junior College. By then I was smoking reefer. The more I smoked the more I slept, until I blew off college. I spent all my money on reefer and acid. When I lost my job at the supermarket, I drove back to my apartment and smoked the last roaches.

A week later I called my parents and returned home. By then they had moved to St. Croix in the

Virgin Islands. My Dad had been transferred down there to supervise the building of hotels. That's where I met Melissa, my girlfriend, and where I learned how to deal weed. There were a lot of old-money-rich-kids there who liked buying over selling, so I took to selling. I was good at it. I went from dealing locally to buying from Jamaicans and selling it to a courier from New York. He brought me acid and pills. It worked out well until the local cops caught on. But by then I was turned on to a big load of hash and had signed on to sail it up to New York.

I WOKE UP WHEN MY CELL GATE SLAMMED open so hard I jumped out of bed and hunkered down into a fighting position. It was too early for the morning count. Suddenly a young doctor marched into my cell. He slowed down when he saw me. "You're the most revolting sight I've seen yet," he said matter-of-factly. He turned to Vespi, who was waiting in the corridor. "I want him and the one across the aisle in my office immediately."

"Get dressed," Vespi said to me. "You're going for a walk."

Feeney, the bank robber, and I were escorted down to the doctor's office on the first floor. We were so pitiful looking we didn't have to wait in line behind the string of nervous junkies gathered for their morning methadone.

The doctor's name was Sobel. He made us both strip down. "Why did you do this to yourself?" he asked, handing me a bottle of peroxide. "Clean your genital area," he instructed and motioned toward my privates.

"I couldn't stand the itching," I replied. "I figured if there was less hair there'd be fewer crabs." The doctor removed a big syringe and filled it from a small bottle. He was just out of medical school, I guessed. I thought he might try anything. I doubted if prison doctors could be charged with malpractice.

"What's that?" Feeney asked. "Morphine?"

I wished. I used to shoot morphine, and just thinking about a shot made my stomach anxious. I'd love to have a big fix and slip into a six-year nod.

"Local anesthesia," the doctor said. "It'll stop the itch." He motioned Feeney to the examination table with a wave of the syringe. "Stand still," he ordered and fully inserted the extra-long needle along a rise of fat just above his cock.

"Christ," Feeney said and covered his crotch with both hands. "That stuff feels as cold as my judge."

"You feel this?" Dr. Sobel asked, and splashed rubbing alcohol over his crotch.

"No."

"Good. Now go stand over the sink and slowly pour it over the inflamed areas." Then Dr. Sobel turned to me. "I want you to rub this over your pubic area," he said, and dribbled the anesthesia on a gauze pad. At first it burned, then my skin became numb and ice cold as though I were washing a piece of frozen meat. The doctor loaded a fresh syringe and I leaned back against the table. Feeney held my shoulders. "Think of your girlfriend," he whispered lewdly, just as the needle slid in.

I wished he hadn't said that. Every night leading up to my sentencing, I had said to Melissa, "I know I'm going to get time so I better leave the country." She would put her arms around me and hold me close and whisper in my ear, "Don't worry honey, I know you'll get probation. I have a good feeling about it." But I didn't have a good feeling. I lay in bed and urged myself to get up, get dressed, and flee to Canada. But when I argued this with myself, I always heard her steady voice, flat with reason. "Don't worry. You'll only get probation. They won't hurt you." I trusted Melissa. She could always think things through better than me. But now I was in prison and she was going to college in Boston. After my sentencing she had said, "Don't worry. You can catch up when you get out. The forestry service won't hold this against you." From where I was now, it was hard to believe I might ever catch up. I would rather start over in Canada. There were plenty of trees up there.

"Okay," said Sobel. "You can open your eyes."

I did. The warden, Mr. Paris, was standing before me, along with his inmate assistant. The warden was a young man dressed in a dark pinstriped suit, and anxious. He rubbed his hands together as he looked me over. "There is a rule against disfigurement," he informed me. "And there is a punishment for breaking the rule."

I held my arms and legs apart so he could get a good look. "It was a medical decision," I explained.

"The parasiticide is for that," he replied. "So use it. We can't have people changing their physical identity whenever they get an itch. This is a prison, not a hair salon.

"As for punishment," he said, "you can delouse the men in solitary confinement." As quickly as he finished talking with me he began talking to his assistant, a man with a face like a newly born animal, wet and pointy. "We have to plan the Christmas entertainment," the warden said. "Let's see what talent we have inside before we book any outsiders."

Mr. Bow, the retired military physician's assistant who worked with Dr. Sobel, took me through a set of locked gates and into the medical wing. "I'll mix up a batch of bug spray," he said. "You get dressed." He unlocked a linen closet and gave me a clean pair of underpants, a pair of white cotton trousers, and a white hospital shirt that had a round neck and snaps instead of buttons. "Even though you're gonna be as sticky as tree sap after you spray these guys," he said directly, "I want you to start out with a shower. If you're going to pull hospital duty you have to look good, and right now you look like pig shit."

He pointed me in the direction of the shower room. I carried my clothes down the corridor and ducked through a low entrance and down a half set of iron stairs into a cement room that was oddly smooth, like a swimming pool. It smelled like rum. I sniffed at the walls. Molasses, I said to myself. A jujitsu instructor arrested for postal burglary had told me about West Street on the way over from the courthouse. "It was Dutch Schultz's old booze factory," he explained.

After I finished my shower, my skin felt a lot better and I put on my clean shirt. But when I put on my pants I saw that someone had drawn, with blue ink, an exaggerated cock and hairy dangling balls on the crotch. I took them off, turned them inside out and put them back on.

When I found Mr. Bow he smirked at me. "Do I have to teach you how to wear pants?"

I showed him the drawing. He shook his head. "This place is full of perverts," he said. "Let this be a warning to you. You're probably the youngest kid in here, and these guys will be after you like tomcats. Around here, it's not a question of sexual preference. It's just sex. Period."

The thought of being boned up the ass flipped me out, but I didn't want to tell him, so I fell back on my manners. "Thank you," I replied.

"You're welcome," he answered and smiled a big doggy smile, then handed me the pump spray can of pesticide. "This stuff will kill anything. It's half malathion and half Kwell. You have to strip them down, spray them all over, and take their clothes and sheets and set them outside the cell."

"Got it," I said, thinking that I was putting myself in a position to piss off a lot of guys. "What about the padded cells?" I asked. I had seen two of them.

"The pads are covered with plastic," he explained. "Most of those guys dump on themselves. But don't worry about 'em. They're empty today."

We passed through the hospital gate and descended a flight of circular metal stairs that led to a basement corridor of dank isolation cells. We walked down to the first cell. The door was solid iron except for a small barred peek window. The metal slot was damp and flecked with rust. I figured we were below sea level. When Bow unlocked and pulled open the heavy door, I saw four men sitting around a hissing transistor radio. "We gotta spray for crabs," Bow said directly. "Everybody strip 'n' dip."

"Hey, I'm a weekender," one of them replied and threw up his hands. He was wearing undershorts with bank notes on them and thin socks pulled up to his knees. "I don't have no schwartzer crabs."

I looked at Bow. I was eager to pull the trigger on the spray nozzle.

"They're all weekenders," he said with regret. "I forgot." He closed and locked the door. "The one with the big mouth is the mayor of Jersey City," he whispered. "Embezzlement."

"What's a weekender?" I asked.

"Family man," he said, unlocking the next cell. "The judge lets them out during the week so they can work and support the wife and kids, and on the weekends they join us. Taxpayer-friendly sentence, we call it. They call it a football weekend without yard work." He smiled and the hundreds of lines around his eyes and mouth curled up. I liked him. He didn't seem as scary as the rest.

When I entered the next cell, I was surprised to find Harrington. His face was long and thin without his saintly beard, the one thing about him everyone found so attractive. When he saw me he gave me the finger. "Fuck you, Jakes," he said, sounding very high and mighty.

He had been the boss of the hash-smuggling operation, and I hadn't seen him since he had paid me off five months before. He still thought I had betrayed him, that I was the one who got him caught, and this is what pissed me off the most. I had been loyal to him. It was Kenny, one of his two-faced drug dealer friends, who had turned him in. If Harrington had listened to me, neither of us would be in prison.

"You really let me down," he said coldly. I was tired of taking the blame, and before he could say more I clenched my teeth and pulled the trigger. I didn't wait for him to undress. I sprayed him up close and jabbed him with the nozzle. He just sat on his wet sheets and curled up slowly, tucked his head between his knees and held his ankles and became more shrunken as if the spray were dissolving him.

"If it wasn't for you, I wouldn't be here," he spat. I aimed for his mouth to shut him up.

"Now take off your clothes," I ordered.

HARRINGTON AND HIS PARTNER, GORDON, had bought the ton of hashish in Morocco. They sailed it to the Virgin Islands, where they hired me as an extra boat hand. Gordon flew ahead to New York to arrange the deals while Harrington and I sailed up the Atlantic. When we got into New York harbor, we knew something had gone wrong. We moored the boat in Flushing, but the dealers Gordon had said would meet us didn't show up. Harrington called Gordon, who was staying at the Chelsea Hotel. He had located some new contacts. The old ones had been busted while we were at sea.

We rented a car, put 250 pounds of hashish in it, and drove up to Woodstock. There we met George, the buyer, gave him the hash, and sat around his house getting everyone high on our samples. George had built his house and all the furniture in it. He had his own style, and I didn't like it. Everything was on a slant: the grandfather clock, chairs, tables, wall hangings. Nothing was properly balanced. I had just spent a month on a rocking boat, and each time I stood up, I lost my balance and knocked into the furniture. It was like one of those trick houses at a carnival.

"One pill makes you larger and one pill makes you small," George sang to me.

"This fucking house should be tipped over," I whispered to Harrington.

"Don't piss anyone off," he cautioned me. "We haven't been paid yet."

We got paid 136 grand. On the ride back to New York a storm broke. The harder it rained, the faster Harrington drove. We couldn't see out the windows, and soon the cars in front of us backed up, so Harrington pulled into the V-shaped grass median and floored it. We slid up and down the slopes like a wet bar of soap while passing everything on the road. No sane cop would have followed us. They'd just radio ahead and have us picked up. As soon as it stopped raining, we pulled back onto the pavement.

"Why'd you drive like that?" I asked Harrington. He looked at me strange and off center. He had that enormous spongelike beard and gray eyes. "Someone was following us," he replied, patting his beard into shape. "Maybe George."

When we got back to the Flushing marina, the manager trotted over to us.

"Funny thing," he started. "During the storm your boat began to drag anchor up river, and before I could do anything, some guys in a power boat went out to it and threw an extra anchor overboard, then took off."

That was the exact moment I knew we were screwed.

But Harrington didn't look distressed. He thanked the man and led me toward the dinghy. "Just do as I do," he whispered. "Trust me."

I didn't exactly trust Harrington, and I was scared shitless, but I didn't want to just bolt and leave behind the $10,000 I was to be paid. And I knew he was not about to abandon the hash. He was already in trouble in England, having jumped a £50,000 bail after the police arrested him with a quarter ton of the stuff in his Bentley. Also, he had borrowed $100,000 at 100 percent interest to finance this trip. I knew you didn't get that kind of money at that interest rate from a neighborhood bank.

When we boarded the boat we just crept around like cats, in and out of all the cabins and closets. I went down into the front cabin where the extra anchor was kept. It had been next to a half ton of hashish. The anchor was gone, and I knew that whoever had put it out had seen what we were up to.

"Not necessarily," argued Harrington. "Once I was coming through customs in England when agents found twenty pounds of hash in my baggage. I just told them it was Egyptian henna, that I was a hair dresser, and they let me go."

"Well nobody's gonna believe we have a ton of henna," I replied.

"So, let 'em watch us," he said with tremendous arrogance. "They want to get the distributors, so they won't bust us until we've unloaded almost all the stuff. So we'll just keep selling until we're near the end."

"Well you better time it right," I replied, " 'cause I'm getting nervous."

Gordon's new contacts were solid. I crisscrossed New York pushing a shopping cart full of canvas-wrapped kilos of hashish. No one paid any attention to me as I made my deliveries. Harrington was making money fast. I told him I figured it was time to move all the hash and ditch the boat. "We've been spotted," I argued. "It's not worth the risk. We can just leave the boat as a decoy." But he liked the boat and wanted to sail it back to England.

"Then why don't you stay on it," I argued. He was now living at the Chelsea Hotel with Gordon, setting up the deals and collecting the money. I had to live on the boat and guard the hash from freaks like George.

"You know I can't let anyone know where we keep the stash," he replied. "Be patient."

I didn't want to cut it any closer. I knew the feds were watching us and figured they'd soon make their move. I asked Harrington for my money and as soon as he paid me, I packed up and left. Two days later he was on the boat loading the last fifty kilos when the FBI arrested him. I was in a grocery store not far from the cabin I had rented in Vermont when I saw a photograph of Harrington on the front page of the *New York Daily News*. He was sitting on a bag of hashish with his head in his hands. I bought the paper and read the article. I wasn't mentioned by name but was referred to as an "as yet unnamed accomplice."

"Greedy bastard," I said bitterly. It was just a matter of time before my name was known. Take off for Canada right now, I said to myself. You're not far from the border. Do it now. Become a new person. No one will know the difference. Send for Melissa. Go to college. Get a job. Live in peace among the trees. Instead of doing that, I talked myself into believing that Harrington would keep his mouth shut. He's no snitch, I said to myself. He's British. He's honorable.

The instant Harrington was busted he started thinking for himself. First, he told the FBI he was only working for the owner of the boat, who was staying at the Chelsea Hotel. So the FBI drove him there. They had all just walked up to the front desk when through the door came three U.S. Customs agents. When they saw Harrington, they pointed at him.

But Harrington was cagey. "Those are the owners!" Harrington yelled to the FBI and pointed right back at the customs agents. The feds jumped the agents, and Harrington ran out the back door. Harrington hailed a cab but jumped out when he got bogged down in traffic. He spotted an Italian barber shop, ran inside, and asked the barber to cut his beard off. But the barber refused. "It's-a too beautiful," he sang. "It make-a you look-a like a saint." So Harrington dashed out of the shop and was captured on the sidewalk. In the meantime the police had cordoned off a ten-block area and had arrested a dozen bearded men who were over six feet tall.

AFTER I SPRAYED HIM DOWN, HARRINGTON looked even worse than before. A plum colored rash began to appear in large irregular spots over his body. "And another thing," he said as he swatted the nozzle away from his face. "You stole $50,000 from me."

"You're delirious," I replied. "I didn't steal anything from you. It was probably your good friends, the ones who ratted you out. Now get off your ass and give me your clothes and sheets."

"My life is over," he said. "This is it for me."

I had no sympathy for him. "All actions have consequences," I said like a talking fortune cookie. I looked over my shoulder. Mr. Bow was chatting to the wing security guard. I picked up the spray tank and swung the bottom edge around. It caught Harrington just above the temple and he went straight over.

Bow and I walked down the corridor. Harrington was right about one thing. I *had* stolen money from him. But only $40,000. I had seen him hide a bag of cash in the cabin, and before I took off for upstate Vermont I took some. I thought I deserved more than $10,000. I also grabbed twenty kilos of hash. In the spring of '78, two months before my sentencing, I gave the cash to my lawyer to put in his safe. I buried the hash in the woods near Hull, Massachusetts.

When we passed another cell, a high pitched voice called to us.

"Please help me," the man cried.

Bow opened his door. A young guy was lying stomach down on his cot. A sheet was pulled up over his back, and there was fresh blood on it.

"What's wrong, Jewel?" Bow asked.

Jewel slithered out from under the sheet. He squatted way down and duck-walked over to us. I noticed blood running down his thighs. I wasn't certain of the problem until Jewel turned around and bent over. Then it was obvious that he had been fucking himself with a light bulb and it had broken. I could see the filament sticking out his butt. I took a deep breath and slowly let it out. It was about the nastiest thing I had ever seen, and it scared me to be locked up with people who did things like this.

"Please don't tell anyone," he whimpered, reaching behind himself and pulling his butt apart with his hands so we could get a better look at the bloody spot. "It just fell out of the light socket and right into my booty," he explained. "Honest." The three of us stared up at the white porcelain light fixture on the ceiling over the bed. The bulb was missing.

Bow stooped down and tried to pick away some of the larger pieces of glass from Jewel's asshole. "Is the metal part still inside you?" he asked.

"Yes," he cried.

"I'm going to need a pair of needle-nose pliers for this job," Bow said, then gave out a low whistle.

"Please don't make me laugh," Jewel begged. "It hurts when I pucker up."

Mr. Bow looked up at me. His face showed a kind of despair I didn't yet know. He had opened a lot more of these spook house doors than I had. "I'll take care of this in private," he said to me. "Why don't you go down to the kitchen and spray around the baseboards. I told them I'd send someone."

"Okay," I said, relieved that I could go.

"Do you think this will work against my parole?" Jewel asked as I walked away.

"Well, son, it just depends if this is judged an accident or self-inflicted," Bow replied evenly.

On THE WAY TO THE KITCHEN I PASSED the warden. "You," he said, pointing at me. "Come here. What are you up to?"

"Mr. Bow sent me to the kitchen to spray for crabs."

"Man, you stink," he muttered, and turned aside to cough. "Go on," he said, still hacking. "Take off. That smell is making me sick."

It was making me sick too. And I wasn't looking forward to working with the Gay Gourmet. He was the kitchen boss, and Ebbers had told me about him. "We smoke dope and jerk off in the storeroom," he'd said. "When he shoots off, he hollers, 'Feeeed the roaches! Feed the lovely lady roaches!' "

I didn't believe him. I figured everything Ebbers said served himself in some perverse way.

"If he likes you, he'll see to it that you eat well. But don't get on his wrong side," Ebbers said. "He's a mean old queen."

I remembered this as I entered the kitchen. I spotted Feeney on the far side, along the wall of chipped porcelain washtubs. He was scrubbing pots and pans with Brasso and steel wool.

"What's goin' down?" he asked.

"I think this spray is dangerous," I replied. "It's giving me a wicked headache."

"It's the food," he said. "Just smell it." On a low stove under a steel awning coated with grease sat three fifty-gallon kettles filled with beef shoulders. The water boiled furiously and the meat bobbed up and down like drowning cats. An inmate skimmed the foamy brown scum off the surface with a utensil that looked like the oar of a boat. The meat smelled foul, and my head throbbed as though I were crashing after a week of amphetamine popping.

"Just look at that morgue meat," Feeney added.

I changed the subject. I told him about Jewel and the light bulb as I sprayed the baseboards. "It looked nasty," I said. "I don't know how someone could hurt themselves that way."

"If they screwed his ass into a socket he'd make a lamp shade," Feeney cracked.

"Sorry I mentioned it," I said, but laughed anyway.

"They gonna send him to an outside hospital?" Feeney asked.

"Don't know," I replied. "I haven't been here long enough to tell."

"Well, he must be thinking of some way to break out." When Feeney talked his eyebrows seemed to underline the important details, so that "break out" looked like *BREAK OUT!*

"Could've been pleasure," I suggested.

"Don't be a moron," he shot back. "Nobody plugs a light bulb up their ass for pleasure."

On the other side of the kitchen, the Gay Gourmet was waving to us. "All kitchen ladies line up over here," he shouted in a windy falsetto. Already a line of men was forming in front of the baker's oven. "Don't be shy, my little Hansels and Gretels," he cried out, shaking an orange feather duster over his head. His face was round and red as a boiled potato. It was a jolly face. A happy face. Feeney and I joined the rest of the guys in line.

"Who stole it?" the Gourmet asked suddenly in a husky man's voice. I was startled, as though he had just ripped off a wig and dress and pulled a gun on us. "Which one of you butt cruds lifted my wallet?" No one stepped forward.

After a moment of silence he turned and opened the oven door. "Okay," he wheezed. "You dicks blew your chance for an easy way out. Now, load the oven." It was a huge rotating baker's oven. Each shelf was as large as a single bed. It was like loading a Ferris wheel. A ferret-faced guy named Parker climbed in and stretched out on his back. The Gay Gourmet handed him a wire brush, then pressed the on button. Parker's shelf rotated up and another came into view. A black postal worker got in. Then a skinny, non-English-speaking Chinese. I got in, and Feeney was the last. Each one of us was given a wire brush.

"Clean the oven!" shouted the Gourmet in his high-pitched voice. "Clean it good my little kitchen thieves, or I'll turn it on!" He slammed the door and the gears began to turn. I lifted my wire brush and began to scratch at the bottom of the shelf just above my face. The others did the same. After a few rotations, metal flakes and carbon dust filled the air.

"Whoever stole that wallet better give it back," Feeney hollered. The large teeth of the gears pinched together. It sounded as if we were trapped in a crippled submarine. We all began to cough and beat against the metal walls of the oven. I pulled my shirt up over my mouth and nose and tried to filter out the dust.

A WEEK BEFORE I WAS SENTENCED, MELISSA and I had visited her aunt and uncle in Baltimore. We were trying to relax the stress between us. I had been pretty tense and argumentative and she was trying to find ways to keep me from dwelling on my court date. Her relatives had a guest room in the basement, and I slept there. The first morning I woke up there, I had a paralyzing migraine headache. I couldn't shift my eyes or head. The slightest movement of my fingers, loud sounds, and bright light sent scratchy waves of pain across my brain. I held pillows over my ears and slowly rocked back and forth across the bed.

Melissa and her aunt stood around me. "What's wrong?" Melissa asked and stroked my head. Her fingers felt like a garden rake. I tried to pull myself together. I squinted up at them. I told them there was a gas leak in the room. They sniffed the air. No. Not one of them smelled gas. I could smell it though, and each time I breathed my head nearly split open. I knew something was wrong with the room. I smelled gas and they were lying to me.

"Just relax," Melissa advised. "It's tension."

I knew it wasn't tension. "I'm being gassed," I whispered to her. "Your Nazi aunt is killing me."

"He's really sick," I heard the aunt remark as she left the room. Melissa had told her about my drug problems and she had been giving me the low-life treatment since I'd arrived.

"You're stressed out because of next week," Melissa said, trying to calm me down. "It's natural." She placed a wet towel across my forehead.

I yanked it off. "Why won't you believe me?" I snapped.

"Because you're being hysterical," she replied, entirely fed up with me.

I lay in bed as though I were strapped into a straitjacket. By that night I couldn't stand it any longer. I was certain her relatives were trying to gas me. They despised me and were quietly hoping I'd get a long prison sentence. They were probably writing bitter letters to the judge asking for the maximum penalty.

Finally, after hours of tiny movements, I levered myself out of bed and slowly wrapped the blanket around my shoulders. I inched my way across the room and opened the basement door and got a blast of air. I breathed deeply. It was clean and cold and filled my lungs. I got as far as a neighbor's yard before I started to black out. My brain throbbed, then emptied. I wrapped my blanket around my head and rolled under a bush.

In the morning, Melissa and her relatives found me. Her aunt woke me up by slowly stepping on my hand. When I opened my eyes my headache was gone. "It was gas," I told them.

"Don't be ridiculous," snapped the aunt. "Now pull yourself together and get up off the ground. The neighbors are watching."

"Okay, okay," I said. I went back into the house, packed my bags, and called a cab.

"Now you're really being ridiculous," insisted Melissa.

I turned away and kept my mouth shut. I went to the airport, got on a plane, and was home in two hours. I should have kept my bags packed and gone straight to Canada, but once again I didn't listen to myself. Maybe I knew it would be the same messed-up me, only in a new location. Maybe I was afraid, or didn't really know what I'd do up there. Whatever, instead of choosing a new life, I waited for Melissa and my old problems to return. In the same half-assed way I'd been running my life, I figured I could smooth things out with her while my lawyer handled the feds.

THE GAY GOURMET STOPPED THE OVEN AND unlatched the door. I rolled my head to the right and peeked down at him.

"Hey, kitchen sweet boys," he sang, smiling in at us. "I think you're done. If you spend any more time in here you'll be overcooked."

"Piss off, you old fag wad," Parker said.

"My wallet or your life," the Gourmet wheezed. He was asthmatic.

"Up your butt, fairy queen," Parker continued.

"Shake and bake," the Gourmet croaked, "an' I helped!" Then he closed the door. In a moment I heard the tick . . . tick . . . tick . . . of the heating coils, then felt a draft of hot air. The shelves shifted into gear and we began to rotate again.

"Who's got the wallet?" Feeney called out. "Give it up."

The shelf began to warm up, and I saw the faint glow of the heating coils. Sweat began to run off my head. I felt it pooling under my eyes.

"Give it up," Feeney demanded, "before we're barbecued."

Suddenly the Chinese man began to scream. It sounded insane. He pounded his shoes against the metal shelf. "Eeeeee! Aiiiiii! Eeeeee! Aiiiii!"

The noise was deafening. I felt a spasm of pain and doubled up and vomited over the edge of my shelf.

"Who puked?" Feeney hollered. The shelves continued to spin. On the next rotation he kicked open the oven door and rolled out in a cloud of rusty dust.

"I hope you rascals have learned your lesson," the Gourmet said as one by one he let us out. "Now where's my wallet?" He leaned into the oven and retrieved it from the bottom. When he flicked it open his jolly face brightened. "What do you know," he chirped. "It's all here."

I had vomit on my face, blood on my head from where my cuts had split open, and was covered with black soot. The Gourmet grabbed my arm and quickly marched me out of the kitchen and down the corridor to the guard's station.

"This man needs to recover," he said. "Take him back to the hospital right away."

WHEN I WOKE UP THAT NIGHT, I WATCHED A burning paper airplane glide across the hospital dorm, crash against the wall, and turn to ashes on the floor. Feeney threw another one. It was a different model. It went straight up, then looped and swooped down and burned.

"Welcome to the world of the living," he said when I sat up.

"I feel crispy."

"Do some exercises," he suggested. "Clean your lungs out. I was coughing up rust dust." He lit another plane. It drifted across the room and skidded to a stop under Kirby's bed. Kirby was staying in the hospital for a presentencing psychiatric evaluation. He had flipped out at his wife and chased her out of the house, then got into his truck and chased her across the lawn. He had missed her and run through the neighbor's bedroom wall.

"Hey, be cool," Kirby said. "I'm trying to jerk off and ya'll be ruinin' my concentration."

I stood up and walked over to the dorm gate. A prison orderly sat at an old school desk reading *Candy*. "Excuse me," I said.

He looked up. "Yeah?"

"I'd like to take a shower."

"Sure," he replied, turning his book over. "Let me get a key guard."

In a few minutes he returned with a towel and fresh clothes. "When you change," he instructed, "put your old clothes and towel in the laundry cart. We still have to boil everything." The night guard arrived and let me out through the hospital gate. I went down to the shower room and turned the water on full blast.

I liked the way the water sounded as it hit the tile floor. The empty room was full of that soothing rain sound, and the hot water leached the sweet smell of molasses from the concrete. The light was dim. There was no one else around. It was the first time I had felt at peace since my arrest. I stretched out on the floor and let the water slap at me. It almost felt like drugs. I wasn't over them. I wanted something soft and rolling. Slow. Like Nembutal. Dilaudid. Heroin.

WHEN I WAS ON THE BOAT WITH HARRINGton, we took turns at the wheel. We had alternating shifts three times a day. I always had the mornings. We washed only our faces in fresh water because the boat had a limited supply. If we wanted to bathe we removed all our clothes and dipped a bucket into the ocean.

After a while, instead of pouring water over myself, I just tied the wheel into position and dove overboard. We had a 100-foot floating tow line in case one of us fell off. I'd knot the line around my ankle and take a bath with a bar of soap as the boat pulled me along. Each time I bathed I went farther and farther out on the line. One morning I went to the end and just held on. I let the soap go free. It disappeared behind me. The waves were high, and at one moment a wave was between me and the boat and I could see nothing but the flagged tips of the tall masts on the fifty-foot ketch. Then gradually I was lifted high up on the crest of a wave, and I looked down on the boat as if I might surf right over it. I knew if I were washed away from the line I wouldn't get it back. But I liked the dare. It was my life I was gambling with, and I was winning. I stayed out as long as I could.

Then one morning I lost my nerve. I had an overwhelming feeling that I was going to be washed away. I imagined the boat moving on as I swam with all my might to chase down the end of the line. But I couldn't catch it and the boat grew smaller and smaller as I became more and more exhausted. I panicked at the thought and, hand over hand, began to reel myself in. When I reached the boat I pulled myself up over the side and never went back into the water.

I SAT UP ON THE SHOWER ROOM FLOOR. "I've learned my lesson," I said to myself. "No more stupid chances. I've got to call my lawyer. I've got to get out of here." I turned off the shower and dried myself. "No more drugs. No more bullshit," I said, "or I'll spend the rest of my life in here. Listen to yourself. Listen."

As I walked up the corridor I passed the laundry cart. I threw in my crab clothes. On top of the pile was a hand-sewn jumpsuit of army khakis. I pulled it out and held it up. It had a big dip collar and gold army stars sewn in a zodiac across the chest. Copper rivets ran down the seams of the legs. I turned it over. Dark green buttons on the back spelled out ELVIS LIVES!

"Elvis has *not* left the building," announced a voice in the back of my head.

M̲R. BOW KEPT ME WORKING AS A HOS-
pital orderly for a month. One morning, after my
night shift in the hospital, I went up the stairs to the
fourth-floor gymnasium and joined a boxer named
Lester Martin. He had had some minor success in the
lightweight class but slipped into drug abuse and
theft when his career thinned. I had met him in the
infirmary when he needed three stitches under his
eye. He was going to teach me how to defend myself.
He had been offering a lot of men the opportunity,
and I thought it would be good for my reputation to
be seen slugging it out with a known professional.

Les was inexpensive. Each lesson cost only two
packs of cigarettes. Now that Melissa was sending
money to my commissary account I could afford him.
Before we got into the ring we ran laps around the
basketball court and did calisthenics. After that we
put on our gloves and head gear and went into the
bathroom. I leaned over the toilet and, as agreed, Les
punched me in the stomach.

"Notice," he stressed. "I am not hitting you in the
ribs, but lower, in the stomach." Then he hit me so
hard my feet lifted off the floor. After I'd thrown up a
few times, he leaned over the toilet and I punched him
in the stomach.

"Harder," he snapped, half gagging. "And watch

the ribs." I thought of kicking him but didn't think he'd understand. I punched him as hard as I could. "Harder," he insisted. I hit him again. "Forget it, Jakes," he said. "You punch like a girl."

We went back out to the gym and got in the ring. "Today I want you to learn to keep your right up," he instructed. "This is the lesson of the day." When he lifted his right I spotted brown blood stains on his gloves.

"Lead with your left and use the right for under-cuts," he said, illustrating the effectiveness of the strategy. Then he gave me an encouraging jab across the chin and grinned. The muscles on his face flexed. I guessed that if his head were cut open it would look as solid as the inside of a golf ball.

I threw my left a few times and then hit him with the uppercut. The left was weak, but the uppercut was a solid punch and left me flat-footed. I stumbled back a step.

"Yeah," I said, and hopped around, picking up the pace. It felt good to hit something that hard.

"That's it," he snorted. He pulled away from me and threw a series of head and body punches at an imaginary opponent. "Now imitate that," he said proudly.

I stepped toward him and threw a series of wild, formless punches. Les jogged in place while watching me throw combinations. "That stinks," he said, low-ering his gloves. "Now watch this." He turned away from me and repeated his last flurry. He was wiry and fast. All his muscles were hard and tailored.

Les began to tease me with his left and cross over with his right. "Watch your gut," he warned me, darting out of the way after hitting me there. I knew he was going to hurt me. That was the lesson. Not keeping my right up or dancing left and right, forward and backward. Pain was the lesson. My arms tired, and he punched my gloves back into my face. A cut under my nose opened. He began to punch my ears, boxing me back and forth as my legs weakened.

"Hit me, hit me!" Les demanded. "Hit me, you bitch!" With each word he grunted and threw a good punch. I knew it was crazy to hit him back since he was looking for a reason to use his knock-out punch. I had seen him practice it in the bathroom mirror. "Death! Death! Death!" he had roared, with each straight right, his thick fist pulling up just short of the glass. He'd rip my head off if he got me just right.

I lowered my head and began to swing out at him. He concentrated on my body. All my punches missed. He kept hitting me, soft then hard, soft then hard. Finally he caught me solidly in the throat, then the belly, and I dropped down on my knees and began to heave.

"You're gonna clean this shit up," he ordered.

I sprang up off the mat and caught him with a solid right on the side of the head. He turned on me with a flurry of punches that set me back on my ass.

"I tol' you to keep your right up," he said, ducking away. "Now you owe me four packs of smokes," he continued, " 'cause today you're gettin' two lessons for the price of two lessons." He held out his gloves. "Help me untie these."

I picked at the knots and loosened the strings. As soon as I yanked the second glove off, he grabbed me by the neck and backed me all the way into a toilet stall. "Shut up or you're dead," he snarled.

I couldn't break away from him, and I couldn't scream with his thumb over my windpipe. He pushed me down on my knees, squeezed my neck with one hand, and tugged at his pants until he pulled out his cock. "Touch it," he hissed. "Do it."

I shook my head, no. He began to rub his cock back and forth across my face as I squinted up at him. My lips were dry and he spit down on them. "That's better," he said, gliding the head of his cock across my mouth. It didn't take him long, and after he came all over my face, he refused to let me wipe it off. Instead, he pinched my nose and waited for me to open my mouth.

"Lick it off," he whispered, enjoying himself. "It's good for you. Make you strong."

I knew it wouldn't make me strong. I had already learned that lesson.

WHEN I WAS IN JUNIOR HIGH SCHOOL, there was a gang of guys that always hung out together. At school they stayed in the bathroom, pitching quarters and slugging each other, toughening up. The rest of us were afraid to enter the bathroom, knowing we'd get punched in the mouth or pushed head first into a toilet. Sometimes the gang broke up into small groups and lingered in dark corners or behind buildings. I wasn't sure what they were doing, but I knew it was something bad. From science class I could watch them walking around the outer edge of the baseball field. Their heavy work boots kicked up the dust behind them, and their cigarette smoke disappeared over their heads.

One afternoon my friend Gary and I were riding our bicycles home from school. We took the side roads that passed through rundown neighborhoods littered with newspapers, broken glass, and stranded cars. Gary was faster on his bicycle even though I had a racing model. He was stronger than me and always rode a half block ahead. We didn't talk much about school except to remark occasionally on some perverse event, such as who had punched the science teacher in the mouth or how chicken bones dissolved in Coca-Cola.

Gary turned a corner by a huge furniture warehouse. When I followed, I saw Gary speeding away while the gang trailed behind him like primitive warriors. Some of them were throwing rocks. One guy had a bow and shot an arrow, which missed. By the time I began to turn around, several guys ran up from behind me and pulled me off my bike. They kicked me and beat me with dead branches from the nearby field of banyan trees. I managed to protect my face and balls by tucking my head between my legs, but they whipped and punched my back and shoulders until a watchman from the warehouse yelled out that he was calling the police. Instantly they gathered up their jackets and hats that had fallen off or had been thrown off. As they fled into the trees I stood up and began to chase after them. "Come back!" I shouted. "I want to join your gang!"

I had never lived anywhere long enough to join a gang. I had never even kept up a lasting friendship. My family had constantly moved about through different countries and towns, following the boom and bust of construction work. I thought all people were this transient, never growing any closer or kinder to one another. I hadn't really known the importance of always being with someone and sharing all my thoughts. I wanted to join that gang because I thought you really had to be tight friends to do all the rotten things those guys did. I chased after them until I caught up with the slowest ones. I followed them through the trees despite their insults and punches. Somewhere in the woods we came to a rope ladder suspended from a tree house. There must have been ten such shelters in that one giant banyan. The gang had taken wooden furniture crates and carried them to that tree. Perhaps, afraid that I might tell the police about their hideout, they encouraged me to climb up one of the ladders.

"So you want to join our gang?" the leader asked. His name was Robby. I thought I recognized him from school but decided it was wiser not to say so. We were huddled together in what was about an eight-foot by eight-foot crate. Carpet samples were tacked to the walls and floor, so that inside it was sweltering hot and all sounds deadened. No one would ever hear me if they began to torture me. Yet, although I was more vulnerable than I had been on the street, I felt less afraid of them. I knew that if they would just give me the chance I could be as callous and brutal as they were. I wanted to be one of them, be part of their family if they'd have me.

"You aren't strong enough," the leader announced after looking me over. The others began to flex and strike tough-guy poses like weight lifters on Muscle Beach. I told them that I'd begin lifting weights and running to build up my strength and wind, and promised that in a short time they could depend on me to be a threat to other gangs. Robby said he had a potion better than weight-lifting. It would immediately make me powerful. If I agreed to drink it, I could join the club. I agreed. He leaned forward on his knees and from under a carpet flap produced a tube of Vaseline. He squeezed some into the palm of his hand. He lowered his pants and began to masturbate, slowly and without shame, stroking himself while rocking back and forth. Once the itch of his cock dominated him he began to stroke himself faster and more steadily. Quickly he opened his eyes and held a cup beneath the tip of his cock. First came a drop and then a thick spurting stream. He gasped and then drew deep long breaths while a pink rash appeared on his cheeks and ears. Laughing, he shoved his cock back into his filthy jeans.

"I've had better ones," he announced.

I marveled that sperm was the ultimate strength

potion. The cup passed around to the other gang members who unhesitatingly repeated the act. Robby then filled the cup to the brim with whiskey. I was so excited at being this close to acceptance into the group that I didn't stall a second, and as soon as Robby handed me the cup I put it to my lips and drank the entire contents. I didn't like it, but I smiled as I set the cup down. I wasn't at all concerned about what the boys stood for or what they were. I wanted to love them all and make them love me.

"You faggot!" Robby shouted. He laughed and the others joined him. I was shocked, as caught off guard as when they had first knocked me off my bicycle. I had thought they would all put their arms around me.

"Get out," said Robby. They lowered the rope ladder, and as I descended they pissed down on me.

That was the first time I felt betrayed after trying to be part of someone else's good time, someone else's gang. I should have just made my own plans and stuck to them. But I didn't. I was always looking for someone else to follow.

LES GAVE ME A PUSH BACKWARD AND I FELL on my ass. "You say anything about this and you're dead," he hissed and raised his fist in the air. "Dead." Then he left.

I TOLD DR. SOBEL ABOUT LES, AND HE AR-ranged for me to work within the safety of the clinic and stay out of population. During the next few weeks he taught me how to draw blood and spin it down, how to do serums and count red and white blood cells. After a while I could work up VD cultures, develop x-rays, and take blood pressure.

"You'll probably be transferred to a real prison soon," Dr. Sobel said. "But until then, we'll keep you with us."

It was early in the morning of my 50th day in prison, and I was drinking a cup of coffee in the hospital dormitory when I heard someone calling for help from the shower room down the corridor. The shouts were rising above a grinding machine noise and a combination of wet slapping and body-dragging sounds. "Help me. Lordy, help me. Mercy, help me," the voice wailed. "Turn it off!"

The shouts continued and I knew I should go down there. It was the right thing to do, to help a person, any person in pain who was calling out for help. But it was also a prison rule to take advantage of anyone who offered you a hand. Help could only lead to trouble.

The calls increased and suddenly stretched into one painful, solitary howl. The machine noise deepened, dug in, then speeded up in pitch like a dental drill. It sounded like torture. "Please somebody help me," the voice cried.

I put on my slippers, passed through the open hospital security gate, trotted down to the shower room, and found an Elvis Presley lookalike lying on the tile floor. His features were mushy, not as sharp and pouty as the young Elvis's but close enough to tell in a glance that he was trying to be Elvis. It froze me. There he was, the King, writhing around on the funky mildewed floor. The cable of an industrial rotary drain cleaner had spiraled up his arm. He wailed and tugged against the cable as it worked and worked, trying to winch his arm off. Already the twisted flesh had puckered into black whirlpools. The sound of the machine labored and continued to swell as Elvis groaned unevenly, twitched, and flopped over and around, his free hand slapping the puddle of inky water. I stooped down and turned off the machine.

"Relax," I said. "I'll get a doctor."

He moaned. I pulled the end of the cable out of the drain and unwrapped his arm. "Easy does it," I said.

"Help! Help!" he shouted.

"Hush," I said. "You'll be okay. We'll take care of you."

"Lordy," he whimpered. "Don't hurt me. Please don't hurt me."

"I'm not going to hurt you," I said. "Believe me."

"Ebbers!" he hollered. "Help! Ebbers, there is a man here trying to kill me."

"I'm trying to help you," I hissed as I squatted over

him. Just then the floor guard arrived, and I asked him to call for a stretcher.

I helped carry Elvis to the infirmary. I looked down on his face as we walked. He looked like Elvis, only out of focus, like a movie flashback. His hair sat up on his head like a big black conch shell, but his brown roots were showing. He silently watched us as we looked down on him. "You'll be fine," I said. "Just chill."

"Another hemorrhoid operation?" someone asked as we passed through the outpatient waiting room, which was filled with men sitting around or trying to sneak a look at the warden's new secretary, Miss Lorraine, the only female inside the front gate. She had skin so translucent you could see her organs function like an anatomy model.

We lifted Elvis onto an examination table. "I don't think the arm is broken," I said to Dr. Sobel. He checked my diagnosis, gently pressing Elvis's arm every inch from the wrist to the shoulder. It was bruised like the skin of an overripe fruit. He shone a light into Elvis's eyes, making him wince.

"He's alive," Dr. Sobel said. "Fill out a chart on him and take his temperature." He went into the x-ray room and started the machine. The walls began to hum, and all the medical gadgets neatly lined up on glass shelves moved slightly forward. At the end of each day I had to push them back against the wall.

Just then Ebbers rushed into the room. "My God!" he said softly. "It's him." About a month ago Ebbers had told me Elvis Presley had been checked in to an isolation cell. At first I hadn't known whether he meant the ghost or the reincarnation.

Since then he had been bugging me each time he pushed the food cart into the hospital dorm.

"Have you seen him? Have you? God, he's the best," he said. "He's so good he's real."

Ebbers was usually dressed in a too-tight T-shirt and pants that hung below his gut. But now he was costumed like a four-star general in dress khakis that were milky with a glaze of starch. The laundry boss charged two packs of Kools per starched item. Ebbers was paying out a lot of cigarettes to look that sharp. "He's my butt buddy," Ebbers said proudly. "We were up on charges together."

Then he asked sadly, "Is he hurt bad?"

"See for yourself."

He leaned over Elvis's flaccid body and wiped a bead of drain sludge off his forehead. Elvis moaned like a troubled spirit. "I've really missed you," Ebbers whispered.

"Don't molest the patients," I said and fastened a chart to a clipboard. "How old is he?"

"Thirty-four," Ebbers replied.

I wrote that down and left the room to get a thermometer. When I returned Ebbers motioned for me to be quiet. He pulled a comb out of his back pocket and began to fix Elvis's hair. He combed it all out, parted it, and patted it into a perfect breaking wave. "I'm so happy to see you again," he sighed, and picked a crab out of Elvis's part. "I'm your number one fan."

"Stay away from me," Elvis slowly replied without opening his eyes. His features were slack. "You're a user. You just want my fame. That's all you've ever wanted. If you had loved me you wouldn't have testified against me. If you loved me you'd take back everything you said in court."

"Don't say that," Ebbers pleaded. "I love you still. I just told the truth is all. I had no choice."

Elvis cringed painfully as he shifted onto his side and looked Ebbers in the eyes. "You're a snitch and a fat freak and you don't care at all about me."

Ebbers stood up and tugged a handkerchief out of his back pocket and wiped the sweat from his own face. "I'm not a snitch," he said. He shook his head back and forth. "I . . . just don't know what to say."

"You had plenty to say on the witness stand," Elvis said bitterly.

"You better beat it," I warned Ebbers. "Sobel's around the corner."

"Just one last thing," he said to Elvis. "Just remember that there is no one in the world who loves you like I do." He lowered his head and motioned for me to follow him out the door. "Keep a good eye on him, Doc," he said. "I'll make it worth your while."

I pushed past him and returned to Elvis's side.

"I wish what he said about love was true," Elvis said, jerking his head away from me.

"No you don't," I replied. "Ebbers is a freak."

"That's true," he said, and sighed. "Still, you need a powerful dream to sustain yourself through prison. It's a hard place to live without hope." His eyes looked shrunken. They gave him an eerie, narcotic look, like the older, fucked-up Elvis.

"Don't swallow this," I said. I stuck a thermometer under his tongue. "By the way," I asked. "How do you know Ebbers?"

His jaw went slack and the thermometer slipped between his lips. "He's president of my Elvis fan club," he said. "We were once in business together. Now he follows me everywhere, even here. He's the fan from hell." He sat up and began to brush the hair from his eyes with his good hand. "You got a mirror?"

I didn't answer. He hopped off the table. "I'm only twenty-nine," he said, and walked out the door. He moved in a jerky way, like a string puppet.

"Hey, honey," somebody said from along the hallway. "When you gonna sing me a love song?"

"What do you care about love?" Elvis replied, and grabbed his crotch. "When you only want my crab roll."

I watched him walk down the hallway. He must have tailored his tight pants himself. The crotch was so high he could only take Geisha-girl baby steps. I returned to the examination room to put the thermometer away. It was gone. I searched the room but it had vanished. I decided not to tell Dr. Sobel. He was very insistent on keeping track of all thermometers.

I did tell him that Elvis had refused treatment. "Fine," he replied. "When his arm falls off he'll be back."

That night I was sleeping when Elvis woke me up.

Dr. Sobel had given him sedatives and checked him in to the hospital dorm. "You have to help me, Doc," he said, breathing hard. "Please," he begged. "It's my arm."

"Can you hold out until the morning?" I whispered.

"You don't understand," he replied. He knew he was talking too loud and he looked over his shoulder. The floor guard was watching the *The French Connection* on television. "I've almost killed the man I love."

"Who's that?" I asked.

"Me," he said. "Come on." He padded back to the hospital bathroom.

I didn't like the idea of following him into the bathroom but I figured I could take him. By the time I ducked into his stall, Elvis was squatting on the toilet seat. The blue lights suspended above the toilet were enormously bright. His ghoulish face was dark and grotesquely stiff, like a carved fist. His arm and shirt were covered with a mist of blood. I saw the problem right away. He had snapped the ends off the stolen thermometer and drained out the mercury. He'd attached a hand ball to the top and shoved the sheared off end into the crook of his arm. Dr. Sobel had shown me a similar set of homemade works in his collection of confiscated drug paraphernalia.

Elvis had hit the vein, but in the effort had simultaneously squeezed the hand ball too hard. The dope had been injected into his arm followed by a ball of air. That bubble was now trapped inside his vein, round and throbbing, but it hadn't traveled past the tourniquet on his biceps. If it did, he was as dead as the real thing.

I removed the works and slipped them into his shirt pocket, then began to squeeze and knead the air back down his upper arm to his elbow. The escaping air hissed like a punctured tire as it came back out. The blood was dark and spurted up each time his heart beat. The vein had split, or maybe he had pushed clean through it. I couldn't tell. I continued to rub my fingers down his arm until I couldn't feel any more pebbles of air.

"I didn't want to do it," he whined. "I didn't want to, but he made me do it."

"Who?" I asked.

"The bad Elvis," he said.

"They found the bad Elvis dead on his own bathroom floor," I reminded him.

"I know," he said fearfully. "Like it's some kind of spooky fate that I might die just like him."

"You ready?" I asked, and before he could reply I unsnapped the rubber tourniquet. His eyes rolled back into his head and he slumped forward. Shit, I thought. He's dead. I slapped his face then felt for a pulse on his neck. His heart was beating. Suddenly he opened his eyes and moaned like a revived cadaver. I jammed my hand into his mouth and waited. I heard footsteps. The guard stood up, changed the channel, and sat back down.

"Go," I said to Elvis. He rose up like Lazarus and drifted out of the stall. I washed the blood off myself with a sock I dipped into the toilet bowl, then sneaked back to my bunk.

In the morning his arm was purple and black and inflamed with dangerous red streaks. I thought he had blood poisoning, maybe mercury poisoning, and told him so. I had seen it before. "It'll kill you," I warned him. "You're gonna have to see the doctor."

"I'm okay," he said quietly. Both his arms looked terrible. "You won't squeal on me?"

"What were you shooting up?" I asked.

"Powdered Valium," he said.

"Do you have any extra?" I asked.

He went into his locker and returned with a couple Valiums he had stashed in a can of talcum powder.

"Elvis loved these," he said.

"What didn't he love?"

"You sure you won't squeal?" he asked again. "I can't afford any trouble. I've got a court date ahead of me." He sat on his bed. He looked like a limp snake propped up on a forked stick. He couldn't even comb his hair. "My lawyer thinks he can get Ebbers out of here with time served," he said. "Right now it's my dream to keep him away from me."

I popped the Valiums into my mouth and swallowed them without water. The bad Ray made me do it, I said to myself. I loved the bad Ray. He always knew how to find a party, while the good Ray just sat with his hands in his lap, waiting for the phone to ring.

THE BAD RAY HAD BEEN AROUND FOR A long time. I was fourteen and I kept pestering that gang of boys until they let me join them. We were called the X-15s, after the black pointy-toed shoes we wore. We also wore beige Levis and black V-neck T-shirts. Every time I put that outfit on I felt great. I'd look in the mirror and know other guys were doing the same thing. And like me, they were thinking, no matter what shit hit the fan, they had someone to back them up. They had friends.

The new clubhouse was an abandoned, half-built house in a housing development that had run out of money. There were about twenty houses laid out in a field, all of them in various stages of completion. Most had the walls up. Some had the trusses set and covered with sheets of plywood. On my first night out, the leader, Robby, announced that each of us was to return to the headquarters with a dead pet. "Cat, dog, or monkey," he said. He cleaned his fingernails with the toothpick he removed from his mouth. "No turtles or goldfish," he warned us as though someone before had made that mistake. He had combed his hair down to his eyebrows and over his ears so that it looked like a German helmet.

I didn't want to spoil my initiation and listened carefully as the more experienced members talked among themselves. I looked around and saw a few new boys standing alone. They looked as anxious as I felt.

"The last one back has to eat a dead whatever," Robby said, and he twisted his dark lips into a purplish sneer. He was bigger than the rest of us. He was the only one who had enough patience to lift weights. "And don't make me wait around all night," he added, poking himself in the chest. "I got something to do later on." He had been fucking Bonnie Three Fingers.

"Now beat it," Robby ordered as we broke up. I jumped on my bicycle and headed toward home. The other boys scattered in all directions. I rode as quickly as I could. I was afraid of Robby's threat and didn't want to be the one to chew on a maggoty dead animal. I pedaled so fast I began to sweat across my upper lip. My teeth ached but I felt good about myself because I seldom sweated, not even when I worked hard in the sun. I thought I must be getting stronger.

It didn't take long to reach my house. I pedaled up the driveway, then struggled to keep the bike moving as I steered across the grass toward the backyard. When I reached the screened-in porch I stopped and carefully eased the bike down. I stood by the back door and listened. Across the canal the parents of the Down syndrome girl were arguing. "It's your turn," the wife insisted. "I've been trapped in this house for weeks." There was no answer. A door slammed.

When I was certain my parents were in bed I opened the back door. I walked through the kitchen and went into the Florida room, where the cat, Simon, slept in an open wicker suitcase.

He was asleep. I petted him a few times. "Goodbye Simon," I whispered, "I'll try to make this painless." Then I swiftly closed the case. He struggled to get out, scratched against the wicker, and cried, but by then I was leaving the house. I felt I had used up too much time already. That gang was a fast group, and I expected them to steal pets from old people who walked their animals on a leash. They'd probably snatch the leash away as they sped by on their bicycles, and then drag the animal along the asphalt until it was skinned down like a potato.

I ran to the edge of the canal behind our house and got down on my stomach. With my right arm, which was my strongest, I swung the basket over my head and into the water. I felt Simon struggling, but he didn't make any sounds. I didn't know how long to hold him down so I began to count. One thousand one, one thousand two. I turned my head to look up at the sky. "I'm sorry," I whispered toward the stars. "If I don't do this, it might be done to me."

I knew that wasn't true. I knew better than to hang around with people who were cruel. I thought that just *knowing better* made me different. But maybe it didn't. Maybe I was just like them. Maybe that's what made people bad — *knowing better* but just not giving a shit.

The couple across the canal continued to argue. During the day they fastened a leash to their daughter's leather harness and let her run around the backyard.

She ran screaming with her arms up in the air, as if chasing after a runaway kite. She could imitate the tinny, carnival sound of noisemakers on New Year's Eve. When she ran out of rope she snapped back like a fish being pulled out of the water. I couldn't bear to look at her, especially her mouth, which was always red and swollen. Maybe they beat her. Maybe she ran into things. I didn't know. It scared me to think that no matter how hard anyone tried she couldn't be fixed. That's how I felt about myself. But I couldn't say what was wrong with me. I just knew I was mixed up about everything. Maybe I'm as bad on the inside as she is on the outside, I thought. Maybe I can't be fixed either.

Once, Kenny Knob, the kid from next door, hid behind a palm tree and threw rocks at the girl. She didn't even notice, but her mother did. She came out of the house with a large soup spoon in her hand.

"Don't you dare throw rocks at my daughter," she hollered. She waved the spoon in the air and with her other hand drew the girl toward her waist. "This is my child and I love her," she said loudly. The houses were close together and I knew the neighbors were watching.

"Sorry," Kenny said reluctantly.

"Next time I'll tell your mother," she said.

"So tell her," he shot back. "At least my mom's kids are normal."

I knew I wasn't like Kenny. I could never have done or said what he did. I was smart enough to be sneaky about the mean things I did. I knew how to be good. I had good manners. I had a nice smile. I could be helpful when needed. I could be upset when hearing about cruelty. I could be anything as long as I could fit in. I looked up at the stars again. They were shiny but cold.

I was thinking about myself and lost count of how long Simon was under. When I pulled him up he wasn't moving. I felt as though I had taken too much time and I wondered if I should go back at all. I didn't want to be last.

I balanced the wicker suitcase on the handlebars of my bike and pedaled as hard as I could. There were no cars out and I liked riding freely down the center of the street. But when I looked up at the sky the stars still troubled me. They looked like pieces of broken mirror. I didn't know how to make shapes out of them and I didn't have time to make some up. To my right, another new boy pulled up on his bicycle.

"What did you get?" he asked. We were both breathing hard. He had a sack in his rear basket.

"A cat," I said. "You?"

"A duck."

I didn't think a duck qualified as a pet. I felt better just thinking that he might be the loser because of this mistake in judgment. Anybody could kill a duck in Fort Lauderdale. They were everywhere, like pigeons. I watched him peddle his bicycle. He was wearing shorts and a sleeveless shirt, and I could see that my arms and legs were slightly stronger than his.

"Where did you get the cat?" he asked.

"Neighbors."

"Which one?"

"It doesn't matter," I said. Just then the cat began to move around. It sneezed, then began to cry and claw the wicker.

"Hold it," I said to the new kid. "This thing's not dead yet." I stopped as quickly as I could without going over the handlebars.

"See you later," he shouted and pumped up and down even harder. "I'm not going to be the last one."

Simon was hysterical by now and I was afraid to open the case. He would claw me and then run off. I was desperate. I looked around by the side of the road. I couldn't find anything to beat him with. What I needed was a sharp stick, something I could drive through both the wicker basket and him.

Time was passing. The other new kid would be at the club by now. If the gang wanted a victim it would probably be me. I had no reputation. I was only let into the group because Kenny, my next-door neighbor, had said I was okay. But he wasn't the type to stick up for me, especially if something went wrong.

I pedaled up the driveway of a stranger's house. A car was parked in the carport. I set the cat case down by the road and my bike further off to one side. All the lights were off in the house. I opened the car door and put the gear shift in neutral, then began to push hard against the fender to get it rolling down the slope. When it started to drift I got into the driver's seat and held the door open with my head sticking out so I could guide the wheels. The back wheel passed over the wicker. Simon cried sharply, but before the front wheel hit the case, he sprang out of the crushed side and ran across the street and into the bushes. The car rolled out into the road and came to a stop. I jumped out, grabbed the cat case, and fled on my bicycle.

When I reached the clubhouse I walked my bike up to one of the back windows. Robby had a fire going on the concrete slab floor. I counted the members. There were ten. I made eleven. Someone was missing. Just then I noticed another member to my right, behind a bush, looking through a window. He was counting out loud. "One, two, three . . ."

I dropped the cat case through the window and jumped into the house behind it. "I got a cat," I yelled. I held the case up for everyone to see. The wicker was crushed down and splintered. The cat pillow was bunched up and wet inside it. In the dark I hoped it would pass for the real thing.

Before anyone got nosy the other kid jumped in through the window. "Mine's better," he yelled and held up a miniature poodle by its neck.

"I'm afraid it's a tie," Robby said. "You'll have to fight it out."

That was a lucky break for me. The attention shifted away from my fake cat to the fight. I wasn't going to let anyone beat me. In one motion I flung the cat case into a dark corner then turned and punched the other kid in the face. He dropped the poodle and fell backward, tripped over a drain pipe, and landed on his back. When his head hit the concrete it sounded the same as when my uncle had let me kill a hog with a sledgehammer.

The poodle kid remained on the concrete. He rocked his head back and forth from side to side like he was saying, "No. No. No."

Robby stepped out of what was to be the front door and returned with a German shepherd. Its back was broken, and I recognized the dog as one that I'd seen dead alongside the highway on my way to school. He must have found the dog first, then thought of the game. Cheater, I thought, but I wasn't going to say so. I was lucky that it wasn't me flat on my back. I had gotten away with my cat trick, and I felt Robby's acceptance for knocking out the other kid. I had gotten what I wanted.

Robby held the dog by its hind legs and draped it over the kid's face.

"Lick it," he said impatiently. "It's late and I want to get outta here."

Because the dog was over his face we couldn't tell if he licked it or not.

"Bite it," hollered Robby. The kid bit the tail. It crunched like walking on gravel, and we all turned away and made faces. "Enough," he said, then walked over to the window and heaved the dog out. He jerked an aluminum comb out of his back pocket and combed his helmet of hair. The kid stood up, spit, and rubbed the top of his head. I kept my fist balled up in case he tried something.

"Now everyone take their animals back to where they found them," Robby said.

We all raced off on our bicycles. On my way home I threw the cat case hard at a house. It hit the striped awning over a window and made a sound like a car hood slamming.

When I got home, Simon was at the front door. I walked toward him. "I'm sorry," I whispered. "Sorry." I bent down and held out my hand to rub his head. He hissed and ran off into a boxwood hedge.

"Well, I wouldn't trust me either," I said under my breath.

ELVIS DID GET BLOOD POISONING. THE swollen veins ran up his dope arm like a bouquet of dying flowers. The other spoiled arm just dangled by his side like a rotting salami, all bloated and ready to burst. Dr. Sobel had put him to work folding the hospital laundry, but after two days both his arms hung uselessly by his sides.

I was reading a book on x-ray analysis when he approached me. "You have to help me, Doc," he said directly. Sweat beaded across his forehead.

"Already did that once," I replied, looking up from my text. "Helping you is too dangerous."

"Look at it," he cried. His face pulled to the side in an effort to draw a line across his pain. He held out his arms like a supplicant priest. They were bad. Saint Elvis, I thought. His hips, his hands, his hair could all be tortured and enshrined in the Graceland chapel.

"Nasty," I said.

We went down the corridor to the infirmary offices and knocked on Dr. Sobel's door. "Come in," he shouted.

"I have a special case for you," I announced. "An emergency."

"Let's take a look," the doctor instructed. He was examining VD smears under the microscope. Earlier I had taken the blood and mounted and dyed the specimens for viewing. The crabs had leveled off, but gonorrhea and TB were spreading.

Elvis shuffled in behind me and meekly extended his arms. His back bowed as if he were holding out a great weight. Dr. Sobel examined them. He pressed lightly against the skin. He felt their fever. "Excuse me," he said to Elvis and motioned me aside.

"Has he been shooting drugs?" he whispered.

"No," I murmured. "Remember? I found him wrapped up in a rotor-rooter."

Dr. Sobel took a step back and gave me an incredulous look. "Well, it looks like a puncture wound to me," he said.

"He was bleeding," I said, lying. "I think the cable stabbed him. I doubt he attacked himself with a rotor rooter just so he could cover his tracks."

"Yeah, well . . . I'm suspicious," he said. "And another thing. Does he look like Elvis Presley?"

"Yes," I said. "Clean him up a bit and he might sing for you."

Dr. Sobel smiled. His teeth looked like a stone fence. His mouth was so huge I thought his nose, eyes, and ears could just fall into it and be swallowed up. "Enough. Let's put him back together," he said.

That's what I liked about Dr. Sobel. He knew which battles to fight and which ones were better left alone. Around here that kind of balance was rare. Everyone ran to extremes.

"One minute," Dr. Sobel said and left the office. When he returned from the pharmacy he had a vial of antibiotics. "Take one every four hours," he instructed Elvis. He wrote up a work release pass for a week. "And stay in bed. Ray," he said, "I want you to keep a temperature and fluids chart on him and see to it that he rests."

"Okay," I replied.

Mr. Bow allowed Elvis to move from the hospital dorm into one of the private hospital cells. It was padded and plastic lined for the psychiatric cases, but it gave Elvis more privacy. After I got him settled it wasn't long before I heard the food cart wheels wobbling down the hallway.

I stepped out of Elvis's room and cut Ebbers off. He was still dressed in his pressed khakis. "You can't come in," I said. "He's resting."

"Is he gonna live?" he asked.

"He'll be fine."

"Does he need anything to eat?" he asked.

"Yes," I replied. "We need chicken soup and a big piece of raw chicken."

"Raw?"

"Yeah," I said. "Half a raw chicken, a plump one."

"Can I see him?"

"Later, after you bring the chicken and soup."

"Remember what I told you before," he said leaning into me. "Take good care of him. He's the reason I'm here."

"Remember what I told you," I replied. "Big hunk of raw chicken."

Ebbers turned and left, pushing the cart in front of him like a hotdog vendor.

What I didn't get is why they were in prison. I was curious about what Elvis had done. Maybe it was a crime to impersonate another person without permission.

When Elvis woke up, he asked me to rub the crust from around his eyes. The lids were puffy and weeping. I did, and picked out a few crabs I spotted in his eyebrows. "And could you scratch my shoulders?" he asked weakly. "I just can't lift my arms."

"I don't mean to be nosy," I started up as I rolled him over and gingerly scratched his back. "But what does Ebbers mean when he says you are the reason he is here?"

"Oh God," he groaned. "Did he tell you that? He's sick. He followed me to prison. I get him off all his charges, then he turns and asks the judge for time so he can be with me. The reason I transferred back here from Morgantown is to return to court and try to get him off *again*."

"Pretty weird," I said. "What's the charge?"

"Embezzlement. Fraud. Conspiracy for just about everything when it comes to taking people's money. Tax evasion . . . scratch a little lower."

"What's that mean?" I asked.

"We're con artists," he said matter-of-factly and arched his back like a cat.

"Ebbers?" I said incredulously. "A con artist? As in talking people out of their money?"

"He worked for me," Elvis said proudly. "He was the setup man and I was the closer. He was the dumb one and I was the smart one. I never should have got him involved, but he did everything I told him to. He's like some kind of loyal dog who occasionally hops up on your leg and tries to hump you."

Ebbers had left the chicken soup and raw chicken with me when Elvis was sleeping. "The soup is room temp," I said, "but you should drink it along with another pill."

"Okay," he replied and sat up.

"Now don't spill this." I held the bowl so he could drink, and slipped a pill between his lips.

"Thank you," he whispered. "You've been very good to me."

"That's my job," I said. "Now try to rest."

He slumped back onto his pillow and closed his eyes. I folded a towel across my lap and clamped the half a chicken between my legs. I removed a straight-edge razor from my top pocket and sliced a cut an inch deep and three inches long across the breast. I needed to practice my triage skills if I was going to pull night duty in the hospital.

As Elvis slept I threaded my suture needle. I looked into the chicken's wound. It was too deep to close just the surface. I would have to sew an interior seam with degradable catgut and then close up the outside with a stronger, nylon thread. I wouldn't need staples. I gripped my suture needle with my locking tweezers and entered the wound. It showed little blood. No need to suction the incision. I looped the hooked needle through the deepest corner of the cut and carefully drew both sides of the pink flesh together. With a second pair of tweezers I held the loose end of the thread and worked the needle to finish off the stitch with a precise knot. I clipped it free with my scissors and began the second stitch. If I had had the rest of the chicken, I'd have had it sewn together and pecking the floor in a week.

"Don't you want to know why Ebbers and I are in on the same charge?" Elvis asked, suddenly sitting up. I knew he wanted to tell me. He was vain. I glanced over at him. His eyelids were crusty and seeping like cracked eggs. His fever was peaking.

"Sure I do," I said, concentrating on my work. "I'm just polite."

"It really was a sharp con," he said. "After Elvis's death there was a lot of frenzy about seeing him anywhere and everywhere, and a lot of Elvis fans had a hard time with his loss. So we provided a service to meet their emotional needs."

"What kind of service?" I asked, clipping off my second stitch.

"Elvis seances," he said. "Ebbers would bring me back from the dead, and I would ask people for a donation. They'd all be sitting around a table, holding hands and chanting, 'Elvis come back . . . Elvis can you hear us . . . Elvis give us a signal,' and I'd appear from a closet rigged with dry ice. It was all very slick, and even though it cost people some money, it made them feel a whole lot better. Really. It was therapeutic."

"So how did that get you busted?" I asked.

"It didn't stop with the seances," he said sheepishly. "We got greedy. First, we started the *Elvis*

AfterLife newsletter and sold subscriptions, with a message from Elvis each month. It was all very positive. Each message was for people to love each other and love rock and roll and never stop believing that Elvis was alive in their hearts. Stuff like that. I wrote the messages, and we had good subscription enrollment. Then I started a 1-800-PRESLEY phone line where people could call up and talk to Elvis in the afterlife. We sold audiotapes of Elvis's voice from inside his casket. We claimed the casket was miked. We recorded some weird backgrounds, and then I would talk as if I was Elvis. I'd have him ask people to look after Lisa Marie. I'd ask to have my name cleared of drug abuse. I'd give advice on how to have fun and who to vote for in elections and stuff. I'd end with a little inspirational note on not giving up your hopes and dreams. We got away with this stuff for years because the law figures if people are dumb enough to fall for it, then they deserve to be taken. There was a rumor after Elvis's death that he had died of bone cancer. I thought that if we could get people to donate money to the Elvis Presley Children's Cancer Research Fund we would upgrade our scam. You know, move in on Jerry Lewis's turf. And we did. At the seances I'd say things like I was being abused by evil spirits in the afterworld and I needed money. I'd show them my jumpsuit and say that the devil had stolen all the jewels out of my designs, and I'd show them my empty rings. I'd tell them that I was recording an album from the spirit world and needed production money. I told them I'd met Jesus and he was a rock and roll fan. I once told them heaven was a very poor place because mostly the meek had made it in and that we needed money to build houses and a recording studio up there. And so people gave us a lot of money. And some gave us too much money and then tried to take it off on their taxes, the assholes, and then the government came after us and the crap hit the fan. And then Ebbers spilled his guts and did me in. He's the most spineless fat man that ever lived. But what's worse is that I confessed to doing everything to get him off and away from me but *no,* he stood right up in court and cried out, 'Your Honor, I'm just as guilty as him and deserve time!' So they gave him time. And now he's back after me."

By the time he had finished his story I had completed the interior string of stitches. I looked up at Elvis. His story was so bizarre. I wondered if he was telling the truth. But then he was so odd, and Ebbers was such a freak, I thought it could just as easily be the truth.

The floor guard stuck his head around the corner. "Jakes," he said. "You have a visitor."

It was Al, my lawyer. I had written and asked him to come down to go over my sentence with me. I was thinking of a possible appeal. I wrapped the chicken up in a towel and slipped it under Elvis's bed. "Get some rest," I said to him. "And if Ebbers comes nosing around, call for a guard."

"No kidding." He turned his head to the side. In profile he looked exactly like Elvis.

* * *

FOUR MONTHS EARLIER, I HAD FLOWN WITH my lawyer from Boston to New York. I was to be sentenced the next morning. "The prosecuting attorney is a young bastard," Al said. "He'll try and send you up." I tried to imagine what I might say to the prosecuting attorney. Nothing came to mind because I didn't feel sorry about anything. It was only hash, and that wouldn't hurt anybody. "Now have a good dinner and get a night's sleep," he said, leaving me in the cab as he got out at the Plaza. I went down to the Biltmore. I checked in. I was so nervous I couldn't sit still in my room, so I went down to the bar and began to drink. Since pleading guilty six weeks before, I had been batting around the same argument in my head. Would I get time? Would I not? Should I take off for Canada and build a new life or take a chance on receiving probation? Now that I was on the verge of finding out, the argument got even meaner. It was slapping me around from one corner of the bar to the next.

As soon as I felt drunk, I became even more restless. The alcohol wasn't working. I needed some narcotics to shut me up. I thought about taking a cab downtown and scoring some dope from the pill dealers I knew. It's the wrong night to go around searching for dope, I said to myself. But I finished my drink and took a walk to see what fate would hand me.

All the theaters I passed were showing sex films. I wanted to go inside but sensed that the audience would be as shifty and beaten as those who stood outside just staring at the posters. *Flesh Picnic* and *School Girl's Lips* were showing at the Modern Theater. I liked the way the poster women looked, their yeasty breasts high on their chests, their panties so clean, their feet gently kicking off those pink fluffy pumps while they meowed, "Catch me if you can." I wanted one of those perfumed women and knew the movies wouldn't help. Melissa always made me feel better, but lately after sex I'd start talking about whether I'd get time, and that tortured us, so now I needed a woman who knew nothing about me. I crossed the street and went into a Zum Zum. When I opened the door I saw a homeless man grab the Jerry Lewis money can from on top of the cash register. He pushed past me and ran out the door and down the street. "There goes one of Jerry's kids," I said to the cashier.

She shrugged. "It happens so often we just keep bottle caps in there."

I sat at the counter and before the waitress arrived, a black man sat down next to me. "Excuse me," he said. I looked across my shoulder at him. The plastic globe of lights hung just above our heads and both of us shaded our eyes with one hand. I recognized him as one of the men who had been milling around the sex theaters. "I don't have any money," he said. "I'm hungry, my little daughter's hungry, could you buy me a sandwich?" His hands mimicked his words like shadow puppets. "Please?" He extended his hand and I shook it. "Cool," he said, perking up. "My name's Marvin.and my daughter's is Rose."

When the waitress arrived I ordered for him. Our ham sandwiches came and he ate half and wrapped the other half in napkins. "For Rose," he reminded me, slipping it inside his jacket pocket. It was a thin jacket, and beneath it he wore a filthy yellow shirt. I was wearing a light blue summer suit I had bought for Melissa's high school prom in St. Croix.

He kept scratching himself, rubbing his joints and stretching, and I knew he was junk sick. My lawyer had said to have a quiet evening, not to walk the streets and feed sick junkies. "So long Marvin," I said as nicely as I could, and stood up. He caught up with me as I paid the bill.

"I'm just gettin' to know you," he said like a junk puppy, and rested his hand on my shoulder.

Outside, the street was wet and the cars passed by with the regular crash of waves. "Let's take a walk," he suggested. I walked faster than he, but every few steps he'd run up in front of me, then turn around in order to talk face to face. I kept stepping around him. He kept asking for money. Finally he gave up and said, "Look, man, I know you want to score some reefer."

We ducked into a bar to talk about it. "How can I trust you?" I asked.

"I'm straight up," he said.

What the hell, I thought and slipped him a ten. When he finished his beer, he took off. I noticed a lot of men looking at me, so I took my beer and slipped into the phone booth. I called American Airlines and asked if they had a flight to Canada. It was 9:00 P.M. They had one to Toronto. I left the phone booth and stood outside the bar. The street was jammed with cars and hustlers. I lit a cigarette and waited, just thinking over what I should do. Suddenly I thought

Marvin might be an undercover cop. I knew this was totally paranoid. He was a beat junky who was taking me off, nicely. Still, the feds had impressed me with their stealth.

The month before, when I had gone with my lawyer to see Mr. Tierney, the prosecutor, Tierney had opened a folder on his desk and leafed through it. He showed me an aerial photograph of the boat with me standing on the deck. I remembered the airplane that swooped down over the boat, the left wing dipping in that friendly movie fashion. I waved back. I saw the pilot. He waved and took pictures. "That's you," Tierney said and tossed the photograph at me. It was me, all right, with an idiot's grin on my face. "We had you tailed from day one," he stated. Then he showed me a map. "And this is the island the stuff was buried on." Before Gordon and Harrington made St. Croix and U.S. Customs, they buried the hashish on a smaller, deserted island, Little Dog. When I left with Harrington, we sailed there that first night. In the morning I rowed the dinghy to the shore. "See if you can find it," Harrington had said over breakfast. It was easy. The gulls hovered around my outstretched hands and pecked at my fingertips. They were used to tourists.

"I suppose you'll plead guilty," Mr. Tierney said. He was feeling pretty cocky.

"We'll see," replied my lawyer.

Mr. Tierney questioned me about other drug connections on St. Croix. He listed my contacts. I told him I didn't know those people. "You're a fuckup," he said to me. "And I'm telling you now I'm going to inform the judge that you are uncooperative. Now give me the names of the people you deal with. Tell me, and I can make things easier. It's up to you if you want things to change for the better here."

My lawyer stood up. "Let's go," he said to me. "There is no reason to take this abuse."

"You're hiding information," Tierney said. "I'll personally make sure you do extra time for not cooperating."

We left.

JUST WHEN I DECIDED FATE HAD SENT MARvin off for good, he returned. "You don't mind if I took a joint for myself," he said, slipping the small envelope into my hand.

"No," I replied. We walked to the corner and I waved down a cab.

"Where you goin'?" he asked.

"Nowhere," I replied. I was thinking more and more that he was a cop and would follow me to the airport.

When the cab pulled up I got inside and as soon as I locked the door, I turned away from him. He tapped on my window and began to plead for money.

"To the Biltmore," I said to the driver. I opened the envelope and felt the dope, then smelled it. It was oregano. Somehow I felt relieved. The score had been a charade. I hadn't done anything I could be arrested for. I shoved the envelope into the crease in the back of the seat. This is a good omen, I thought. I'll stay and take my chance on probation. After I paid the driver, I went directly to my room. I turned on all the lights and searched the place. Everything was fine. I turned off the lights, carefully removed my clothes, folded them over chairs, then lay awake until morning.

THE GUARD STOPPED ME BEFORE I ENTERED the visiting room. He patted me down and snapped ankle cuffs above my shoes. The chain was short, and I hobbled over to the table where Al greeted me.

"You look pretty good," he said, all cheery.

I nodded. He was lying. I had lost twenty pounds, my hair looked like it had been cut with lawn shears, and I had broken out with acne.

He flipped open his briefcase. "Basically," he stated, "since you pled guilty, you don't really have an appeal. You gave up your right to have a trial. But," he said, "there is one approach you can take. You can write the judge directly and ask him to change the sentence. It's called a prisoner's appeal. In a way it's better than a lawyer petitioning the court. It's more sincere for the judge to hear your words."

"This sounds like the bottom of the barrel when it comes to sentence reduction," I replied. "What are my chances?"

"Not very good," he said, and frowned. "More than likely you're going to do at least a year or two."

"When do I see the parole board?" I asked.

"I don't know," he replied. "Usually you get a caseworker who handles these things. You'll have to check."

"Al," I said, looking up at him, "I need your help. I'm in limbo *here*. There are no caseworkers *here*. The parole board never meets *here*. This is a transfer center and I've been stuck here for four months. They keep saying they're sending me somewhere, but they haven't."

"Maybe you should see the warden," he suggested lamely.

I was back where I'd started. Nothing I said was getting through. I'd never get out. "Al, you've got to help me here. Nothing is happening. I'm telling you I'm stuck in this no-man's-land."

"I'll check into it," he said and pursed his lips. He was pulling back. He was drifting further out of reach. The line at the end of the boat had slipped out of my hands.

I leaned forward and looked into Al's wide face. The bags under his eyes sagged like funeral bunting. In a minute he would walk out of here, flag down a cab, and find a quiet, expensive restaurant. "Al, do you still have the money?" I whispered.

"I had to take some for expenses," he replied. "But the rest is in the safe."

"How much is left?" I asked.

"Over forty grand," he said.

"That's my future," I said to him. "That's all I have. Don't fuck it up."

He stood. "Don't worry," he said and waved to the guard. "Something will happen soon. I'll look into it."

I DIDN'T LIKE THE PRISON DENTIST, DR. Buchelle, because once a week I had to lance boils on his back, abscesses as large as small breasts that, when pricked open, squirted out a thick pus that smelled like sour milk. His blackheads were the size of peppercorns. I used an instrument like an apple corer to pop them out. He was just out of dental college and working in the prison as a way of paying off his government school loans. He sat around all day making fishing flies out of medical supplies. Still, I thought I had better get my dental work done in prison while it was free.

I sat tilted back in the elevated dentist's chair as Dr. Buchelle shined a flashlight into my mouth. He smelled of tinned fish and his eyes were red-rimmed, like tiny lips. He decided to remove my wisdom teeth.

"It won't be easy," he warned me, as he mindlessly squeezed a pimple on his neck. "They're impacted."

"Just make it painless," I replied.

Dr. Buchelle went directly to work and injected eight shots of novocaine along my gums. I could feel the needles scratching against the roots of my teeth as he pushed them in and out as if he were sewing up a leather wallet. I don't like needles in my mouth. It reminds me of a junkie I knew whose veins were so collapsed he had to shoot under his tongue while looking into a mirror. He tied himself off around the neck with a dog leash. "Cut meh looth," he'd slur when he got his hit. "Cut meh looth!"

"I think that will do it," Dr. Buchelle said after the last shot.

Suddenly everything changed. My cheek twisted into a knot. The skin tightened across my chin and around my eye. "Ughh," I moaned, and pointed at my face.

"How unusual," he remarked. He examined my face, poking it in various spots, then left the office and returned with Dr. Sobel.

"Look at this," he whispered.

"Must be an extra nerve," remarked Dr. Sobel.

"Wa ere you lookin ath?" I asked. The dentist held a mirror in front of me. My lips were pulled toward my ear. No one who knew me in the past would ever recognize me now. In one way this new identity is exactly what I wanted, but I couldn't stand to look like a freak. Even if I was twisted up inside, I didn't want to show it on the outside.

"Don't panic," said Dr. Buchelle as he patted my shoulder. "Just relax." I grunted. He filled another syringe, jabbed through the gum, and thrust deep into the hinge of my jawbone. "Do you know how to meditate?" he asked while easing in the plunger and pulling back on the needle. "Just think of the sound of one hand clapping."

My face twisted another quarter turn. "Why didn't that work?" asked Dr. Sobel.

"I missed the nerve again," he said. "Damn it."

Sobel handed Bushelle another syringe and he repeated the last shot. Still nothing happened. My eyes began to tear. "I've never seen anything like this before," he said, sounding stumped. He gripped my lips and attempted to pull my mouth across my face and back into place. He struggled with it as though it were a shoe that wouldn't fit properly. It wouldn't budge and finally he gave up. "Anyway, you won't feel a thing," he assured me.

"You should give him some Demerol," suggested Dr. Sobel. "At least let the muscles relax."

I nodded my head. "Yeth," I slurred. Bushelle fixed the syringe and shot me in the arm. I felt the Demerol gathering in my back, then drifting up into my neck and over my head like warm bathwater.

"You okay?" Sobel asked. Over his shoulder I watched the dentist prepare his instruments. They looked sharp, crooked on the ends and heavy. I wanted more Demerol and so tried to act unaffected. I straightened up in the chair and focused my eyes but then drifted forward and rocked back and forth. "Fine, fine," I moaned.

"He's had enough," Dr. Sobel said.

I woke up in the hospital. My head felt beaten, pushed in like an old hat. The neck of my undershirt was crusty with dried blood. I looked about the room. I closed my eyes very slowly, then one image occurred to me over and over again. Sometime during the operation I had regained consciousness. I wanted to ask for more Demerol. I opened my eyes just long enough to see the dentist holding a chisel in my mouth with one hand while in his other he held a chrome hammer that in a blur slammed into the chisel. I felt as though I had plunged into a swimming pool and hit my head on the bottom. I began to squirm in my chair. I opened my eyes and watched him once more lower his hammer. I jerked my head back and he hit me on the chin.

It took me a long time to gather the strength to get out of the hospital bed. I went to the toilet, sat down, and passed out. When I woke up I vomited several times, then I went downstairs to Dr. Buchelle's office. He changed the cotton wadding inside my gums and checked the stitches. I looked in the mirror. My face was still pulled to the side and slightly blue, bloated I thought, like a drowned person's.

"Come back tomorrow," he said, writing out a work release pass for a day, and he gave me a packet of barbiturates. I couldn't talk, but I could see that the shoulders of his shirt were stiff and brown where several boils had drained.

I left his office and went across the hall to Dr. Sobel's. "Sit down," he instructed. He examined my mouth.

"This is ludicrous," he sighed, easing open my jaws wide enough to get his penlight inside. "What a butcher." I nodded. He went out of his office and returned with a packet of codeine and another of antibiotics. "Take one every four hours," he said. "And don't worry about your face. It's my guess that it will straighten back out."

I left his office and went into the x-ray room and

wrote "I'm in pain" on a piece of paper. I gave it to Mr. Bow. In a minute I had another packet of barbiturates. I swallowed a couple as soon as he turned his back. I felt oddly energetic and climbed the stairs up to the gym. Les was dancing around the ring, showing off his flashy style and begging for fighters. No one was interested. My mouth was numb with novocaine and I knew I wouldn't feel anything he hit me with, so I stepped into the ring. "I back," I slurred. "An I gonna kick your ath."

"Bring it on," he shot back and smacked his gloves together. "I loved the way you kicked my ass the last time."

I knew Les could outbox me, but I felt strong enough to brawl with him. I had been watching him. Men who weren't afraid of taking two or three punches in order to get inside and give one of their own could knock him around. Of course those guys were twice my size, but the drugs were on my side, and my face was already ruined. I slipped a cup into my pants, then adjusted the protective gear around my head. An inmate stepped forward and wrapped my hands in Ace bandages, then pulled the gloves down over them and tied the laces.

An older man was referee. He called us into the center of the ring, recited the rules, touched our gloves together and backed off. Les danced around me and I got into a crouch to hide my belly. He jabbed at me as I walked toward him. I dimly heard the crowd cheering me on. I pulled my chin in and threw looping punches over my head. I could feel his punches landing squarely on top of my head and I could feel some of mine landing on him, but I wasn't certain what I had hit. I threw a hard punch, hit nothing and stumbled forward into the ropes.

When I untangled myself I went after him. I chased him around the ring and flailed out at him. I hit him a few good solid punches and the crowd cheered. My performance was ridiculous. I kept slipping and throwing myself off balance and slamming into the referee. I knew Les was growing angry because it wasn't a pretty fight and he was being ridiculed for not being able to handle me.

I made it through the first round and felt a lot of men slapping me on the back and offering advice.

"Take it to him, man. Work the body over. Stick the overhand right. Fuck it, just kill him." I was spritzed down and pushed back into the ring for the second round. Instead of trying to punch me, Les kept stepping up and pushing me back until he pushed me into the corner, then he leaned into me. I didn't have any novocaine in my belly and ribs, and each punch smashed into me. My forearms, my shoulders, my hips throbbed. My arms dropped to my sides. I felt like one of those soldiers who, being machine-gunned to death, couldn't fall down until the bullets stopped. When Les stepped back, I slid down against the corner. The fight was called and I was carried out of the ring. When I regained consciousness, one man was lifting my shoulders and another my feet.

"You okay, kid?" the old ref asked as they propped me against the wall.

"Yeth," I groaned. "Hep me ge' the 'love off."

"You got a pretty bad cut on your face," he said, and pressed a damp washcloth over my right eyebrow.

"Noth a prob," I replied. "I can fix tha' up."

"Nice goin', kid," a man cracked as he walked by. "I've pet cats harder than you hit that guy."

"Don't mind him," the ref said. "He's in here for grab-assing a nun."

WHEN I RETURNED TO THE HOSPITAL, EBBERS was in Elvis's room. I heard him before I turned the corner, and stopped before he could see me.

"Say I was your partner," Ebbers hissed. "You better say it, Elvis, or I'll get you bad."

"Leave me alone," Elvis wailed.

I peeked around the corner.

"I don't want to leave you," Ebbers said. He picked up the suture needle off the nightstand and jabbed Elvis in the arm.

"Ouch," Elvis cried and jerked away. "You're sick. Settle down."

"If you don't tell them I'm guilty, I'm going to tell them all where you have your Elvis stash."

"You wouldn't dare," Elvis spat back. "If anyone should take back what they said, it should be you."

"You pussy," Ebbers said and jabbed him again. Elvis winced. "If you don't stop lying 'bout me I'll blow everything. I'll call the Elvis museum an' tell 'em you sold 'em fakes."

"Fine," Elvis snapped. His anger seemed to run through him like good medicine. He lifted his arm and pointed his finger at Ebbers's face. "Then maybe I'll stay in here for life and away from you . . . you fat, smelly, pathetic idiot!"

I thought Ebbers might react violently to that so I turned the corner. "Okay," I announced. "Vithitin' hours are overth."

Ebbers glared at me. "Fuck you, mush mouth. If you think your face looks bad now, just wait 'til I finish with it."

"I've go' to give 'im an enema," I said, and pointed at Elvis.

"He'll take that with a side of Vaseline," Ebbers replied, then he pushed past me. He turned around at the door. "Just remember what I said," Ebbers threatened. Then he blew Elvis a kiss. "Love you, baby."

Elvis looked despondent. He slumped back onto his pillows. I lit a match and held the flame up to the suture needle Ebbers had just used on Elvis. I didn't want to get any of Elvis's diseases. I threaded the needle with catgut left over from my practice session on the chicken. I looked in the small wall mirror and jabbed myself just below the gash, then worked the needle up and through the rim of skin above the cut and out. A thin line of blood ran down from the puncture.

"That's not love he feels," Elvis said of Ebbers. I looked over at him with my one open eye. "He's taking advantage of me. He's killing me. This is just like the real Elvis. His friends did him in, too." He

"You know, what bugs me," he said, starting up again, "is how people have jumped on the anti-Elvis bandwagon. They call themselves academic musicologists, but they're just lowlife Elvis bashers. And you know why? Because Elvis had *real* talent. These losers can't bash the really great Elvis, the real singing Elvis. They can only take potshots at the cheap newspaper version of Elvis. I hate people who put others down to build themselves up."

I clipped off another stitch.

"Sure he was poor. He made it. He blew it. If I study him and learn not to make his mistakes, then I'll walk out of here someday and not have to do myself in. When I get out of here I'm going to avoid the pitfalls Elvis fell into. The early years are the good lessons . . . working hard, following your big dream . . . working your way up the ladder . . . establishing yourself . . . this is good."

"You know," I lisped and tied off another knot. "I don' know much 'bout music."

"Hey," he shot back. "You don't have to know a thing to dig Elvis. Heck, people who first heard Elvis in the early fifties didn't know a thing at all."

"How do I look?" I asked, turning toward him after I had finished all eight of my stitches. The clipped thread arched up over my eye like a fuzzy caterpillar.

"You have to stop hating yourself," Elvis answered. "I used to hate myself. My looks, my voice, my hair. Then I turned to Elvis and stopped hating myself."

looked away from me and composed himself.
you what my dream is," he said to me, quietly
get out of this. To stop being Elvis. I've got to
up. Look at me," he said, holding out his b
pockmarked arms. "I'm even killing myself. I
Sick in body and sick in mind." He looked aw
me and exhaled loudly. He sniffed and pinch
some tears. "You know," he started up again,
one thinks they can make fun of me. Just like
the real Elvis. It's mean. It's like being mean
Elvis is a national pastime. But he wasn't a jo
was great. Heck, I'm from Tennessee, and in
high school there must've been a dozen of us.
an Elvis club and every member had to be a
impersonator. We loved Elvis. He was a g
Sometimes people get all mixed up and think
the same genius. I like that."

I looked over at him and tried to compare
the real Elvis. His face wasn't as full, his lips w
as dark, and from his illness his cheeks were dra
and wrinkled like dried fruit. His hair was brow
black. The skin across his forehead was pitted
acne scars. His movements were awkward and
not deliberate and robust like the real Elvis's
Elvis with a big heart and soul and that raw,
voice. This Elvis wasn't even close, but after liste
for a while, I realized this Elvis had his own talen
could talk some serious shit.

I took a deep breath and slipped the ne
through my skin, then looped it back into a
knot.

[

"I don' hate mythelf," I said and squatted down beside him. My head was pounding. The novocaine was fading. I reached into my top pocket and swallowed two more barbiturates.

He leaned toward me and combed the hair out of my eyes with his thin fingers. "You know," he said, "with a little voice work and some makeup and hair dye, I think I could turn you into a junior Elvis."

"Not me," I replied, and laughed at the thought. "I'd 'ave a heart a'tack if I woke up lookin' like Elvith."

He turned toward me. "Wow," he said. He paused and grew thoughtful. "Maybe that is what happened to Elvis that last night in the bathroom. He was just sitting on the toilet and looked into the wall of gold-flecked mirrors and in a flash realized that there was no way in the world that anyone could understand just who he was. No one, not Ginger, not Lisa Marie . . . not even himself. Just that thought killed him. Boom! It hit him. He was no longer the Elvis he knew."

"Maybe," I said, thinking more about how the cut above my eye would scar and give my eyebrow a permanent question mark. I'd go through life looking as if I were puzzled by the simplest idea. People would not only think I was a criminal, but that I was stupid, too. I didn't want that, but I was too tired to change the sutures. I'd open it back up in the morning and start over.

"You know what would have saved him?" he said.

"If he 'topped takin' drugs an' got rid of his awful friends he could'a pull' through."

"You know the King was a DEA agent. Made so by Nixon."

"I thaw the photo of 'em at the White Houth," I said. "Elvith looked methed up to me. Like he could'a arrethted himthelf on the thpot."

"You laugh," he said. "But if Elvis wasn't so pressured to be himself he might have quit singing and become a cop. Had a career change."

"You don' believe tha'?"

"I do," he shot back. "Elvis wanted out of the music business. And he had enough money to walk away from the movie deals. He thought that being a drug agent would be great. This is one of the reasons I'm going to give up my Elvis thing. At this moment, our lives are exactly parallel. But if I don't pull away I'll end up just like him, dead. I'm going to be the ultimate Elvis impersonator by doing what *he* should have done . . . I'll move on. And it will be the hardest thing I've ever done. Because really, if you knew who I was, just some small-town nothing driving a milk truck, you wouldn't give a rip about me."

"Not true," I said.

"Don't lie," he replied. "You only know me as an Elvis impersonator. Heck, I've only known myself this way since I was in grade school. So naturally it scares the crap out of me to think that I'll give up this Elvis thing before it makes me kill myself."

"But you already tried to kill yourthelf," I said.

"Not so," he protested and wagged his finger at me. "I was trying to get high. I was doing my Elvis thing. That's what he was doing when he fell off that toilet. He escaped to death, but I have to find a different exit. I told you," he said pointing a finger at me, "You got to have a powerful dream. And I have that powerful dream . . . but I can see that you don't," he said. "You're happy just poking along, living a lie, chasing that dope and dollar."

I didn't know what I would become, whether I'd be a forest ranger or a dope fiend, but I didn't want this guy, an Elvis freak covered with blood blisters, to look down on me. "That'th na true," I said. "That'th in the patht."

"That's not enough," he said. "You need a dream to get you through this place, and that same dream has got to carry you into your future or you won't have one."

"Enuff of thith *dream* talk," I insisted.

"No," he shot back. It's time you faced facts. You're like one of Elvis's flunkies just hanging around lookin' for handouts. You need to *move on*, buddy."

I knew I wasn't looking too good at the moment. My cheeks were swollen, my face was cut up, but I knew I was better than some Elvis wanna-be. And I did have a dream. I wanted to get out of prison, get my money, work things out with Melissa, carve out some kind of future, and be left in peace.

Elvis smirked. "I can read your mind, Doc. And when a bullshitter shits themselves, they don't have a dream. They have a *fantasy*."

I stood up. "I'm thick a thith talk. I'm goin' to bed. Thweet dreamth," I lisped, then drifted down the corridor toward the dormitory.

A WEEK LATER I WAS WAITING IN LINE TO go up on the roof for fresh air. The guards allowed only twenty men up at a time, for half an hour each. Every time they lifted the hatch the sour prison air whistled out as if from a steaming kettle. The roof was six floors above ground, and after a stretch of time inside the building it seemed worth it just for the chance to jump. Some time before, a man had braided strips of bedsheets into a rope and wrapped it around himself. He scaled the roof fence, secured one end of the rope with a homemade grappling hook, and began to rappel down the building, but his rope snapped and he didn't come back. There were fences around the roof's perimeter, with barbed wire on top and an orange guard shack in the middle. Two guards stood there, back to back, with pump-action shotguns held casually across their arms.

Finally the first group descended the circular iron stairs and our group was led up. The sky was gray and gusty. I squinted and held my hand out over my eyes. Manhattan was crisscrossed with Christmas lights like a fallen Gulliver. The World Trade Center's twin towers were his upturned feet. I couldn't see his head in the dark Bronx, where I guessed the lights were smothered. The wind blew right through my cotton army jacket as I circled inside the fence. We were close to the Hudson River, and between two buildings I watched a rusty cargo ship glide across the slate water. A few blocks downtown on West Street, men in white uniforms unloaded a shipment of beef. They snared the shoulders with bloody meat hooks and flung them down a basement chute. Watching them made my shoulders hunch up, made me think of Les creeping up on me.

On the other side was an office building. I looked into the windows and watched people working at dull tasks that suddenly seemed romantic: typing, carrying papers, talking and drinking coffee. Why couldn't I be like the office workers—normal and ordinary and content? They were so close. When they spoke to each other I saw the expressions on their faces, the gaps between their teeth, the rings on their fingers. They were different from us. They looked so relaxed. Their faces looked true to their feelings. I wanted to climb the fence and leap across the alley, through the window, and join them at the water cooler.

I turned and walked away. DuBoise, the guy who'd tried to electrocute himself, was in front of me, and I tried to avoid him. His teeth were black. They had abscessed to sharp points. He was always after me for sleeping medication. "Sleep's no good for me, Doc," he'd slur, his breath hot and foul. "It fucks me allll up." When he did fall asleep in his chair he'd wake up like a belt snapping, his face wet and folded in like an accordion. He claimed his dreams were serialized. "Like the God damned TV," he said. "Everyone I ever met is in them. My whole fucked-up life's in these dreams, and they don't like me. I need a drug, any drug. I got to keep these people away from my sleep." When he wasn't on Thorazine he got flippy.

"Five more minutes," one of the guards shouted down at us from the shack.

"Hey, Jakes."

I turned as the warden put his hand on my shoulder.

"Yes?" I said. My face was still asymmetrical, but I had regained my voice.

"Is that Elvis impersonator well enough to go on stage?" he asked.

"I'll find out," I replied. "Why?"

"I'm putting together an Xmas show and thought he'd be good entertainment," he said. "So check him out for me."

"Sure," I said, pleased to do him a favor and hoping he would return one. The last time I'd spoken with him he'd said I'd be sent to either Morgantown, West Virginia, or Ashland, Kentucky. I was hoping for Morgantown. It was the latest experimental prison for marginal offenders. It was coed, without fences, and worked on the honor system. Before he could break away, I asked, "When is my transfer coming?"

"We're waiting for a bus," he said. "Don't get impatient."

That was easy for him to say. I still had no idea how much time I'd do. I had to turn away from him. If I said anything, I knew it would explode out of me and just make things worse.

I went downstairs to check on Elvis and find out if he was willing to go on stage. He was sitting up in bed, propped up by three pillows and reading a book on astral projection. "I'm going to think my way out of here," he said, tapping a finger against his temple and squinting sagely. "I'm going to will all the cells in my body to unlink and drift out of here and link up again on the outside. Just like they beam people up on *Star Trek*, only I'm going to do it with the immense power of the brain."

I gave him a skeptical look. "You know," I said, "you're not ready to give up your *Elvis* thing just yet."

"Oh yes I am," he replied.

"No you aren't," I said. "You sound just like him. That's probably the same trash he was reading when he fell off the toilet."

"He was reading an illustrated book that showed the proper sexual positions according to your birth sign," he said, correcting me.

I set a package wrapped in brown paper on his lap. "I have a present for you," I said. "It will change your mood."

"What's this?"

"Your cure," I replied. "You're about to check out of this padded cell."

He slowly opened it. "Yes!" he shouted. He hopped out of bed and held the ELVIS LIVES! jumpsuit against his body. He looked at me, "Where did you get it?"

"I found it in the infested clothing bin and had it sterilized."

"I made this in Morgantown," he gushed. "They made me throw it away when I checked in here."

"It's how I knew you were here," I said.

"Wow, Elvis lives," he sighed.

"He does live," I said. "And here's why. The warden wants you to put on an Elvis concert for the Christmas show."

"Here?" he asked. "Here? I can't do it here. Look at my hair, my roots are showing. I haven't seen a bottle of L'Oréal Excellence Blue Black in months. I don't have any makeup. I don't have a guitar. I haven't seen my voice coach in a year. No, I can't do it. I've lost too much weight. I look more like the Tupelo Elvis, but this jumpsuit is from the Vegas Elvis. I'd need early Elvis clothes, something with pink and black combinations."

"It might just be easier to fatten you up," I suggested.

He ran his hand slowly across his face. "And I have acne," he said. "It plagued Elvis, too."

"I can help you with that," I said. "Look, I can see this has caught you by surprise. Why don't you think about it and let me know later, and then we can work on the details. Okay?"

"I really need to think about this," he said, shaking his head. "I need to calm down and get in touch with my feelings. I thought I had given this up."

"You do that," I replied, "and I'll see you later."

As I walked down the stairs I was thinking that this was good for both of us. Elvis could stop wallowing in his sorrow, and the warden would think of me as a man he could count on to deliver. And just maybe I could count on him to deliver me out of West Street.

Dr. Sobel's door was open. He was filling out medical records. "What's wrong?" he asked. "I can tell you're smiling, even if your face is crooked."

I explained about the Elvis concert. "But we have a problem," I said. "We need a guitar and some other stuff. Can you help?"

"Sure," he replied. "I have an acoustic guitar and some Elvis tapes. But maybe you should ask Miss Lorraine about the cosmetics. The only stuff we have here is a wax kit for cadavers so when people get beaten and slashed to death we can spackle up the holes with Flesh Wax."

I strolled down to Miss Lorraine's office. "Certainly," she said, "I've always been a big Elvis fan. I can get whatever he needs, but who's going to pay for it?"

I went down to the warden's office on the first floor. The last time I had tried to meet with him it had taken three weeks to receive an appointment. But once I explained to his assistant that I was working for Elvis, he escorted me directly into the warden's office.

"No problem," Mr. Paris said, having put a phone call on hold. "You work out the details, give us a list, and I'll do whatever I can."

Amazing, I thought. We can't get decent food, warm clothes, or even the proper medications, but for Elvis everyone is tripping over themselves to help.

"Any news on my transfer?" I ventured, while I had his attention.

"Nothing yet," he replied. "We're waiting for your court records, to see if you'd be better suited for Morgantown or Ashland." Then he waved me off as he returned to his phone call.

By the time I got back to Elvis he had a list of necessities. "I'll do it," he said. "But only if I can do it my way."

I looked over the list. I was ahead of him. "By the end of the week we should have the supplies," I said. "Now we need to work on your body. Do you have any money in the commissary? I want you to eat a lot of junk food."

"I don't like junk food," he said with a pout. "I want a platter of fried peanut butter and banana sandwiches. I want some bacon and some cheese-burgers and fries. I want some *Elvis* food." He rubbed his belly.

"There are limits," I replied. "I'll see if we can get some peanut butter and bananas from the kitchen but don't count on the rest."

"I also want a poster announcing the show," he said.

"You're in prison," I replied. "Get real."

"I want a poster," he whined. "Or I won't do it."

"I'll see what we can do."

"I'll also need a makeup artist. There are a lot of queens in here, I'm sure you'll find one that has had theatrical experience. And one more thing," he added, smiling. "I want you to open for me. Elvis always liked gospel music as an opener. You'll have to sing 'How Great Thou Art.'"

"No," I said. "Absolutely not."

"Then forget it," he said and threw his hands up in the air. "Tell the warden. No opener, no show."

"Okay, I'll try," I conceded. I was fair at singing hymns from church, and I didn't want the warden to take it out on me if Elvis pitched a star fit.

I had seen a man on the third floor who wore only red bikini underpants and a little vest he'd made from a khaki shirt. His face was always poised when I watched him sashay by, his ass marking time like the pendulum of a clock. I guessed he might know something about makeup.

I stood outside the locked gate of his cell. "Excuse me," I said tentatively. "May I speak with you?"

He was hand washing his faded underwear in the sink. He jerked his head to one side and raised an eyebrow. He looked like a cockatoo in a cage.

"I know you," he said. He snapped at the waistband of the tiny shorts that were stretched tightly across his cock and balls. Whatever was in there kept twitching. "Les told me what he did to you. He's a client of mine."

I blanched. That was the kind of public news that would set perverts to daddy me every time I entered the shower room.

"You should have bit it off," he whispered, and mimed a big hotdog bite. "You had the upper hand, considering the circumstances." He smiled. He had a husky voice. "Then you should have spit it out."

"I thought he was going to kill me," I said. "I'll get him back."

"Sure you will," he lisped and winked at me. "Now what can I do for you?"

I explained. "I'm here to find Elvis a hairdresser and makeup artist. He's going to do the Christmas show."

He raised an eyebrow. "So," he purred, "Ebbers says you and Elvis are *married*."

I groaned. "Ebbers is just going through a jealous phase."

"Well, honey," he drawled out, and shifted his legs again, "I'd keep an eye on that fat man. He doesn't like *the Doc*."

"Let's stick to the point," I said.

"Okay. Honey, my name is Troy, and you have just hired the House of Troy, home of Helen, the Face That Launched a Thousand Ships. Most of my friends call me Helen, but you can call me Troy." He framed his head in his hands and struck a pose.

"Hi, Troy," I said. "Let me get right to it. Elvis needs a cut, a dye job, a steam facial, a manicure, a pedicure, acne therapy, makeup, and wardrobe assistance. Can you do all that for free?"

"Free?" he parroted.

"Prestige," I said.

"I love prestige. When do I start?"

"I'll be in touch," I replied.

"In touch?" he purred.

"You'll hear from me," I said and walked away.

THE NEXT FEW WEEKS WERE HECTIC. I found someone to draw a picture of Elvis wearing a

Santa Claus outfit. The warden's assistant xeroxed it and sent one of the office inmates to tape copies up.

I was a little worried about my singing. I couldn't play the guitar, and since I was singing a gospel tune, the visiting priest offered to accompany me. We practiced together a few times. He gave me a lot of encouragement, but I wasn't very good. Still, I thought it would be better to sound dreadful. In contrast, Elvis might sound outstanding.

On the day of the concert, Troy took care of Elvis while I took care of the gym, which had a stage. I taped up big gold glitter letters spelling out ELVIS PRESLEY LIVE. I cut Elvis pictures out of a fan magazine Miss Lorraine gave me and taped them up around the auditorium. I lined up the chairs. At best, the place looked like prom night in a school cafeteria.

When I returned to the hospital ward to get ready, I watched as Elvis washed his skinny body in the shower. Troy patted him dry with talc-sprinkled towels. Elvis looked like a sugared jelly roll, all red and powdered, before gingerly wiggling into his jumpsuit. He faced the mirror and Troy combed his jet black hair, careful to imitate the King's swelling wave that curled from front to back. Mascara and eye liner were applied. Rouge. Lipstick. When the perfect look was reached, Elvis jerked his hips back and forth, working out the kinks. He removed a folded handkerchief from a zippered pocket and tucked it into his crotch. He molded it into the correct shape. I gave him a questioning look.

"Hey, they all do it," he said. "Little Richard even used a banana."

When the time was right, I gathered the two VD patients, the brain-damaged paint sniffer, DuBoise, and the anorexic I had to feed through a nose tube, and marched them into the auditorium. I wanted to make certain that Elvis had some audience. The Christmas show was not a mandatory activity. I lined up my patients in the front row. "Cheer at everything he does," I instructed. "Or else I'll stop your medication."

I went backstage. Troy and Ebbers were setting up the equipment. Elvis was practicing.

"Howdy," he said, striking a sultry pose. "My name is Elvis Presley and I just want to sing a few songs for y'all."

I noticed that his voice had changed. He sounded like a bad Presley, but not meek or afraid, and when he began to sing "Heartbreak Hotel" into his fist, he looked so heartbroken that Ebbers began to moan. Elvis ignored him.

"I'm set," Elvis announced. "I've got the feeling."

At noon I stepped out onto the stage. "Welcome to the West Street Christmas Concert," I announced to about two hundred inmates. They looked up at me. For so long I had tried not to attract any attention and suddenly I was attracting all the attention. Bank robbers, murderers, drug dealers, thieves, and the rest all looked directly at me. Men I normally wouldn't look in the eye, men I would avoid standing next to, men I would swerve away from in the corridors, all stared at me, sizing me up and wanting me to make their day better. "We have a great show for you today," I said.

I glanced over to the stage wing. Elvis wasn't watching, but Troy impatiently tapped his foot. "Get on with it," he hissed.

"Yeah, get on with it," aped DuBoise from the front row.

I hoped *his* medication had kicked in. "And so," I continued, "tonight we are graced with the second coming of Elvis Presley."

A loud cheer went up and I felt a little better.

"As an opening number, Elvis has requested that I sing one of his favorite hymns." From the wings, Troy gave Father Ryan a little push. He strolled out with the guitar and struck a G chord.

"Aw fuck," DuBoise yelped loud enough for everyone to hear, "not the singing nun."

"Flying nun," Troy yelled from the wings.

Father Ryan strummed loudly and gave me a nod. I came in on the next phrase. Right away I could hear the boos. What am I doing? I thought. This is nothing but trouble. I should be singing out in the woods where the worst that could happen is some squirrel might pelt me with nuts. With every line I could hear snatches of "give 'im the hook . . . put a cork in it . . . jam this guy."

Finally I reached the end and stopped. "Thank you and enjoy the rest of the show," I said and quickly walked off. There were more boos, but they gave way to a mounting chant of, "Elvis! Elvis! Elvis!"

"They're a tough crowd," I said to Elvis when I'd slipped backstage. "I took a beating."

"They are only tough when you open for the King," he replied and winked at me. "You did fine."

"You're on," I said.

"Let 'em want me," he slurred and closed his eyes. Troy combed his hair one last time. His coif gleamed with pomade so thick the tines from the comb left grooves along the sides. He patted the wave in front.

"Purrrr-fect," Troy said.

"ELVIS!" the crowd shouted. Just then the warden pulled aside the curtain and pointed at us. Elvis stood up with his guitar and trotted toward the stage. The crowd let out an enormous roar.

"Good evening, folks," Elvis gushed, "I sure am pleased to be singing for y'all tonight. I'd like to start out with a ballad I fixed up just for you, 'In the Ghetto.' And then he leaned into the microphone and slowly struck his first chord. "As the snow flies on a cold and gray Chicago mornin' a poor little baby child is born in the ghetto. . . And his mama cries . . ." Now he sounded just like Elvis. The crowd sat spellbound. The warden stood with his face gone flat from disbelief. They were cheering before he finished. "Elvis lives!"

He held up his hand and the crowd calmed. "Now you all might have seen me in a little movie called *Jailhouse Rock*."

He had them. "Well here's a little number called, 'I Wanna Be Free.' "

The crowd groaned. What a tease, I thought. We

all thought he was going to kick in with "Jailhouse Rock." When he finished, he stopped just long enough to sneer at the crowd before getting funky to "Viva Las Vegas."

"Just remember," Elvis said, striking his pose, one hand pushing down the neck of his guitar, the other creeping towards his padded crotch, "you got to follow your dreams. You can't let a little setback like prison keep you from reaching for the stars."

"Yeah, right!" a big man in the back shouted. "What's the dream for somebody doing thirty to life? Huh?"

"That you still have a life," Elvis said with boyish sincerity. "Yes, sir," he said. "If you still have a life, you always have hope and God."

"Then there ain't no hope for Elvis," the man shouted back.

This is the beginning of the end, I thought. They're going to turn on him, and this place is going to blow. But Elvis just waited it out. He looked down at his feet, the toe of his blue shoe drilling the floor, boyish, innocent, misunderstood.

"Blue suede shoes," Elvis yelled and sprang alive. He danced a funky jig then suddenly stopped to strike a classic Elvis pose. "If only I had a camera," Ebbers lamented. "I'd love a picture for my scrapbook of him singing in prison."

Then Elvis pulled tissues out of his jump suit pockets, kissed them, and tossed them into the audience. The crowd let out another cheer. "Elvis! Elvis! ELVIS!"

Then he did it. He stepped to the front edge of the stage, spread his trembling legs, threw back his head, and struck the first chords to "Jailhouse Rock."

It was beautiful. I stood to the side of the stage doing a little rockabilly dance as two hundred men wiggled in their chairs, sang along, and pumped their arms in the air—and all without a fight. The guards stood lined up against the walls, their eyes scanning the faces, waiting for something to go wrong. But nothing did. It was remarkable. And on the other side of the stage, in the wings, the warden stood clapping his hands to the beat and looking out at the crowd.

I started to think that this was going to be good for my parole, that I was going to get a big bonus. But the warden was thinking something else.

Part Two

X-RAYS

I WAS PROMOTED TO FULL-TIME X-RAY technician because the previous technician had been sent to Lewisburg for ten years on bank robbery. Now I was shooting all the x-rays in the prison and doing all the preliminary blood work, cell counts, and venereal disease checks on the new arrivals. It was a job that kept me busy most of the day and often at night. I liked to be busy, but the real benefit was the visit to a downtown hospital where a radiologist reviewed my work. Because of my x-ray technician status, I had been reclassified as a minimum security risk so I could leave the prison with supervision.

When Dr. Sobel first walked me out the front gate I didn't know what to expect from myself. I thought I might throw down the x-rays and run. Years before, I had walked directly into a store and picked up a stereo receiver, then just as quickly walked out with it under my arm. Robby had told me this was the best method when shoplifting. But once I was beyond the main door, two men followed me. "Hey kid, come back here," one of them said. Like all fat men in Florida, he had sweat through his shirt before noon. "Come on," the other said, "we just want to talk with you." I had already begun to run. They chased me across the parking lot. I threw the stereo down and ran until I saw they had given up.

But I knew prison guards would never stop chasing me. And when I thought of running, I couldn't think past charging crazily down the street, pushing people over and leaping dangerously in front of cars, perhaps getting hit by one, perhaps not, but I knew I would end up stretched out on the pavement, exhausted, with my mouth full of dirt, then handcuffed and thrown into the hole, with my sentence extended for another year or two.

When I walked out the front gate, I was stiff. I stayed by Dr. Sobel's side as we crossed the parking lot. When we reached his car, I had to break away from him to get in on the passenger side. I knew the width of his car was the length of my head start. I could probably sprint to New Jersey before he turned the corner, but he could stop and take a cigarette break, have a meal, a nap, live an entire life, and I would still have to keep running. When he opened my door I hopped in, snapped on my seat belt and pressed down the door lock. I removed a cigarette and lit it.

"There's a white smock in the back seat," he said. "You can put it on if you'd like." I changed out of my camouflage shirt as we drove through the warehouse district on the West Side. The buildings were old and mostly abandoned. We passed by the Hudson River. The docks had rotted away and fallen into the water. Still, there were people everywhere. Most of them were sapped lushes and dope fiends. This is what they looked like when they came to West Street. By the time they left they had seen a doctor, received treatment, and put on weight. Even though they were off to do an average of twelve years in a federal penitentiary, they were the only people who looked *better* after leaving prison. I was looking better myself. I had kept the crabs at bay. I hadn't gained any weight, but my hair had grown back so that I could comb it over.

Once Dr. Sobel had parked the car, we entered the hospital and marched through the corridors until we arrived at the radiology department. He was well known by the other doctors and nurses, and I expected they knew I was from West Street. A receptionist greeted us and we followed her into a viewing room. I arranged the x-rays on the light table and the specialist, Dr. Wong, looked them over. His eyes moved rapidly from top to bottom as if he were reading a book.

"These are very good," he said to me after he had reviewed the stack. "You could have a future in this. The technicians here start at around $28,000 a year."

"I'll consider it," I said, nodding smartly and feeling like a prize pupil.

"Let's go to my place for a drink," Dr. Sobel said as we left the hospital.

"I'd love a drink," I replied.

We walked the couple blocks to his apartment. It was surprisingly large and empty. In the bedroom he had a bed and a dresser and in the corner a round pillow in front of an altar with candles, an incense burner and a picture of a mantra that looked like a television test pattern. "I believe in meditation," he said. "It relaxes me."

"I believe in medication. That does it for me," I joked.

"That's what it says on your records," he said. His voice was disapproving.

I wanted to know more about my records. I was eager to learn anything about my future. "What else do they say?" I asked.

"The usual stuff," he added casually and moved into the kitchen.

"Like what?"

"Don't put me in a bad spot," he replied. I knew I had just located the boundary between us.

I followed him, knowing he didn't want to tell me. He opened the refrigerator and removed a bottle of wine. Maybe that will loosen him up, I thought. He poured two glasses and gave me the one that was fuller. Suddenly I thought he might try to get me drunk and blackmail me into having sex with him. He might be thinking, "This will loosen *him* up." There was no controlling my thoughts. One minute I was grinning like a loon from the slightest compliment, and the next I was overwhelmed with paranoia.

"To your future," he said, holding his glass above his head. We tapped them together and I took a sip. It was good. I told myself that if he touched me I'd punch him out, tie him up, and take off in his car.

"Relax," he said. "This is a treat."

"Do I look nervous?" I asked.

"Jumpy is how I'd describe it," he replied.

I felt so self-conscious I couldn't speak. I figured he could read my sick thoughts. I took another sip, then stood near the window and looked out. It relaxed me to know what I might do even if I knew I wouldn't do it. Or would I? Would I really punch him if he touched me? Would I really take off in his car?

"How much longer do you have left?" he asked as he drifted toward the living room. I followed him. There were only two hard chairs and a wooden box for a coffee table.

"I don't know," I replied. "I'm in limbo. I'm like The Man without a Country. Without a caseworker to help me set up a parole date, I have no idea how long I'll be in."

"I see," he said. He was trying to be nice and friendly but we were just so far apart.

I got up and walked into the kitchen. "This is the first wine I've had in six months," I said happily. "I like to drink it."

"Bring the bottle in here," he said, and when I did he held out his glass. I filled it. There was just a little left in the bottle and I held it up to my mouth and drank it off even though my glass was still full.

He gave me a worried look.

"Do you have a radio?" I asked.

"No. I find it distracting," he replied. "How are you holding yourself together?" he asked. "You can talk openly with me."

I shrugged. I didn't know what to say. "It's not something I ask myself every day," I told him. "I don't want to be dick-whipped, or beat up or driven crazy, and I want out. It's pretty simple, really."

"What were you like before you were sentenced?"

"Pretty mixed up, I guess. I wanted to go to college, have a girlfriend, screw around, plus be a drug smuggler. It wasn't a life I had charted on graph paper, if you know what I mean. But I sure didn't expect to go to jail." I could feel the wine and I wanted a radio and I wanted to stand around in the middle of the floor and drift and slow dance and not talk about my life, which had kicked my butt.

"That's why I meditate," he said. "It helps me to know myself."

I really didn't want to hear about his problems. They couldn't begin to compete with mine. I looked around the room. The light filled it irregularly, in green and gray streaks. I waved my hands in front of the window and the shadows moved about like large fish in an aquarium. The wine moved through me in the same way. There was one picture on the wall of an enormous green apple that completely filled the room it was in. I caught him looking at his watch.

"Is there anyone you'd like to call?" he asked. "Don't worry about long distance."

I went into the bedroom and dialed Melissa's number in Boston. I got her machine. "Hey, honey," I said, trying to sound cheerful. Things weren't great between us, and I thought if I sounded just how I felt she would flee and not leave a forwarding address. "I got a chance to make a call and so you are the one. I miss you. I'm thinking of you. Things here are going okay. I'm fine. I'm actually on the outside having a drink. Don't worry, I'm not doing anything wrong. Wish you were here. Think of me. Love ya."

Back in the car I closed my eyes and felt the wine and wondered if I could just throw open the car door and run away. That's how Parker, the parole jumper, had done it. He was being transferred out of Morgantown. Since there were no fences at Morgantown, they didn't handcuff him in the car. But as they drove through the middle of a corn field, he opened the door and jumped out. He didn't hurt himself and hopped up and ran into the field. The guard stopped the car and stood on the side of the road shouting for Parker to come out. Said he wouldn't report him, would keep it a secret. But Parker kept running. By the time the patrol gathered to search the fields, he had made it to a small farming town. He spotted a quiet house and slipped through a basement window. He found some home-canned food and hid in an old coal bin. After two days it was Sunday. He heard the family leave for church, then went upstairs. He found the keys to their second car and fled.

What a great feeling it must have been, I thought. Just to try to escape. The desire went through me and I wondered if I might do the same. I felt I would if given the chance. But I knew that the great feeling would be preceded by the crazy feeling, like the week before when I was shaving in the shower room. The mirrors were all steamed over and I had to wipe the glass with one hand and shave with the other. The blade was dull and I unscrewed the safety razor to change it. Suddenly I was hyperventilating, and just like that I knew I was going to slit my wrists. It was as though I was predicting the action in a movie before it happened. I saw exactly what those deep pink cuts would look like all the way to the bone. I held the blade in my hand and knew I couldn't do it smoothly, but would do it more like a kid drawing wildly with a crayon, coloring all over the page at once, just thrilled with the bloody spree. I had seen a Latino guy do it that way. He snapped and must have hacked himself fifty times. We had to staple some of his cuts back together. Suddenly I was afraid for myself and embarrassed, and I threw the razor into the sink and turned and took a shower so cold my body cramped up. My throat closed and I ran out and back to my bunk, afraid to talk to anyone. I crawled under my covers and pulled them up over my head, but the darkness only drove me deeper into myself. I whipped them off and looked around the ward. At that moment I was as mad as the padded cell types.

"THANKS," I SAID TO DR. SOBEL WHEN WE pulled into the West Street parking lot. "That was real nice."

"We'll do it again," he replied. "We'll get Chinese takeout next time."

I held on to my box of x-rays and walked side by side with him toward the prison and then he held up so I could enter the front door first.

"How'd it go?" asked the door guard as I began to strip down for a search.

"Beautiful," I replied. "They miss me out there."

*   *   *

A FEW DAYS LATER I WAS THINKING ABOUT how different I felt. Dr. Sobel had treated me like a human being and I was still high from Elvis's performance. Because I was feeling so good, I thought just maybe something good might happen as a result. Maybe if I change my attitude, I reasoned, the whole world will change. It was a thought.

I was standing against the entrance to the third-floor shower room. Parker was in the back, and I was watching out for him. He removed a kitchen salt shaker from his towel and poured salt onto a piece of trouser cloth, then rubbed it forcefully over and around the tattoo on the outside of his left shoulder. The picture was of a standing woman with a tape measure stretched across her misshapen, jumbo breasts. Her name was "NANCY" and her breasts were "SIZE 44."

"Magnums," he said fondly. The picture was poorly executed, shaky like police chalk drawings of murder victims scratched on concrete sidewalks. "So long, cock tease!" he said grimly, and pressed even harder.

"You should just change the name," I suggested, while still thinking good things were coming my way. "Write your wife's in. Be a lot easier."

"Won't work," he shot back. "*You* got more chest than she does."

I looked down at my chest. It was pushed in like a dented can. I had been smoking too much. There was so little to do that it seemed as exciting as sex each time I struck a match and lipped that chilly smoke through a fresh Kool.

I scanned the corridor. Parker didn't have access to the hospital wing, so I had to meet him up on the third floor. "Hurry," I said, "I don't like it up here."

Home-applied tattoos were gruesome and we were always disinfecting botched jobs. Van Hinde, a Pennsylvania Dutch kid in for forgery, did most of the work in West Street. He used long sewing needles and wrapped them firmly with cotton thread, leaving just the point free. For ink he burned toilet paper and mixed the ash with water and ballpoint pen ink until he got the right pigment. He prepared the skin surface with a wash of Aqua Velva, then jabbed the needle repeatedly along a handdrawn blueprint while the blood drizzled out. When the pigment dried up in one needle, he dipped it back into his tin can of ink and started with another. Van Hinde used Li'l Abner gals for his models.

"Aw man, this stings," Parker hissed. He unscrewed the top of the big kitchen salt shaker and poured a mound of salt onto the cloth, then continued to grind it over "NANCY." Everyone claimed that repeated injections of buttermilk along the tattooed lines would eventually dissolve the ink, but we didn't have buttermilk and it was almost impossible to get a syringe and clean needle. So Parker clenched his teeth together and rubbed harder. It was like scrubbing the peel off a potato, and it didn't take long for the skin to wear away and blood to begin to snake down his arm and along the side of his body.

"Come over here," Parker said. "God! Lord!

Jesus!" he muttered as I scratched away the layer of salt. The flesh was rough, nappy like suede. He slapped at the wall. "This really sucks. Are you sure it works?" "You'll have to go deeper," I replied. The water bloomed red as it ran across Parker's flesh, but I could still see her breasts topped with erect baby bottle nipples. "Fuckin' Nancy!" he said, "and to think I paid for her boob job." He gritted his teeth then poured more salt on the bloody cloth, some directly on the wound, and rubbed even harder. "You got to do it for me," he said, "I can't stand the pain." He was paying me a carton of cigarettes to watch out for him and change his bandages every day. I knew he'd want his cigarettes back if he went through all of this pain then still had the tattoo.

"Just a little more," I said. "Now really dig in. You can handle it." I forced myself to sound hopeful, because I knew that once it healed the new skin would look thick and gummy, like melted cheese when it cools. They'd soon be calling him Pizza Hut.

Parker suddenly found renewed strength and pressed down hard on the cloth as the blood spun away. I wanted him to finish. We could both end up in the hole, although I would deny everything and Parker wasn't a snitch. Just as putting tattos on, sanding them off was viewed as an attempt to disguise the body through disfigurement. It was also dangerous because the open wound usually became infected as it was hard to keep clean. Still, the sanding was better than watching Parker burn the lines out with a lit cigarette, as he had done with a set of dice on his forearm. It would take a stick of Dr. Sobel's Flesh Wax to fill in those holes. I had some hydrogen peroxide and gauze bandages in my locker and was hoping I could at least keep the infection out.

Just then I saw the warden walking toward us. When he saw me he smiled and lifted his hand in recognition. *Yes*, I thought, my transfer has come through. *Unless* he spots Parker.

"Be cool," I said. Parker quickly wrapped a towel around his shoulder and kicked the salt under a stool. I stepped forward to cut off the warden's view.

"Jakes," he said, "I've got really exciting news. I talked with some other wardens, and they want Elvis to do shows at their prisons. I told them he was sensational, just like Vegas, only cheaper. So how would you like to go on the road? Be his stage manager. You know, keep an eye on him. You seem to handle him pretty well. Talk to Elvis and give it some thought."

"Yes sir," I replied. "But what about getting a caseworker? I really need to see the parole board and it's impossible to do that on the road."

"You do this Elvis thing for a few months and I'll get you a caseworker and on track," he said.

"Is that a promise?" I asked.

"You bet," he replied. "I'll take care of you." Then he winked at me.

I winked right back. "Thanks," I said. "I'll work on it." Suddenly the good things I had hoped for were going to happen. Yes, yes, yes, I thought. A road trip with Elvis and then I'll be on a road trip home.

The warden walked away and I turned and told Parker what had happened.

"Who's gonna take care of this?" he asked, nodding toward his shoulder, which had already bled through the doubled-up white towel.

"You are," I replied. "I'll get you the supplies." I checked the corridor, led him back to his bunk, and examined his arm.

"She's still with you," I said. I could see her nipples, faintly, like a constellation. "But don't worry, the scar tissue will cover it over."

"Man, I thought you claimed this would work." He was pissed. "The last time I escaped, this tattoo is how they said I could be identified. I was coming out of a grocery store and when the cops grabbed me they went straight for my shirt, ripped it off, and said, 'Gotcha, lover boy.' Then they called me 'Nancy' all the way here."

"This was your idea," I reminded him. "I'm just trying to help." I patted the area dry then quickly rubbed on an antibiotic cream over the wound. "Come see me tomorrow," I instructed him. "I'll keep it clean."

ELVIS WAS ECSTATIC WHEN I TOLD HIM about the tour. "Comeback concert 1979!" he shouted and pumped his fist in the air. "This will be great, Doc. You and me on the road. What a team. You'll be a one-man Memphis Mafia."

"Please don't call me Mafia," I said flatly. "I'd like to get out of here someday."

"I need some black leather," he said running his hands down over his hips. "Elvis loved his leather."

"I always thought of him as a black velvet man myself," I said.

His head snapped around. "Don't you dare start in with smarmy comments about Elvis. I'm not going to put up with some drug smuggler mocking my Man."

"Sorry," I replied. "It just slipped out."

"Well, honey," he said in Elvis's low, sexy voice, "put it back in your pants because we are going on the road."

I began to think about being Elvis's road manager. The travel sounded exciting compared with West Street. Plus, the warden said he would give me a hand. I was doing all I could to help myself, but one snap of his fingers and I could have an exit date. Maybe that's what he meant when he winked at me.

I WAS SLEEPING WHEN THE FLOOR GUARD woke me up. "Hurry and pack up all your stuff," he said. "They're waiting for you downstairs."

I quickly put on my clothes and grabbed the letters from Melissa and my toiletries, then followed him to Receiving and Discharge.

Elvis and Ebbers were going through the clothes closet searching for costumes. There were a lot of unclaimed outfits from the early 1970s. I'd always pictured men going to court in jackets and ties, but there was lots of fake orange fur, leather, sequins, and puckered silk. A lot of men who commit crimes dress like celebrities. One evening we would see them on the television news wearing leather and the next evening we'd see them in their cells, dressed like me.

"Just go for the funky fabrics," Elvis said to Ebbers. "I can tailor anything myself. Just make sure I have a needle and thread."

The warden was filling out our transport papers with a federal marshal. "Are we taking the bus or a car?" I asked.

"Car," the marshal replied.

"Good," I said. They locked your feet in floor cuffs on the bus.

Ebbers looked sullen but dutiful. He turned to me. "I have to do everything for him," Ebbers said. "If it wasn't for me he'd never practice or show up on time or get his costumes together or anything. I should be going with him, not you."

"Hey," Elvis said to him. "Doc here has spent time trying to heal me, not hurt me like you. Besides, I need to train a new manager since you'll be leaving soon. Once I testify for you, you'll stroll on out of here."

"You're in love with him," Ebbers said in a pout. "I've seen it before." He turned toward me. "You better watch him or you could end up like me."

"He should be so lucky," Elvis said bitterly. "Look, I'm giving you the gift of freedom. I'm letting you out of here and you treat me like this. Get it right, man. Can't you see that the greatest love you can give someone is freedom?"

Ebbers hung his head. "It's true," he mumbled, "that you're doing me a big favor. I'm just hung up on you being in love with the Doc."

I stepped in. "Look," I said, "I'm a friend of Elvis's but we are not lovers. I'm not that way. Don't worry, this is business."

"You just wait," he replied. "He has a way of getting what he wants in business *and* pleasure."

"Come on," Elvis said and rolled his eyes. "We got work to do. Now give me a hug good-bye."

I turned and walked away. When Elvis caught up to me, he put his arm around my shoulder. "You played that beautifully, man," he whispered. "You're a natural."

"I just told the truth," I replied and pushed his arm

off my shoulder. "That's all this is. We're just going on the road to do concerts."

"Every con man thinks he's telling the truth. That's what makes them great. Your natural con is that you are so sincere. People love that shit. You can't fake that sincere element in a good con. You're like me, totally honest. We'll make a great team."

I looked at him. "Are you conning *me?*"

"Nobody can con you," he replied. "You're a natural. You'll make a million with your talent."

A million, I thought. I wondered how I could turn forty grand into a million. Water into wine. But Elvis has the touch, I said to myself, stick with him.

The chains and manacles around our ankles slowed us to a shuffle. My handcuffed wrists had a foot of chain between them. A length of chain, starting from my wrist cuffs, coiled down through my belt loops and continued down to lock on to my ankle cuffs. I couldn't raise my hands above my shoulders.

"Just take your time," Officer Trout groaned. He was carrying Elvis's heavy suitcases. "Just one little baby step at a time." His large black mouth was pulled down at the corners, like his shoulders, from having to help rather than just herd us along.

Officer Jensen drew his pistol and held it flat against his thigh, more like a machete than a gun. "Move slowly toward the yellow Ford," he said from behind us.

Elvis was decked out in a silver lamé shirt and a pair of black leather bell-bottoms that were folded up inside his ankle cuffs. He walked unsteadily, as if on a high wire. I was wearing blue jeans, a denim shirt, and an old plaid car coat. The manacles hadn't fit around my cowboy boots so I took them off and hobbled over to the car in my socks.

I stared out the window as we drove off. It was a good feeling watching the city so early in the morning, seeing people eat donuts and drink coffee as they sat in diners. Simple, useful acts of waking pleasure. People being so much themselves that even the most modest gesture, the use of a napkin, the wave of a hand, the nod of a head, can say, Get to know me. And soon, maybe I *would* get to know them.

My window only rolled down an inch, but the stream of air felt cool across my face. There were lots of people about, and it seemed easy to tell the good ones from the bad ones. The bad ones were dirty and idle, with active eyes sizing up the clean people, who were occupied with thoughts of their day's responsibilities. But I knew the world of good and bad wasn't that simple, so I figured it was best to distrust all of them. I looked over at Elvis. He only dealt with being the *real* Elvis or the *fake* Elvis. I envied him. I was stuck on good and evil and a fear of never quite defining the line between them.

The traffic was light. We left the city and got on the highway heading north to Connecticut. Parker's story of escaping into the corn field kept returning to me, but it was impossible to run in the chains. In a way I was glad to have them on, as they kept me from trying something stupid. I could think about escape all I wanted, but I couldn't do anything about it.

DANBURY IS A WHITE-COLLAR PRISON FOR men who have committed nonviolent crimes and are serving less than ten years' time. There are checkpoints and watch towers with rifle ports, but the guards dress in gray slacks and blue blazers. The prisoners address them as "Mister," and the guards respond in kind. But once we were inside and unchained, we were strip-searched.

"Thank you," the guard said after I had bent over and showed him the empty crack of my ass.

"You're welcome," I replied.

Elvis's costumes were searched without wrinkling them any more than necessary, and we were assigned a prisoner escort to see us to a holding cell.

My friend Austin had been sent to Danbury. He was one of the New York distributors who had been tracked down after Harrington was caught. Austin and I had been in court together. He had also pled guilty, and he went up for sentencing just before me. The judge gave him a straight five years, which meant he had to do twenty months before he saw the parole board. That's when I knew I was going to get time. When the judge said to Austin that the entire country was disgusted with drug scum like him dealing to kids on the street, I knew I was in trouble. I got my zip six right after.

On our first night in West Street we were assigned to a large tank, D-10, for new prisoners. There were thirty-six of us in the tank and eighteen bunk beds. I was so full of fear I moved as if I were naked in freezing weather. If I didn't concentrate on holding my cigarette with three or four fingers, it dropped from my hand. It was November and bitter cold inside. There were two open bunks. I took the one on top in the corner under a light fixture. Austin was left with a bottom bunk far away in the middle of the tank.

I slept with my clothes on. I was so terrified that when a man grabbed the toe of my boot during that first night, I kicked out at him. I could see he held a dinner fork in his hand. "What do you want?" I hissed.

"Are you funny?" he asked. He was black and slender.

"What?" I didn't understand.

"Funny," he repeated. "Are you a funny boy?"

I couldn't figure out what he meant. He twisted the fork at me. I brought my leg back and was ready to kick his face with my heel. From the top bunk I figured I had the advantage. I could hold him off and holler until the guards arrived. "I don't understand," I repeated.

"Funny," he said. "You know. Funny, like your friend."

"No," I said. "I'm serious," I insisted. "I'm a serious person. Leave me alone."

"Then you better talk with your friend," he said, and just as suddenly as he arrived he slipped away into the long rows of dark bunk beds. I sat up the rest of the night, my head buzzing with fear, waiting for him or someone like him to return. No one did.

Austin didn't do so well. He was sleeping when a gang of men jumped on him, shoved a bath towel between his teeth, and took turns raping him. They gouged his back with their nails and pulled fists of hair from his head. I didn't hear a thing.

The next morning Austin avoided me. I called his name and he turned away. I noticed the dried blood down the back of his pants. "I'm sorry about last night," I said. I had heard about it from another man in the tank.

He leaned his head against the bars and cried. "I miss my wife and kid."

"Don't cry in here," I said. "Don't give these fuckers the satisfaction." I felt we should stick together because we were in on the same drug deal and knew each other on the outside. "Is there anything I can do to help?" I asked.

"Man," he said and wiped his face with his fingers. "I just want to do this time, then get out and be straight with my wife." I had seen her in court as she stared at him, their new baby in her arms, bewildered that, for the second time in his life, he was receiving a prison sentence on a drug charge. Five years before he had spent a year in Greenhaven.

That afternoon she visited him. When he returned, we sat on the edge of his bunk. He spoke softly, without inflection. His movements were carried out slowly as if each step or each precise dip of his hand were measured the way a dope dealer measures each spoon. I thought he might be on medication.

"How's your wife?" I asked, trying to make conversation.

He looked bitter. "She's leaving me," he said. "She's moving to Jamaica. I don't think I'll be seeing her again." That afternoon he was transferred to Danbury and I was sent down to C Cell House which, at that time, was referred to as the crab trap.

OUR HOLDING CELL IN DANBURY WAS MADE up like a country cottage. The metal bunk beds were carefully painted to look like knotty pine, and patchwork quilts were folded neatly at the foot of tightly made-up beds. The walls were painted light blue, the ceiling a soft white, and there was no graffiti. A painting of a sailboat in a hand-carved frame hung on one wall and a painting of a collie on another. There was a magazine rack with magazines next to a lamp and easy chair.

Elvis was wide-eyed. "And look at this," he said, pointing to two sets of new shower shoes on the floor.

"I don't get it," I replied. I looked hard at the mirror on the wall. Perhaps we were being studied through a two-way mirror.

I began to wash my socks in the small sink above the toilet. Elvis was lying across his bunk whistling "Young and Beautiful" when the warden arrived.

"Greetings, Elvis," he said through the bars. "I'm a big fan of yours."

Elvis smiled back at him. "Why thanks, warden."

"Here's the setup. Tomorrow night is movie night. We've rented *Clambake*—"

"I hate that movie," Elvis snapped. "It's gruesomely fey."

"It's not that bad a movie," the warden replied. "The men like it. There are women in it, plus it's got an upbeat attitude. Now, before the movie we want about a half-hour set. Then on Saturday we have a family day scheduled, and we want you to do another short set there. Something wholesome. Any problems with this?"

"Yeah," Elvis replied. "What about musicians? A sound system. What kind of stage setup do you have?"

"We got the best," the warden said and smiled. "We have a fantastic band here and they've been practicing some of your songs, so they can provide backup. We've got a fine sound system and a stage, so just relax."

"What about my guitar?" Elvis asked. They had taken it from him when we checked in.

"We used to have a stand-up piano but the wire kept showing up around guy's necks. Suicides," he said with a sigh. "But I'll see that you get your guitar back in time for the show."

After the warden left, Elvis turned to me. "You know, he looks like one of the Monkees. The cute little one."

"Bizarre," I remarked. "I feel like taking up knitting."

"But that *Clambake* movie can be an inspiration," he mused. "Elvis should have said *no* to making that beach blanket trash but he said *yes* and gave away his nasty sexiness, his rock an' roll black soul, and took the first step in the long slide downhill to the white bread basement of Anglo sellout. By the time he finished screwing himself on screen, there was no coming back. He had his 1968 moment, but then Vegas gassed him. He took the *pipe*. Traded his soul for rhinestones. So you know what I'm going to do?"

"What's that?"

"I'm gonna say yes to *Clambake*. Elvis should have known then to quit when he was making that shit. It's a signal to me, too. I'll only sing shit and then I'll quit. It's like heavy drinking. You only give it up after it has totally fucked up your life and you hit rock bottom. You *never* give up the bottle when you're ridin' high. And *Clambake* is the bottom."

"The guys may not like listening to shit songs," I suggested. "You're better off sticking with the hits."

"You're missing the point. I'm gonna do all the losers. So fuck 'em. I hope they riot."

AFTER BREAKFAST I WENT TO CHECK OUT the stage and make certain it was in order. Behind the curtain I spotted Austin with some other men. He was blowing scales on a trumpet. I went up to him. "Hey," I said, "how have you been?"

He looked at me sideways. "Okay," he replied,

and shook the spit from his horn. "But I really don't want to talk to you."

"Why? You don't think I ratted you out, do you?"

"No," he said. "I'm trying to get my sentence reduced. I might be able to get back with my wife, and one of the stipulations is that I never speak with or see any of the people I was in drugs with. So it's nice to see you but I'd rather not talk." He turned his back to me and blew a few jagged notes.

Jesus, I thought, it's not like the parole board is going to come down on him for bumping into prisoners while in prison. But I remembered how nasty it was when he got pumped up the ass, and figured he had a lot of fear left over.

My fear was building with Elvis planning to actually sing the soundtrack from *Clambake*. It built even more when I saw the first inmates. As soon as they passed through the door they broke rank and raced each other for the front-row seats. They turned the metal chairs around and sat backwards in them, their forearms crossed above the curved backs. But when I looked at them closely I saw they were neatly dressed in pressed khaki slacks and shirts, and they were smiling.

One of them spotted me. "I've been looking forward to this all week," he hollered.

I closed the curtain and walked over to where Elvis was strumming his guitar. "Have you changed your mind?" I asked. "I'm not convinced that singing crap is what they want."

"Hell no," he said, grinning. "I'm gonna give them

the ten worst Elvis songs ever written, and if they want an encore, which I doubt, I'll give them 'Rock-a-Hula Baby.' "

As rehearsed, I opened with a hymn. I sang, "O Lord my God! When I in awesome wonder . . ."

A man stood up. I looked at his hands to see what he was going to throw. But he crossed them over his heart and joined in.

I looked up at heaven. ". . . Consider all the worlds Thy hands have made . . ."

I pressed on, and by the time I finished, half the room was singing along with me. The band, which was set up on risers to my left, came to a ragged stop. The horn section sounded like a traffic jam, but they received a standing ovation. I shook my head. "And now," I announced, "I present to you the one, the only *true* Elvis Presley!" I turned to the stage entrance and waited with a big smile plastered across my face, my arm extended. "Elvis Presley!" I shouted again and marched across the stage. He was standing just behind the curtain, watching me, smiling, lanky.

"Get the fuck out there," I said.

"You're doing a great job of warming them up," he replied slyly, and gave me his practiced sneer.

"Your knack for sarcasm is gonna get you killed," I snapped back.

"Let it be a lesson to me," he said, then slowly shuffled his way onto the stage to a combination of cheers and catcalls.

"Good afternoon," he said flatly. "I've made a bunch of fucked-up movies in my career and I just want to sing some of the worst, most humiliating, dick-sucking songs I know."

The audience was momentarily stunned. Then Elvis struck the first chords and sang some Louisiana trash, "I saw three shrimp in the water, two were old and gray..."

Some laughed. Some booed. Some cheered. Some even sang along. Maybe he can't bomb, I thought. Maybe just being Elvis gives you a built-in safety net. I breathed a little easier, and still felt that good things were headed my way.

Then Elvis followed with "There's no room to rhumba in a sports car..." He didn't even move when he sang. No hip shaking, no wiggling, no splits, not even a sex-crazed swoon. And the crowd loved him. Half the men sang along. The warden must have been an Elvis freak, I thought. He must have rented all of those insipid, happy-go-lucky Elvis movies to show in prison.

When Elvis came off stage he was shaking his head. "Shit," he spit, and swung the guitar at a pillar.

"Don't!" I grabbed it.

"I don't care," he said ruefully. "I gave my worst performance ever, and they still liked me. They thought I was a comedian."

"Don't get down on yourself," I said. "I think you can find a way to sink lower. You can always sing his Christmas album."

AFTER A WEEK OF SITTING AROUND OUR guest cell in Danbury like an old married couple, Elvis and I were returned to West Street. My pal Parker was living alone in a two-man cell on the third floor. There were only three of these small cells on the floor, and they were generally considered a luxury and were snapped up by the strongest men. The hospital ward had been made off-limits because a New York cop, turned informant against corrupt cops, was being kept there. The warden didn't want anyone around the cop, since his life had been threatened and they wanted him to live to testify in court. They didn't want to anger him by putting him in a private isolation cell, so they gave him the next best thing to a suite of rooms: the entire hospital ward.

Elvis returned to his previous padded cell, and I was bumped into population. The second bunk in Parker's cell was empty and I moved in.

"How'd you get this cell?" I asked.

"Pull," he answered, meaning vaguely that he had either paid for it or kissed ass. Everyone knew there was no such thing as pure "pull." Pure pull meant you owned the warden; that he answered to you. Pull usually meant cashing one favor in for another, kissing up to a guard, or, worse, getting pay back for ratting out another prisoner. Pull *never* meant you got something for free.

After I had settled in, Parker asked me to check his shoulder. He had made bandages by tearing the sheets into strips.

"Don't let anyone see you ripping sheets," I warned him. "They'll think you're making a rope."

I unwrapped his shoulder and didn't like what I saw. The scab was unformed and the swollen wound was spongy with a membrane of cheesy pus. When I touched around the wound's furious edge, he pulled away in pain. "I'll take you down to see Dr. Sobel tomorrow," I told him. "But we'll have to ask him not to tell anyone."

"Okay. You take care of me and I'll take care of you," he said, alluding to his "pull."

I wrapped the shoulder with fresh bandages, then went to sleep. I woke up some time later when I heard Parker making hacking noises as though he was chopping cocaine with a razor on a mirror. When I looked down on him I saw he was using a kitchen fork to examine his shit, which was piled up in a hard plastic cereal bowl. He was going through it carefully, a section at a time, breaking it away and mashing it before flicking it into the toilet bowl.

"What are you doing?" I whispered.

I caught him by surprise. "Just don't look," he shot back. "Just turn over and I'll tell you about it later."

In a few minutes the toilet flushed, then he told me that his wife had visited him last week. She had put a piece of hash in five separate balloons and fed them to him when the guard turned away. "But it was so disgusting," he said. "She coated each balloon with Vaseline to make it easier, but it was like swallowing garden slugs. Man, I had to cut the visit short 'cause I thought I'd ralph 'em up in front of the guard."

I had never smuggled drugs that way. I knew a woman who carried three ounces of cocaine from Bogotá to New York in her vagina. It was a regular route for her. I had read in the newspaper about men who swallowed condoms of cocaine. One guy's stomach acid dissolved the condoms just as he was passing through customs. He collapsed and died of an overdose.

"The hash won't hurt you," I told him. "But you probably won't shit for a while."

He grunted. "I'll give you some if you help me get to it."

Suddenly I had a little pull with Parker. "I'll see what I can do."

In the morning I checked in at the hospital.

"Hey, buddy," Mr. Bow said and slapped me across the back and smiled. "We missed you around here."

"I missed it myself," I said. "This place feels more like home."

"Even I know this place should *never* feel like home," he said. "But I know what you mean."

The chest x-rays had backed up, and Mr. Bow kept a steady stream of men in front of my machine. I spent the rest of the morning developing the x-rays in the darkroom. As arranged, Parker met me in the lab at lunchtime. Dr. Sobel was waiting for us. I unwrapped Parker's arm and explained how he had sanded off the tattoo with salt. "I won't lie to you," I said. "This is my fault, too."

Parker had a nervous way about himself. He always came off looking like a weasel. "My wife said looking at Nancy's big tits was ruining our sex life," he said. "I was only trying to help her out."

Sobel didn't encourage this line of thinking.

"And I'm worried about it spreading into the muscle," I said. Dr. Sobel agreed, and after conducting his own examination, he left the office and returned with a two-week supply of penicillin.

"Give him one four times a day," he said to me. "And make sure he takes them, or I'll write him up for this."

"I won't do it again," Parker said apologetically.

"Please don't," Dr. Sobel said sternly, "because if I don't get to you first, your arm will rot off in the hole." He wasn't just trying to frighten Parker. It was true that medical problems were ignored when punishment was being carried out. Once I had seen a prisoner brought up from the hole with a bone infection in his left calf. He had been shot when first arrested, and placed in an outside hospital. But when he tried to escape, he was brought to West Street and put in solitary. After sixty days of isolation he was finally given medical attention. The bone had atrophied from infection. He was rushed to a hospital, and his femur and tibia were shortened by an inch. The extra muscle sagged down around his ankle and gave him an elephant foot.

When we left Dr. Sobel's office, I brought Parker into the x-ray room and turned on the fluoroscope. We weren't supposed to use it because of the amount of radiation it leaked. "Quick, lift up your shirt and drop your pants," I said. He did and slipped behind the screen. I couldn't spot the hash and had him take a deep breath and move his stomach around like a belly dancer. I held a mirror up for him to watch as his organs swelled and released. His abdomen was filled with lumpy shit and it was difficult to tell which dark shadows might be the balloons. "Now suck your gut way in," I instructed. He did, and I spotted the lumps. They were dark and pressed together like a map of Africa.

"Oh man," he groaned. "It all looks like something you see in a swamp."

That evening when I returned from work, I gave Parker a present. "Something I found unchained," I said and tossed it toward him. He opened the small box and removed a plastic bottle with a long nipple on top. The label was printed in bright red. Hospital Disposable Enema.

"Thanks," he replied. "You're a four-square guy."

After dinner I made a deck of cards out a stack of Our Lady of Guadalupe religious cards I had found in the chaplain's office. We played hearts until the white lights were turned off.

"I'm gonna use that thing now," he whispered. I knew he wanted some privacy. I climbed up onto my bunk and waited a few minutes until I heard him pull his pants off. I peeked over the edge of my mattress and stared out between the bars and into that blue-tinted darkness. The televisions in the thirty-man tanks were turned off, and most of the men were smoking bedtime cigarettes. The embers glowed like fireflies. Their shadowed faces were blue and damp as clay. Layers of smoke curled loosely around the bars and drifted upward toward the ceiling and took on a radiant cobalt tinge. When the ventilators kicked in, the clouds of smoke floated across the ceiling like a gang of ghosts.

I looked down on Parker to see how he was doing. He set the enema upright on the floor and held it steady with one hand as he squatted down over it until the nipple was well inside him. Then, with one hand still holding the bottle in place, he tilted forward on his knees.

"Take your time," I whispered. "Squeeze it gently every few minutes."

"Man, just don't watch," he said, annoyed, his other hand waving awkwardly back at me. He hobbled over to the toilet and sat down.

Just then the floor guard walked up to our tank. "Jakes," he whispered. "You awake?"

I waited a few seconds. "Yeah."

He unlocked the cell. "They want you in x-ray."

When I got down there, I saw that the informer cop had a nasty gash across his skull and blood was running through his curly black hair and down off his nose and chin. His eyes were dilated. He was slumped down in my desk chair, his mouth working to breathe.

"Did you give him anything?" I asked and turned on the x-ray machine.

"Don't worry," Mr. Bow replied. "He's almost unconscious."

"You should give him something," I said. "He looks bad."

"I said he doesn't need anything," Mr. Bow repeated.

It took four of us to get the cop into position across the x-ray table. He was a big man. The blow had left him speechless, but he could squirm. When I developed the shot I was pretty sure I detected a head fracture, but the image was slightly blurred because he had jerked around.

"Should I take a second shot?" I asked.

"No," said Mr. Bow. "He'll be fine. His head isn't swelling up enough."

"What about calling Dr. Sobel?"

"No need," Mr. Bow said.

I looked at the cop's head. It was dented. The furrow was deep enough to plant seeds. "What hit him?" I asked. "He was by himself."

"Mop wringer handle," replied a cell guard I had never seen before.

"The same one you're holding?" I asked.

"Evidence," he said coldly. "He must've got too close to the bars and someone reached in and gave him a wacky."

I didn't say any more. Guards are cops, too, I thought. Nobody likes a snitch. I shut my machine down, and they dragged the cop upstairs.

When I returned to my cell, Parker was lying in bed. He winked at me. "Everything is cool," he said.

"Except for the smell," I replied. I washed my face and hands, then climbed up into my bunk.

"Look under your pillow." I did and found a gram of hash. It smelled nasty. There was no possible way to smoke it. I popped it into my mouth and swallowed it whole.

I ATE A LOT OF HASHISH WHILE WE WERE sailing the boat to New York. I had brought along a pipe, and when we first went to sea, I smoked as much as I wanted. But I soon began to eat the hash instead. It was much easier than trying to light matches in the wind, and the effects were amazingly potent. In the beginning I cut gram-size pieces off the kilo block I kept in my duffle bag. As the days passed, I ate more and more. After three weeks of sailing I had gotten up to eating about an ounce a day. It didn't seem to affect my sailing ability, and with little else to do, it seldom occurred to me just how high I was.

The night we moored in Flushing, I sat in the cabin and listened to the radio. Harrington was once again asleep in his cabin, and I sang along with the radio, a word or two behind on the rock and roll songs I hadn't memorized. I ate a few grams of hash and then shaved some more off my kilo with my boating knife. I kept shaving the kilo until I had a pile the size of a salt shaker. I sang and looked through the sailing magazine I had earlier bought on shore and smoked some of the powdered hash in a pipe. I got up, fixed some soup, ate more hash, read, sang, smoked, and repeated myself. At some point I passed out.

I awoke without reason. The cabin was unlit except for the reflected light that came in through the portholes. When I opened my eyes, I felt a sharp rip behind them. My entire body was in great pain, nothing like the rapid adrenaline fear of being too high, but something physical like bad cramps, or scalding water. I thought I would move about to distract my mind, but when I sat up, an incredibly sharp pain in my head, like a snapped bone, stopped me. I lay back on the couch. I closed my eyes and tried to wait it out. But the pain grew in intensity, just as something grows larger as it approaches.

I had to take a piss, so I lifted my legs and dragged my body forward until I was on all fours. I twisted myself around until I faced the ladder that led to the upper deck. I groped at the ladder, and after a struggle, I made it to the top. I heard the sounds of distant motors, the waves touching the boat, and the whistling wind. I tried to stand, but fell over on my side against the boom. The harbor lights were as shiny as hot glass, and boats sped by, throwing up enormous wakes that rocked the yacht and jerked it around at its mooring. I reached the rope railing with my hands, pulled myself up and stood there flat footed, legs apart, trying to balance myself, trying to pull down my pants and trying to unscramble my hallucinations. I pushed my pants down and began to piss and it felt like it should, warm and starting out from below my belly. I pissed for as long as I could and it felt good, so I stood and peeked out over the water and saw a blue light that I fixed on. That blue light suddenly took off like a rocket, and I clutched the railing and felt myself being launched in some direction, like the feeling of falling unexpectedly into a hole, only this time the hole was over my head. I hollered and fell backward. I hit the deck hard and felt it rotating and wobbling.

In the morning I woke up facedown, and all day I could barely function. Harrington was annoyed with me. I figured out that I must have had about two ounces of hash. I told myself to give it up, and for a few days I did quit. But slowly I worked my way back to it.

"YOU FEEL IT YET?" PARKER ASKED. I DID, and I watched the blue light above my bed and tried to get that drifty feeling back, to be so high I didn't know where I was.

"Yeah," I said quietly.

In the morning, I was still high. I ate breakfast and went down to the hospital. In the hallway, I passed the usual half dozen men who were waiting for their chest x-rays. I rushed them through, then took their blood. I had to concentrate on exactly what I was doing, otherwise my attention drifted and I caught myself staring at the technical pictures in a medical magazine instead of loading new film into the x-ray cases.

When Dr. Sobel dashed into the lab, he grabbed me by my arm and pulled me aside.

"What's wrong?" I asked.

"Where's that cop's head shot from last night?" he whispered. I took him into the darkroom. "Close the door," I said, and flicked on the red developing light. I gave him the x-ray and he held it against the light and squinted.

"What's up?" I asked.

"That cop can't speak," he said. "He's had a stroke from a blood clot, and he's lost half his left-side motor coordination."

"Looks pretty hard for him to testify."

"No kidding. Look," he said. "Slip this shot between all the chest shots and let's go downtown. I want to have this looked over by a pro."

The moment he left, the warden dashed into the lab. "Do you have the head shot from last night?" he asked. He seemed a little nervous.

"Sure," I said. I went over to the files and pulled out a head shot from when some nut had set his hair on fire and tried to put it out by banging his skull against the bars. I handed it to him. He smiled.

"Thanks," he said and glanced at it. He didn't know what he was looking at.

"Do you think I could see a caseworker and parole board anytime soon?" I asked and handed him a large manila envelope, so no one would see him leaving with the shot. "I'm still waiting. You said before that if I helped with Elvis, you'd help me out."

He slipped the x-ray into the envelope. "I'll check into it today and see where we are," he said. Then he left.

Dr. Sobel opened my door. "Hurry," he said. "I squeezed in an appointment with the radiologist."

I grabbed my x-ray box and we walked downstairs to Receiving and Discharge. He signed me out, and we raced to the hospital.

Dr. Wong, the radiologist, was waiting for us. I gave him the head shot and he examined it. "A bit blurry," he remarked.

"He squirmed," I explained.

"But it's clearly a fracture." He pointed it out for us. The break paralleled the natural expansion line of the skull. "He took a hard blow."

I walked with Dr. Sobel to his car. When I got in I realized I was becoming more high. Sometimes the hash takes a while to break down, and now I felt that it was just peaking.

We went back to his apartment.

"Here's what I'm thinking," he said, pacing back and forth. "That cop was nailed by one of the guards and then they let him lie there all night long without calling me so that he would get worse, and he did. Now I don't know what to do. Should I blow the whistle or just let it pass?"

I drifted off.

"What's wrong with you today?" Dr. Sobel asked. I turned toward him. I felt as though I was being called away from a dream.

"Oh, just thinking about my girlfriend," I replied, trying to recover.

"Something wrong?"

"Hard to tell," I said. "I think she's at the end of her rope." I was bluffing.

"You seem really depressed," he said.

I didn't want him to guess that I was high, so I just tried to appear moody. "Don't worry," I said. "Once we have a little time together we'll work everything out."

He went into the kitchen and returned with a bottle of sake and two glasses. "You know," he said, "I chose to work in the prisons. I could be working anywhere, but I chose the prisons because I thought I could make a medical difference. But this is political, and it boils down to if I have the balls to go up against the system."

"Take my advice," I said. "I went up against the system and now I'm doing a possible six years. They're tougher than I ever thought. You're outnumbered and they are sneaky. Don't take them on just now. Wait for your moment and then put it to them. You know what I mean?" The hash was making my thoughts fade, and I wasn't sure I was making sense.

Dr. Sobel looked away in thought. "You're right," he said quietly, then fell silent. I didn't want to go back to the prison just yet. "Hey," I said cheerfully. "What about that Chinese food you promised?"

He glanced at his watch and jumped up. "I'll call them. They're just around the corner. Do you like shrimp or pork?"

"Shrimp."

I finished off my glass and poured another.

"I think you should just let this x-ray thing drop,"

I said again. "You can't afford all this high-minded stuff. The guy's a cop to boot."

"But he's a human being," Dr. Sobel said. "As human as any of the prisoners who have done even worse things in some cases."

"Yeah, but after a few months in prison, Old Testament justice rules."

"I know, but I'm supposed to be above all that."

"Then just think about it carefully," I said. "Once you blow the whistle, they'll flip."

"Okay," he said. "You're right. I've got to think it through carefully. After all, I can't prove anything. I don't know if a guard hit him. All I really know is that they neglected to call me when it happened. It could have just been bad judgment."

"It will be hard to prove otherwise," I said. "You'll draw attention to the case but nothing more. You've got no proof."

"You're right," he said. "But I'll be watching them. For now I'll just stand pat."

The buzzer rang. "The chopsticks are in the kitchen drawer," he hollered over his shoulder as he opened the door. I stood up quickly and felt the sake in my head and legs.

DR. SOBEL AND I DIDN'T SPEAK UNTIL HE pulled the car into the West Street parking lot. "Look," he said quietly, pursing his lips together. "You really helped me out today with this x-ray thing. And I know you have problems with your girlfriend." I nodded and he continued. "So maybe I can help you. Maybe we can work out a furlough visit. I could take you out and then drop you off with your girlfriend so you'd have some privacy. You guys probably need to work out some stuff, and that visit-ingroom is a bad place to do it. What do you think of that?"

"That'd be great," I said. "Man, that would really help. We aren't getting along too well and some time alone is just what the doctor ordered."

"Well let me know soon," he replied. "It takes a few days to get the paperwork in on a furlough."

I went back to the x-ray lab and stood quietly in the dark developing room. I had to find a place to hide the cop's head shot. A place no one would find even if they took the room apart. I felt for the trash can with my foot. I turned it over and stood on it. I pulled apart one of the joints in the galvanized vent pipe over the developing tank. I rolled up the x-ray and slid it into the pipe, then put everything back together. I stepped down off the trash can, then sat on it with my head spinning between my hands.

BEFORE I COULD GET BACK TO DR. SOBEL about the furlough, Elvis and I left West Street for the big federal penitentiary at Lewisburg. Once again we were assigned to Trout and Jensen. They were annoyed because they also had to transport Marchers, a spent junkie who was in for passing counterfeit money. They were taking him as far as Lewisburg, and other marshals would take him from there to Lexington for the heroin cure.

We were somewhere in Pennsylvania when Marchers threw up on the floor between his feet. It smelled like battery acid. His methadone was wearing off.

"Shit," Trout groaned. "Can't you do that out the window?"

When Marchers had first come in to the West Street hospital he was high. "What are you in for?" I asked as I took his x-ray.

"See this vein?" he said, pointing to a short black vein on the top side of his hand. "It's paved with gold. You hear me? Gold!" A good buck bought him ten bad ones, and he used the counterfeit money to buy the junk.

Marchers slumped over onto Elvis, then spit up some blood.

"Just relax man," Elvis said calmly. "Just be cool."

He stroked his back and neck. "We'll get you some help."

"A freak and a junkie and a drug smuggler," Jensen said bitterly. "You're all worthless human scum."

When Trout spotted a blue road sign for a hospital, he took the turn. "We can have him checked out here," he said reluctantly.

We started down a country road.

"If he doesn't get something soon he'll mess in his pants," I said. That remark worried Trout. He stepped on the gas.

The road became more heavily wooded on both sides. Marchers continued to moan and gag.

"Hospital Zone. Quiet!" read a sign as we passed through a set of open iron gates bordered by a high brick wall on both sides.

"What kind of hospital is this?" Trout asked. No one knew. We continued up another long driveway until we reached the entrance to what appeared to be a shabby estate. The hedges were unkempt, and the swimming pool was empty and filled with rotting leaves. We saw some people walking around dressed in white gowns, with hats on their heads, tight like bathing caps, and white air filters over their mouths and noses. I couldn't tell if they were male or female.

"Check it out," Jensen said in a scared voice. He pointed to a partially shuttered window on the second floor where a few others dressed the same way had gathered.

"Emergency Room in Rear," read another sign. Around back a man dressed in a black suit with a filter over his mouth and rubber gloves on his hands was waiting for us. Jensen pulled up next to him.

"I'm Dr. Hamm. What can I do for you?" the man asked. His voice was muffled.

"I'm a federal marshal," Trout explained and held out his badge. "I've got a sick prisoner who needs some methadone treatment."

"Treatment," echoed Jensen derisively. The doctor ignored him.

"We don't stock methadone," he said.

"Say, man, just what is this place?" Jensen asked.

"It's a state-run TB sanitorium," he replied. The patients had begun to approach the car and peer into the windows.

"I don't want no fucking TB," Jensen said under his breath.

"I'm hip," replied Trout.

"One minute," Dr. Hamm said. He went back inside and we continued to watch the patients as they watched us. A few of them waved. I waved back. They could probably escape if they wanted to. Just walk away and go find a peaceful place to die. They were worse off than I was but they didn't seem angry. As Elvis said, when you still have your life, you have hope. I guessed that's what they had. Hope. It made me think I should keep hoping that things would get better.

The doctor returned and gave Marchers two pills and a paper cup of water.

"I got cramps," Marchers said to the doctor after closely examining the pills. They looked like Libriums. "Can't you do better than this?"

"What's the charge?" Jensen asked when Marchers handed back the empty cup. There wasn't one. The doctor slipped Trout an envelope of pills and we pulled away.

LEWISBURG WAS BUILT TO HOLD AND PUNISH nonrehab career criminals. They were there for a long time, and they didn't give a shit about anything but tattoos, pumping iron, playing cards, and surviving their sentences. We were strip-searched and run through a metal detector, then hustled into a cell made out of riveted boiler plate. Before we could unpack, the warden came down and told us to get ready. "You're on in an hour," he said. "And no funny stuff. I won't put up with anything that promotes drugs or violence. I'll give you the hook in a New York second. Got it?"

"As you know," Elvis said arrogantly, "I don't cotton to drugs and violence. Richard Nixon made me a DEA agent."

"Just don't fuck up," the warden advised, and marched off.

"You know," I said when the warden had turned the corner, "I think you ought to do the good material."

"Nooo," he whined. "There's something in the air here. Something evil. Something painful. This might be just the blowout I need to quit." He poked himself hard in the chest. "I need the Elvis kicked clear out of me, and I think this is the place to do it."

"Think about it," I said. I didn't need my head kicked in. "This is a very serious prison."

"Hey," he replied, dropping into his husky, southern croon. "Nobody tells the King what to do."

He propped his hand on his hip and lowered his head and looked out at me through his eyebrows. "You just don't get it, do you? I'm the boss and you're not."

I didn't want to argue with him when his head swelled up and he thought he *was* Elvis. "Just think about where you are and what your audience wants," I said. "This isn't Carnegie Hall."

In less than an hour I was on the stage singing "How Great Thou Art." A lifer with a harmonica was my accompaniment. Halfway through, a man with a bandanna tied back over his head jumped up and yelled, "I came to hear Elvis, not his sweet-boy flunkie." A guard was on him in a moment and led him away. "I don't want to listen to this lame shit anyway," he hollered over his shoulder. "Put me in lockup. Just get me away from this fuckin' racket."

I cut my song short and announced Elvis as quickly as I could. He stepped out from behind the curtain looking as though the blood had been drained out of him. The guitar hung around his neck like a rock, and he had his hands shoved down into the pockets of his boxy shantung jacket. He was putting on the indifferent act and I was hoping it was just going to be an opening mood before he turned on the charm. As I passed him he curled his lip and whispered, "I've seen worse crowds in Vegas."

Then he turned to the audience and stood there staring out at them, judging them, teasing them with a little wiggle of his hips. He jerked his head to one side and groaned. "Jesus, you guys are the biggest bunch of losers I've ever laid eyes on, so I'm gonna sing you your theme song." Then before they could figure out what was going on, he started up with "What a Wonderful Life." Then for no reason at all he began to whistle and trill and tap out a bongo beat on the belly of the guitar. He looked out at them, smiling, daring them to act up.

Suddenly a man sprinted down the center aisle like an assassin. He sprang up on the stage and ran directly at Elvis. "Home boy!" he hollered.

My God, I thought. It's a second Elvis.

He had the black speedboat hairdo and was wearing a white kitchen outfit, cheap white shoes, and a little white cape. "Give to me that git-tar," he said to Elvis in an exaggerated southern drawl. "And let me show you how it's done."

"Get the fuck off my stage," Elvis sneered and slapped his hand away.

"Then let's duet," the man bargained. "The early Elvis versus the later Elvis. How 'bout it, battlin' 'Hound Dog's?" He turned to the audience and pumped his fist in the air. "How 'bout it? Duelin' Elvises?"

The crowd loved it. The guards moved closer, a bit

confused. They may have thought this was part of the show.

My Elvis slapped his double across the face. "Duet that!" he cracked. "And get your ugly nonsinging ass off my stage."

Someone in the audience hollered. "It's the battle of the Elvis impersonators!" The auditorium broke into laughter and boos.

"Git him, Hal," someone hollered out. "Grab him by the hair and show 'em who's the real King!"

Elvis wheeled around. He grabbed his crotch and gave it a tug. "Suck my cock," he shouted to everyone in general. "You all are good at that I bet. You cum-sippin' butt-lickin' losers."

I ran onto the stage and grabbed Elvis by the collar of his jacket.

"Come back!" the Lewisburg Elvis beckoned as I steered Elvis away. "Let me play your guitar."

"Fuck you," Elvis hollered and then shot everyone the bird. "Fuck all of you," he yelled.

I hooked my arm around his throat and yanked him off his feet. "Shut the fuck up," I shouted. "I don't want to die with you."

The guards behind the curtain and along the aisles ran onto the stage and stood between Elvis and the men. Two more guards shoved us backstage, through a door, and down a corridor into the Discharge office. We were put into chains and escorted to Trout's yellow Ford.

"What about my costumes?" Elvis protested through the car window.

"We'll mail them to your next gig," a guard cracked, and we pulled out, just two hours after we had arrived.

ON THE WAY BACK WE STOPPED IN WASHINGTON, Pennsylvania, for the night. Trout checked us in to the local prison. It was a soot-streaked Victorian structure with a portcullis and crenelated towers. "See you in the morning," he said after the paperwork was complete. Elvis and I were led up to separate cells.

" 'Night," Elvis said. "Thanks for saving my butt."

"Next time," I replied, "when you want to die, do it by yourself."

"I don't want to die. I just want the Elvis kicked out of me."

"Where do we go next?" I asked Elvis. "Atlanta?"

"Home," he said, "Memphis. This is it for me."

"Home? What do you mean?"

"There's something I didn't tell you," he said shyly. "I made a deal before I agreed to do this Elvis tour."

"Deal?"

"Yeah, with the warden. They cut some time off my sentence. The prisons are overcrowded. If you have a nonviolent crime and can come up with a reasonable offer, you can get out."

"What about me?"

"You'll have to make your own deal," he said.

"With what?"

"It'll come along. You got to be patient. A good con artist takes advantage of any situation," he said.

"Something will come along, and its up to you to milk it."

"I've been waiting," I said. My voice tightened. I could feel the hurt in my throat. "You should have told me about this. I've worked just as hard as you. Christ, I could be getting out too."

"Be patient and wait for your moment," he advised, and put his arm around my shoulder. "The moment will come, and when it does, you gotta go for it."

He stepped into his cell and I went into mine. The floor guard pulled a lever and the gates slammed shut.

It was hot, and I stood by the window to get the breeze. In the distance were a row of small houses that looked like the salt and pepper shakers I had once won at a carnival. A religious radio show was coming through a metal wall speaker in the cell. The preacher was saving sinners. He asked them their names and their sins or ailments. Each life story was pathetic, filled with immense pain and suffering. "Well, my friend," boomed the preacher. "Close your eyes and think of Jesus' face on that cross of pain. Look at his hands. The blood. Touch the spikes in his hands and feet. YOU have killed him. YOU! YOU! YOU!" Suddenly the preacher began to speak in tongues. It sounded like an epileptic fit, and then he snapped out of it and you could hear the wet slap he gave the sinner across the face and the sinner crying out, "I saw the pure light shining in God's eyes!" I could picture the scene exactly. When I was a kid I used to watch those shows on television and imagine false ailments and how I would be saved from my hunchback or blindness through a miracle. I loved being saved, and when the preacher slapped an invalid, I'd close my eyes and fall back onto the couch. I thought of the reverend's hand slapping my face and knocking the bad Ray out of me. But now I didn't see angels or stars or heaven. I wasn't saved or free or even a better person. I just fell back onto my bunk and lay there waiting for sleep.

WHEN I RETURNED TO WEST STREET I told Dr. Sobel that I wanted the furlough visit with Melissa. "You were right," I said quietly. "I think it will help us." I could tell he was pleased with himself.

"I'll go down to the warden's office and fill out the forms," he said. "Why don't you use the phone and give her a call?"

His was the only phone I liked to use. It was a direct line outside — you didn't have to pass through the switchboard.

Melissa answered. "Hello?"

"It's Ray."

"Where are you?" she asked. "Boston?"

"I wish. But guess what? I've worked out a furlough."

"Really?"

"I can't wait," I said. "I've really missed you."

"Are you coming to Boston?"

"No, you'll have to come here."

"I don't have the money," she said.

"No problem," I whispered. "Just go to Al's office and get what you need."

"Are you sure?" she asked.

"Absolutely," I replied. "I really *miss* you." .

"Well you just let me know what you need and I'll be there," she said. "Champagne. Chocolates. Me."

"I love you," I sighed. "But I have to go for now. I'll call you back when I get the details."

"I know you've gone through hell," she said. "But we'll get through this."

"We will," I said. "I know it's been rough on you, too. But this will help us both."

When I put down the phone I spotted my file on Dr. Sobel's desk. I flipped open the folder, hoping to find a letter from the warden to the parole board, requesting my release. My work report from Mr. Bow was full of praise. Dr. Sobel had written a note asking for my minimum-security status so I could travel to the hospital. And then I found something curious. It was a letter from the judge responding to my request for a sentence reduction. My lawyer had told me to file for a prisoner's appeal. I had, but when I hadn't heard back, I'd figured the courts were just clogged. But the judge had denied my request over two months ago. What was worse was a letter from the prosecutor, Mr. Tierney. He had filed a petition asking the parole board to give me the maximum sentence. He called me unrepentant, and suggested I complete at least forty-eight months. My head started reeling.

I flipped through the rest of the papers. The warden had no response to the letter. He hadn't written me up for my work with Elvis. There were no letters about where I would be sent. Nothing. It was clear that if I wanted out, I would have to do it myself. I put the file away and slipped through the door. My heart was pounding. Stay calm, I said to myself. Just think slowly and clearly. One step at a time. As Elvis said, I had to find my moment.

I was lying in bed listening to Parker. He was talking about life in Canada when the escape plan hit me. It was perfect, simple and clean. A dream escape. I'd instruct my lawyer to give Melissa $2,000 in cash. Then after Dr. Sobel dropped me off with her for a couple of sweet hours, I'd tell her I had to go back to West Street. I'd take my cash and a taxi to the airport, where my ticket would be waiting at the airline counter. I'd be in Canada before they began to search for me, and then after things cooled down I'd send for her. It was a smooth plan. I wouldn't be leaping off roofs or climbing fences or jumping out of cars. None of that sloppy physical stuff. No. It's all a confidence game. I'd just walk out of here, in plain sight, with a big grin and everyone's blessing. That's how it could be done. I could con my way out with my sincerity as collateral. Just like Elvis said, I'm a natural.

"TELL ME MORE ABOUT CANADA," I SAID TO Parker. I was searching my pubic hairs for crabs, again. Every time I was put in population, another family of them camped out around my cock. I didn't want Melissa to spot them and blow our evening in paradise.

"What?"

I had to speak up. He only had one good ear. The other looked like a piece of dried apple. He had passed out at a party and someone stuck a firecracker in his ear and lit it. "That woke me the fuck up," he had said with a sick grin.

Parker was sixteen when he was first arrested for bank robbery. He stole his uncle's business key to the night deposit box of a Providence bank. He opened it up and taped a bag to the inside money chute, then locked it back up. He hid and watched as people drove up, dropped their money in, and drove away. When Parker finished his last cigarette, he opened the depository, untaped the bag, and began to walk home. "Hold it right there," a cop ordered, stepping out from behind a hedge. Someone had noticed the bag and called the police.

"I just kept walking," Parker said. "I still couldn't hear much and I had a big bandage around half my head. It wasn't until he tapped me on the shoulder that I knew I had been tagged. He scared the crap outa me."

For that job Parker got two years in a youth center. The time he escaped, he was being transferred out of Morgantown. Another bank job had been traced back to him. Not handcuffed, he had jumped out of the car and taken off through the corn field.

"How much time did you have left?" I asked him.

"About six months," he said.

"Then why'd you chance it?"

"I don't know," he said, flipping through a magazine. "I didn't plan it. I was young and they were getting close to figuring out that I had done a number of bank jobs. When we drove through that corn field was the first moment I thought of jumping, and two seconds later I jumped. It was that quick."

After they caught him, he did another year in Danbury, then went out on parole and violated that with a drug possession misdemeanor. That's when he moved to Canada for two years. But he got caught after his wife became pregnant. She wanted to have the baby in Providence where her mother lived, so she left Canada in her seventh month. When she gave birth, she called him, and he drove down. The baby was a girl, and they were full of love and happiness, except for the wife's parents. They didn't think Parker's past and future as a father looked good enough for their daughter. So they called the FBI and had him picked up for the parole violation. He was sent to West Street and had been waiting to go to a penitentiary for over a year, but it was unlikely he would go, since he was soon going to the parole board for the second time and would probably catch a release date in a few months. He was already calling himself a short timer. "But I need insurance," he said. "I need to let these assholes know I've turned my life around." He had applied to a few auto repair schools to make himself look rehabilitated.

"Look at this," he said, and showed me a picture of his wife and child. "This is how I want to spend my future."

I didn't understand how anyone could devote his life to what I saw in the photograph. She looked like the type of slack-assed woman you see drifting up and down grocery store aisles with a screaming kid on each spreading hip.

"I love this lady." He kissed the photograph. "And

I love my baby, an' I'm gonna spend my life with them."

I looked at my watch and jumped down from my bunk. "It's time to take your penicillin," I announced, and held it out in front of him. "Then I'll check your bandage."

I unwrapped the gauze around his shoulder. The scab from the tattoo removal was thick and crusty like the sole of a shoe, and I tapped at it with my fingernail.

"What's it like living in Canada?" I asked, changing the subject as I rubbed an antibiotic cream around the edge of the scab.

"Why? You thinking of going?"

"Just interested."

"Well, for one thing, there's a lot less heat," he said. "People mind their own business. If you hurry up, I'll show you some pictures." I finished quickly. He opened his locker and removed a tattered envelope stuffed with photographs. We sat on his bed and he showed me the first one.

"This is where I lived," he said. "It's *the* place to live in Toronto." The picture showed a large apartment high-rise, an old building with large windows and copper trim. The grounds were well kept. It resembled a hotel with a lot of taxis in front and a doorman. "The cops couldn't bust anyone there without us knowing it," he explained, pointing out the doorman. "He'd call us when our connections or buyers came and warn us if the cops were hanging around."

The next photograph showed him dressed like a

pimp in an orange suit and black fur coat. He leaned against a powder blue Cadillac. Through the tinted windshield was the vague image of a woman's face. "My wife's in there," he said. "You can't see the Chinese in the back seat, but they were some bad dudes, man. You could clean up in that city," he said knowingly. "People there got lots of money and nothing to do with it."

In the next picture he was holding a stack of fanned-out one-hundred-dollar bills in each hand.

I loved the look of that money. I told him so.

"Did the feds ever try to get you up there?"

"You are thinking of going, aren't you?" he asked, testing me. "Aren't you? Come on, you can tell me." He put his arm around me in confidence. "Because if you are, I can help you get started."

"I'm only thinking about it," I said.

"I still have all my contacts there," he said. "I could get you set up with new ID and papers and you would have a clean slate just like that." He snapped his fingers. "That's the trick, 'cause if you don't pay taxes nobody knows you exist, and I love that feeling."

I did too. "I'm only thinking about it," I said, as if keeping my hand on a half-moved chess piece. "I need to think it through."

THE NEXT DAY DR. SOBEL LET ME USE HIS PHONE again. I called Melissa and told her to get $2,000 in cash from my lawyer and $500 for herself. Reserve a room at the Plaza, I said. Bring my credit cards and ID.

"Why do you need so much extra money?" she asked.

"So I can pay for correspondence courses in forestry." I didn't want her to think I was going to jump, otherwise she wouldn't help. And also, even in my own mind, as I spoke to her, as I heard her voice charming me, I thought, Don't jump. Just stay with her for the night and make everything all right and come back to prison and do your time and move on to a better place in your life. Be smart.

"I'll see you soon," she said. "I've missed you."

"I can't wait to get my hands on you."

"I bet," she said.

"Party time," I sang. "We're gonna have a *good* time."

After we hung up I was feeling great.

While Dr. Sobel was doing his rounds I called the airlines and got the flight times to Canada and made my reservation, then called my lawyer and arranged to have the money ready for Melissa. It was a snap.

"How'd it go?" Parker asked when I returned from work. He was polishing his shoes.

I told him about the phone calls I had made. "Can you think of anything I haven't thought of?" I asked.

"I envy you," he replied. "I should have gone up there when I jumped out of the car. But I just ran around like a dickhead till they caught me. You're doing the smart thing."

As he talked, I took all my letters and photographs and ripped them up into small pieces, then flushed them down the toilet. Parker wrote me out a list of friends and their phone numbers.

The next few days passed slowly. I had little to do. I went to the barber and had my hair trimmed back. I paid the clerk at Receiving and Discharge five packs of cigarettes to let me into the clothes room so I could pick out what I'd wear. I found a two-piece blue wool suit, a pair of black leather shoes, a nice white shirt, and a silk club tie.

Elvis had been sent down to C Cell House. It was common practice to isolate men who were leaving. The ones who were institutionalized would start fights; the ones who were leaving were afraid someone would pull something on them to mess up their discharge date. Some men never talked about their "date." They just did their time until one day you woke up and they were gone.

I asked Dr. Sobel if he would take me to see Elvis during his hospital rounds. I wanted to say good-bye. He agreed.

I hardly recognized Elvis. His hair was brown and cut short. He didn't have any makeup on and his face once again was soft and undistinguished. He wore a khaki uniform. He was reading the newspaper when I surprised him.

"Just checking out the job listings," he said as he refolded the paper. Even his voice had changed, had become direct, sincere.

"You look good. I'll miss you, buddy."

"I'll get it together," he said. "I'm going to keep it simple, do the right things, and get my life in order. I can't wait just to have a good clean life where I wake up every morning and I'm not looking over my shoulder for people I've fucked over. And I'm only going to keep good friends around me. You know what I mean?"

"I know what you mean," I replied.

"That's my advice to you," he said. "I love you, man. I want you to be my friend on the outside. You're a good guy." He gave me a hug with the bars between us. "Gotta go," he sang. "Gotta go become myself. Gotta go meet that stranger and make him my friend."

"See you soon," I said.

"Soon?"

"Yeah," I said. "I'm feeling pretty confident I'll be out before too long."

"Hey," Elvis said. "Confidence is the key to the dream. I've got confidence in myself, and that's why I'll never be Elvis again. Never."

I wanted to take him into the corner and tell him just what *my* dream was. But he was standing there with his ratty haircut holding the want ads down by his side, and I couldn't tell him just how dull his life was going to be and how great mine was about to become.

"I have one more question," I said. "What's your name?"

"Seth Zimmer. I'm in the Memphis phone book. Come visit sometime."

"You bet," I said.

My FRIEND ROBBY AND THE X-15 GANG had broken up a few years earlier. Most of the guys were older than me, and when they got to be high school age, they dropped out. They had dreams of running a criminal empire, but they didn't get very far. I would find them working at gas stations or stocking shelves in supermarkets. Only Robby still wanted to get mixed up in stuff. For a while he went on a car-stealing spree, but that ended when he was caught delivering luxury cars to a chop shop in Atlanta. He only did three months' time, and when he got out he decided he wanted to be a hit man or a body guard and stand around in an Italian red linen nightclub in a shiny suit with a gun pressed against his ribs. He began to hang out at the skin and drug clubs in Dania, Hallandale, Pompano Beach, North Miami, and Fort Lauderdale. But he didn't know how to get recruited into someone else's gang. Everyone had always been drawn to him and *his* gang. So as he sat at the clubs by himself, smiling up at naked women or looking over the top of his beer bottle with hard blue eyes, he was just another underage customer, another bar tab. And he didn't like it.

His girlfriend, Bonnie Three Fingers, was gone, his pals were gone, and he was alone, drifting and picking up petty arrests. He did some breaking and entering, some shoplifting, public drunkenness, vandalism. None of it big enough to make the newspaper. I wouldn't have known about his troubles if he hadn't told me himself. Once everyone else was gone he started to come around more often.

He made me nervous. He'd say things like, "Did you see the Big Daddy's Liquors down on Wilton Manors?"

"No," I said.

He seemed disappointed.

"Well you should have seen it," he said. "I threw a cinder block through the plate glass window and grabbed a few bottles."

"The really giant display bottles?" I asked.

"Yeah. Why?" he asked.

I knew those bottles were just filled with colored water.

"Did you drink it all?"

"Was shitfaced for a week," he said.

"Yeah," I said.

Once he sold me a portable stereo, and when I didn't want to buy a long silver chain, he gave it to me anyway, saying, "What the hell. The pawn shops won't give me shit for it."

A few weeks later he knocked on my bedroom window. It was two in the morning. "Ray." Tap. Tap. Tap. "Ray. Come here."

I pulled the curtain back with my hand. The moon reflected down Robby's long chrome zipper and off the studs on his leather jacket. "Ray."

"What's up?" I asked.

"Come on out," he whispered. "It's beautiful tonight. It's a full moon. We'll go down to the duck pond. Man, it's fucking beautiful."

I looked up at the moon. It *was* beautiful. "Be right out," I said. I pulled on my jeans and sneakers. I tiptoed down the hall, pulling a shirt over my head, and slipped out the back door. I kept a fishing rod in the utility room. I grabbed it and met him on the street. The tar was warm and the breeze was cool. A good mix, I thought.

"I'm glad you could make it," he said. "The rest of the bums I know are asleep."

"Yeah," I replied. "Maybe we'll get lucky and catch some fish."

"Yeah. Hey, look at that," he said and nodded toward one of those painted Negro lantern holders some people put on the end of their driveways. Its arm pointed at us. "If I had a gun I'd put it in his hand."

"What have you been up to?" I asked.

"Jail time," he replied. "But I'm out on bail now. My old man left me in for two weeks before he posted it. Said he'd give me one last chance to get my shit together. What about his own shit? Hasn't had a decent job in a lifetime." He reached into his jacket and pulled out a cigarette. "Want one?"

"Yeah."

We cut across Broward Boulevard and entered the woods that were part of the abandoned golf course. The moon was so full, the trees were dark blue under the silver light. Our faces shone like coins. My ears were swollen with every sound, every footfall, every snapping twig. We marched forward, up over the now-bushy greens and through the tall sawgrass covering the fairways. Abandoned cars hunkered down in the sand traps, their smashed glass sparkling, soft orange rust taking over where fires had blistered the paint. We passed one and the sharp smell of piss off the soggy upholstery burned my nose. I turned my face into the wind and breathed deeply. The moon was sinking. The thin necks of the pines, the oaks, the cottonwoods blew yes, then no, then yes. When we arrived at the duck pond the air throbbed with the pitch of crickets and frogs.

I unhooked my line from the cork handle on the rod, slipped on the rubber worm, placed the bobber an arm's length above it and cast out into the pond. Plop. About thirty feet, I thought. I ran the line over my finger to feel for bites. I liked to fish. It was like getting stuff for free.

"Remember the time I let you have my sister for a carton of cigarettes?" he asked. "Those were good times."

Since then his sister, Suzie, had been sent off to a home for unwed mothers.

I looked over at Robby. He was picking leaves off an oak tree and floating them on the water. He placed a pebble on each one for cargo. Or maybe they were people. After he launched an entire fleet he picked up a big rock and held it over his head. "Bombs away!" he said and threw it into the water. The fleet sank. There go the fish, I thought.

"Did I get Suzie pregnant?" I asked. I had never dared ask the question before because I didn't know how he'd react. On the one hand he would pimp for his sister. On the other, he'd kick your face in to protect her reputation. Even though I had paid for her the first time, I had seen her again for free and thought I was in love with her. I had never been with another girl that way and wanted her to be my girlfriend. But that was out of the question. Robby had claimed her for his own business. Still, I just wanted to know if I was part of some baby, somewhere.

Shortly before Suzie was sent off, we had met by accident at the Thunderbird Drive-In. They showed porno movies after midnight. It was easy to sneak in through a hole in the fence. I saw her when I went to buy a soda at the concession stand. A lot of married people brought their kids and made them play outside the car. They were running all over the place, imitating the action. "Hi," I said to Suzie. "Remember me?"

She was standing in line with a giant Coke in one hand and a tub of buttered popcorn in the other. It smelled really sexy, salty and habit-forming. It made my tongue roll over my teeth. She had on a tank top and white cutoffs. They were bleached so white they glowed. I wanted to kiss her and go for more. I didn't know much, but I knew that dizzy feeling in my belly. Her lips were so glossy they reflected the overhead lights.

"Hi," she said. "Are you here with Robby?"

"No," I said. "Alone. And you?"

"One of Robby's friends," she said and looked away, over the rows of waxed cars, checking for her "friend." Then she turned back to me. "Well, you know what that's all about," she said, and shrugged.

I took a chance. I thought I still loved her and that she wanted me to love her, even save her from Robby, although I didn't know how I might do that. "Can I see you later?" I asked. "Right here. Like you can tell him you forgot something, cotton candy, cigarettes, or something, and come back."

"Sure," she said. "Yeah. I'll meet you out back by the rest rooms." She smiled. Then, aware of the time, she marched down below the first row of cars and beyond the glaring concession stand lights. I watched her walk toward a truck all the way down in the front row. She drifted up and down the wavy parking lot as though she were strolling across the ocean. She was fourteen.

It wasn't long before she returned. "Told him I forgot to pee," she said. "He wanted me to pee in a cup. I don't know where Robby finds them."

I held out my hand and she took it. "Hurry," I said. We went and hid among a line of fir trees that ran along the fence and blocked the screen from passing cars. We hugged, kissing each other on the ears and neck. I smelled her hair. Buttered popcorn. I ran my hand under her shirt and up her smooth back. She grabbed what was in my pants and we dropped down. It was over in a shudder, my hand pressing down on her left shoulder, my chin on the other. After a minute she squirmed and said, "You were the first one tonight." Then she edged out from under me and trotted off, slapping at the dirt and twigs on her rear. Over the next months, I only saw glimpses of her before she was sent away.

Now, I wished I was with her instead of Robby. I reeled in my line and recast it. Plop. I'd be with her, holding her, kissing her. Instead I was trying to catch mullet with a rubber worm at three in the morning.

"I do have a gun," Robby said, sliding it out of its place between his belly and belt and pointing it at me. "Would you like to die tonight, man?" He raised his arm and aimed for the moon. "Would you? Well, if you ever thought of just pulling out the plug, this is the night. I'll do it for free. Free death, one night only," he hawked. He laughed. His teeth were wet and shiny.

I looked over at him. His eyes were filled with little moons. "Don't fuck around," I said. "Put that away."

"I'm just going to shoot ducks," he said.

"Don't. People will hear us and call the cops."

"You're right." He slipped it into his pocket. "Seriously. Do you ever think of ending it, just blowing yourself away?"

"No," I said. "I always think of blowing other people away."

"Let me do it to you," he said.

"Don't fuck around," I said. He looked at me and shrugged his shoulders.

"Then *I'll* do it," he replied impatiently. For a moment, I thought he'd kill me just for being afraid to die. Or maybe I did get Suzie pregnant.

But he held the barrel to his own head. "Is this the right angle?" he asked.

I dropped my rod and stood up. I adjusted his hand so the bullet would travel from temple to temple. "That should do it," I said and stepped back. "But don't."

He fired. I jerked my head from the flash. When I opened my eyes he was flat on the ground. His leg kicked out and he sucked once at the air then let it go. I leaped across his body and felt his neck. There was a pulse. Suddenly he jumped up.

"Tricked your ass," he shouted. "I only have blanks."

I was scared shitless. I stumbled back and stepped into the pond. "Oh man," I moaned. "Oh, fuck."

"I'm dead," he said. "I'm gone. No more Robby. I'm takin' off for Canada. I'm not comin' back either. The cops can grow old and die before they catch me up there."

My heart was still pounding. I stepped out of the pond and squatted down to get my breath back.

"You wanna come with me?" he asked. "We can start fresh up there."

For a moment I wanted to go. Just leave school and my dried-up family behind and take off. But I couldn't. I didn't have any money and I didn't have any idea how to make money.

"I can't," I said.

"Well, if you ever change your mind," he said, "that's where I'll be. Once I'm up there, I'll send you my address."

I walked home alone that night. I never saw him again and I never heard from him.

He must have gone up there. He must have made it. Otherwise, I figured, I would have read about him in the "Police Report" column of the *Fort Lauderdale News*.

Now, six months after I got thrown into West Street, I lay in my bunk and thought, if Robby could do it, I can do it. I was always smarter than him. Fuck yes, I thought. Canada. It's a go.

As I MADE UP MY BED I THOUGHT: THIS IS the last time I'll do this. "I'll send you a postcard," I said to Parker.

"Don't put a return address on it," he replied.

At breakfast, when I passed the steam table stacked with soggy eggs, I knew it was my last. On the way to the infirmary I passed men in the hallway and thought, I won't see your ugly faces again. No more bars. No more "yes sirs" and "no sirs." No more nothing unless I said so.

I didn't want to talk with anyone, because I was afraid I would blurt out my secret. It was the same fear as feeling I'd fall over the edge of a cliff while I was still ten feet away from it. The new admissions were waiting for their x-rays, and I was pleased to have work before me. I lined them up and one by one had them stand with their shirts off in front of the film case.

"Take a deep breath and hold it," I said, listening to the whine and click of the machine as I pressed the button and took the shot. Blam! I thought. You're dead and I'm outta here.

When I thought I had finished, Mr. Bow brought Les, the boxer, into the lab. "Lester here needs a VD test. Says he has a sharp pain in his prick. Isn't that right, Lester?"

"Yeah," he said, and gave me a mean look with his head bobbing up and down as though he were ducking punches.

"Lester's been stickin' that thing in the wrong end of the business," Mr. Bow said. Then just before he left he said, "You don't have to check his rear, I did and his prostate is okay."

"Thanks," I replied. I had no intention of sticking my finger up Les's ass. A hot poker, yes, but not my finger. When Mr. Bow left, I had Les drop his pants and sit on the examination table. "Now grab your cock and squeeze the discharge toward the tip," I ordered.

"You know," he said slyly, "we could be friends again."

"No, we can't," I replied. "No way in hell."

We didn't have cotton swabs in the hospital. Instead I used a wooden-handled instrument that held a strong but extremely thin wire about four inches long with a tiny loop on the end. I had to run the wire down the urethral canal and pull it back out. The sample was trapped in the loop, and that's what I used to make the culture.

During my spare time I had made another, similar instrument out of a paper clip and tongue depressors. The real medical wire was made of a particular metal that cooled instantly after being sterilized over the Bunsen burner. The steel paper-clip wire retained the heat. I turned on the Bunsen burner and looked up at Les. He was playing with his cock so that it was half hard. I remembered very clearly what he had done to me.

I removed the medical wire from the Bunsen burner and waited for the redness to disappear.

"Okay," I said. "Milk that stuff up."

"No fuckin way you're using that on me," he said, pointing at the wire.

"Relax. It's cool," I explained. "Feel it, it's a special kind of wire."

He did. He gave me a puzzled look.

"Science," I said.

"Okay. But be careful. I'm not supposed to enjoy this."

You won't, I thought.

Once more I turned around. I put down the medical wire and picked up the steel wire. I passed it through the flame until it glowed red. "Take a deep breath," I said over my shoulder. "And close your eyes." I turned, held the head of his cock with one hand so that the pink target showed, then shoved the entire hot wire into that tight hole. He yelled and jumped back. I jigged the wire out and slid it into my pants pocket then grabbed the other wire.

"Oh fuck!" he hollered. "Fuck!"

"Let me see." He held it for me to examine. A blister had puffed out on the tip of his prick and I knew it must have burned like that on the inside, too. I knew that blister would pop and every time Les pissed it would burn and sting and bleed a little. It would take a long time to heal. Maybe it would fuse together.

"Got you back!" I said to him. "Don't you ever fuck with me again. Ever."

"You're dead," he snapped and took a half swing at me.

I stepped back. The pain in his prick overwhelmed him and he just sat there with it in his hand, rocking back and forth.

Mr. Bow came in and wanted to know what had happened. I was holding the medical wire. "A freak accident," I said.

"He tried to kill me," Les hollered.

"You keep your dick outta boy's assholes and it won't get scorched," Mr. Bow said to him. I brought him some burn ointment. Mr. Bow dabbed it on the head of Les's cock. "This will help. Come back in a few days."

When Mr. Bow left, Les turned to me. "I want to kick your ass again," he said. "Let's get back in the ring. You and me, white trash."

"How about tomorrow," I said eagerly. "Around noon? And bring all your money."

"You're a dead man," he said. "I'm gonna kill you. I'm gonna teach you to respect me."

"I can't wait," I said. "I'm really looking forward to it, Mister Lester."

AT LUNCH, I THOUGHT EVERYTHING through again. At four o'clock I'll be waiting in my office for Dr. Sobel to finish with his last patient. We'll go down to Receiving and Discharge and I'll put on my street clothes, careful to conceal the list of names and numbers Parker had given me. Dr. Sobel will drive me across town to the Plaza. I'll hop out and thank him and tell him not to worry, that I'll be back before the midnight curfew. I'll see Melissa. We'll say sweet things, drink champagne, and make love. I'll tell her I have to go back to West Street, then take a taxi to the airport where I'll pick up my ticket. I'll board my plane at ten o'clock. I'll land in Toronto by midnight. I'll stay in the Packard Hotel and call Parker's friends and step into my new life.

After lunch, I opened my x-ray room double doors, which were lined with lead. I aimed the x-ray cone down the hallway and retreated behind my control room door. I looked out through the lead glass window, and each time someone passed by I fired at them. Zap! It didn't matter if it was a prisoner or a guard. They all seemed dangerous to me. Zap! Now that I was getting out, I could feel the anger rise up in me. It wasn't enough to just escape into a new future. I wanted to destroy the past too. I didn't want any trace of this left inside me.

The warden was chatting it up with a guard down at the other end of the hall and I was beaming them with a steady dose of x-rays when Mr. Bow walked by. "What are you doing?" he asked.

"Fixing the sights," I replied. "I think they're a little off."

He shook his head. "Don't monkey around. That stuff is dangerous," he said, and walked off.

"I better stop this shit," I warned myself. "I better act normal before I do something stupid."

I turned off the machine and went into the darkroom to develop the morning x-rays when there was a knock at my door.

"Jakes," called Miss Lorraine. "Doc Sobel wants to see you."

"I'll be right there," I called back.

I looked at my watch. It was early. I washed the developing fluid off my hands, took a deep breath, and flung open the door.

"Sit down," Dr. Sobel said when I opened his door. He stood up, then sat down and positioned himself with his elbows on his desk. "Something very disturbing just happened," he said tightly.

"Is this about the head x-ray?" I whispered.

"No," he replied. "I just now received a call from the warden, and he claims you intend to escape tonight."

My heart took off. I didn't know what to say. I felt like Les was hitting me over and over with his death punch but I couldn't show it. Dr. Sobel looked toward me and waited for a reply.

"Someone may have told him that just to get back at me," I said, trying to remain calm. "This shit happens all the time."

"You mean someone is jealous because I'm taking you out?" he asked.

"Of course," I said.

We looked at each other across the desk and it was obvious he wasn't falling for it.

"I'll have to speak to the warden," he said, hedging.

"Give him a call," I suggested. "He'll tell you the same thing."

"Yeah, give me a minute." He nodded toward the door and I stood up.

"Do you think we'll still go out tonight? Or should we clear this up and do it tomorrow?" I had to ask.

"It's up to the warden," he replied frankly.

For a moment he closed his eyes and looked pained. We were both in trouble. When he opened his eyes he jerked his thumb toward the door. "I need some privacy," he said coldly.

Almost immediately a guard came and escorted me down to Warden Paris's office. Parker was sitting in a corner on the other side of the room. When I looked at him, he cringed.

"Parker says that you're planning to take off tonight," Mr. Paris said matter-of-factly.

"I don't know what he's talking about," I replied. I didn't have time to think up another story. I didn't think there was one that would explain it. "He's lying," I said with all I had in me. "I don't know why he's saying that. I'm just going out for a visit with Dr. Sobel."

"Dr. Sobel already told us he was going to drop you off at the Plaza Hotel," Mr. Paris said.

"Now you know," I replied, lifting my arms and letting them slap down against my hips. "But that was to see my girlfriend, not escape."

"What else don't we know?" he inquired.

Parker said nothing. He looked down at his hands, then up at Mr. Paris, who was looking back and forth between us.

He already knew the answers. "Parker says that

you have plane reservations and money and plan to fly to Canada tonight instead of returning here," Mr. Paris said calmly. "Isn't that what you said, Parker?"

I looked over at him. He looked at me, then over at Paris. "That's exactly what I said, sir."

"We're checking with the airlines now," Mr. Paris said. "And we're tracking down your girlfriend to see where she stands in all of this. As you may know, aiding in the escape of a convict is a felony charge." He smiled curtly.

There was a knock on the door, and Mr. Paris was called away by the assistant warden.

I lurched forward and held my fist in front of Parker's face. "So this is how you get your *pull*. By being a fucking snitch?"

"Hold on," he said, with his hands in front of his face. "I've been thinking that it would be better if you didn't do it, man."

"You just want to turn my ass in so you make parole," I shot back. "I'm the insurance you needed. But now you better straighten this out. The whole prison will know you're a snitch and you'll have your ass kicked."

"It's for your own good," he said. "Really. Just calm down and think about it. You would never be able to come back to the U.S. again without doing time. Sooner or later it would all catch up to you."

"That's not what you said before."

"I was bragging," he replied. "Honest, man, I've given this a lot of thought. Don't do it."

"You set me up so you could rat me out," I shot

back. "If you didn't want me to do it you coulda' just said so."

I cocked my arm back and swung hard at his face. I don't even know if I hit him. He hopped up and I pushed him back over Mr. Paris's desk and began to punch him. He was weak because he was so wrong, and I didn't give a shit. I felt insane. Instead of trying to punch back, Parker grabbed at my arms. All the fear in me turned mean, and when I saw a small cactus on the desk I grabbed it and shoved it hard into his face and twisted it. He moaned and thrashed around, and we slid off the desk onto the floor. I kept swinging at him. One solid punch to the face after another. The guards rushed in, pushed the desk and chairs out of the way, grabbed me around the chest and pulled me off him. He was covering his bloody face with his hands and crawling on his knees and elbows toward the door.

"Snitch," I yelled. "You're fucked." I struggled to get at him again, but the guards had me in a choke hold. I couldn't break away or see all the men who watched as I hung my head and hissed like a punctured tire as they led me down to the hole.

I SLEPT. WHEN I WOKE I LISTENED FOR noises to distinguish morning from night. The same meal of milk and a cheese sandwich was delivered through my door slot twice a day. I didn't know if it was breakfast or dinner. My basement isolation cell was blacked out except for lines of light that poked through cracks around the door. I squinted up at them like a cat. The cell was empty except for an army blanket and a bucket. There was a damp odor of piss and disinfectant. I folded the blanket so half was beneath me and half was on top of me. When I rolled onto my right hand it hurt. Cactus spines had been driven into my palm and fingers. They were infected. My hand was swollen and sticky with pus. I held it close to my face and sniffed. It smelled sweet.

I carefully picked at the spines with the fingernails of my left hand. When I could get a firm grip on the head of a spine, I pried it out. It seemed to me that even among those hundred other spines I could feel the individual relief from the one just removed.

I heard footsteps. Leather soles stepping swiftly across the gritty hallway. Keys jangled. A padlock was unlocked, and my peek window slid open. A beam of fuzzy light, like a projected movie, shot across my cell. I looked up at the slot and blinked. A mouth appeared.

"We have a little problem," Warden Paris announced.

"Yes?" I replied.

"It seems that Dr. Sobel and Dr. Wong are saying that there is an x-ray that proves the informer cop had a head fracture. They're bringing a lawsuit against us for negligent treatment. So when I showed them the x-ray you gave me as proof that his head was fine, they laughed. It seems you gave me the wrong picture."

"So?"

"As it turns out, Dr. Sobel does not have the x-ray, nor does Dr. Wong. No one seems to have the proof."

I began to think of Elvis. Be patient, he had advised. Your moment will come. I had gone for the wrong moment. I had been impatient and it hadn't worked out. Now this might be another chance. I stared at the mouth. I thought, Speak to me. Tell me what I can do for you. I'm ready.

"I think you know where that x-ray is," Mr. Paris said. His voice was even, reasonable. He wanted to do business. "I want that picture."

Want to destroy it, I thought. But I said, "What's it worth to you?"

"A date," he replied. "If I had that picture, I could run a Special Progress Report through the parole board and have you out of here in two weeks. That's what it's worth to me. And here's what it means otherwise, just to give you some perspective. You'll stay in this meat hole and do the entire six years here. Right where you are. You'll be shitting in that bucket for another five years. You'll have a ring around your ass when you leave. No visits. No books. Nothing but time to think about what you should have done with that x-ray. I'm willing to forget that you gave me the wrong x-ray the first time. I'm willing to forget about your little escape fantasy. I'll let it all drop if you just do the right thing."

As he spoke, I watched the little patch of light which framed his mouth. I couldn't see his eyes, just his lips and chin. "I guess you've already looked for it," I said.

The little mouth jumped into action. "I wouldn't be here otherwise. So this is your chance, take it. There won't be another."

"How do I know you won't trick me?" I asked.

"I'll get you the date in advance. Your lawyer can look over the papers, and then you can get me that picture," he replied. "Fair enough?"

"If you try to fuck me over," I said, "if you give me false papers or trick me in any way, I'll testify for Dr. Sobel in court. I saw that cop's head. I even saw the guard who hit him and I saw what he hit him with. This isn't a slip in the shower room we're talking about."

"Look, you don't have to threaten me. I just want the picture and you can be out on parole. That's the deal. No loose talk, no court testimony, no deposition, no nothing, because we can have your parole officer yank you back in here for jaywalking if you get out and begin to talk."

"Okay," I said. "It's a deal."

"Good." The edges of the little mouth curled up like a canoe.

"I need something too."

"What?"

"A pair of tweezers and some alcohol."

"You owe me a cactus," he said. "My daughter gave me that for Father's Day." He slid the panel across the hole. I heard the padlock click into place.

They hadn't found it! But I knew they'd double their efforts. They knew it had to be there somewhere if I had made a deal to get it. Maybe that's all they wanted to know, if it *was* still around. I should have told the warden I sent it to my lawyer. Now they'll rip the lab apart looking for it.

Just before I left St. Croix to smuggle the hash up north on the yacht, the local cops figured out I was selling drugs and tried to find my stash. A group of black detectives began to follow me around in an old green Volkswagen. Once I parked my car along the Fredericksted pier while I waited in a bar for a connection. When I returned to the car, it had been broken into. They got my drug case, which contained a bottle of blotter acid, some reefer, a prescription for Seconal, and a few hundred dollars. I had kept it hidden under the back seat, which could easily be pulled out. Later, I went over to see Melissa. She lived with her parents. The front door had been forced, and when I pushed it open with my foot, I saw her father going through a closet. He saw me and kept searching. "They got my guns," he said bitterly and kicked at a broken lamp with his shoe. "They got all the jewelry and some cash."

I walked through the kitchen and out to the back patio. They kept a big freezer back there filled with meat and fish. I heard the father stomping up the stairs and so I opened the freezer and quickly moved aside some large packages to uncover what looked like a fish wrapped in aluminum foil. Inside the package were all my sheets of blotter acid rolled up in a bundle. I wasn't certain if that was why the house had been robbed, but I kept the thought to myself. I put it back in the freezer and closed the door.

"Do you know anything about this?" he asked when I went upstairs to look around.

"No," I replied. "Any clues?"

"Someone said they saw a green Volkswagen pull away from here, that's all. You know any locals with a car like that?"

I couldn't think of any, I said. Just then the police arrived. We went down to show them the damage. When they saw me they gave me a suspicious look. I didn't pay much attention to them. They were commonly known to dislike white people.

Two nights later I was driving through town on my way home. I passed the police station on Center Line Road. Those same cops were sitting on the front porch and gave me a look as I went by. In my rearview mirror, I saw them run down the stairs. About half a mile up the road they caught up to me. There were seven men and a woman in an Impala squad car. I pulled over and stepped out onto the road.

"You taillight be out," the driver said, casually pointing toward it.

"Yeah," I said, "I know. I'll fix it tomorrow."

The other cops began to walk around my car and stick their arms through the open windows. At first they kept their hands to themselves, but then one of them opened the back door and began to dislodge the seat.

"You can't do that," I said. "You don't have a search warrant!"

"Don' be so damn stupid," one of them said nastily.

They pulled the seat all the way out of the car then bounced it on the road a few times hoping to dislodge a secret stash. A couple others shone their flashlights into the vacated space below the back cushion.

"Which one of you has a green Volkswagen?" I asked.

One cop looked up at me but said nothing. The driver had been writing out a ticket and when he finished, he handed it to me. The other cops bickered over who would slide into the front seat of the squad car. There was a lot of laughing and name-calling, then they slowly pulled away. All of them looked back at me as I stood leaning against the fender of my Oldsmobile.

I threw the seat in the back, drove home and fixed the taillight. It was a loose connection. Then I drove back to town and took a side road up behind the police station. There was a green Volkswagen in their parking lot. I parked my car a block away and walked down. I wasn't certain what I was going to do. I was so angry I felt invincible. I kicked out the back two taillights, opened the driver's side door and lit a book of matches on the front seat before I strolled off to find a beer. "Fuck you, too," I thought.

The next day Melissa showed up at my house. She had the blotter acid wrapped in foil.

"Man," I snapped, "don't let that thaw out. It'll fuck it up."

She threw it at my feet. "You're such an asshole," she said. "You hid this at my house. You let us take the risk. I hate it when you do things like this."

It took a while to calm her down.

Now, I was wondering how she had reacted when I didn't show at the Plaza. Suddenly the peek panel on my door was unlocked and drawn open. "I have a present for you," the warden said. His closed fist came through the hole. It unfolded and revealed a pair of tweezers. I reached for them. As soon as I touched the tweezers, his hand grabbed me around the wrist and pulled my left arm through the hole. He twisted it and pushed down against the elbow.

"Where is it?" Mr. Paris asked.

"I hid it."

He twisted harder.

"Where did you hide it?"

"No way."

He pushed down on my arm with more force. "I'll break it."

"Nobody . . . can find . . . it."

"I'm going to snap it and you won't get any medical attention."

"It's . . . safe."

He let up on my arm. "Does that feel better?"

"Yes."

"Are you going to tell me where it is?

"Not right now."

He pushed down again. "Where is it?"

"It's safe!" I hollered. "Don't worry."

"It'll be safe when I have it." He pushed harder.

"Don't break it," I said. "Please."

"Please give me the x-ray." He pushed a little harder.

"Don't."

"Please?"

"Don't break it," I begged. "Please. Don't . . . I can't give it to you now. Get me the date and I'll give it to you . . . like you said, I swear."

"Let's hear you swear," he said. He raised my left arm and slammed it down against the edge of the window. The elbow snapped backwards.

He let go of the arm.

"You fuckin' broke my elbow," I wailed. I staggered and slowly began to work my shoulder back from the window. Inch by inch, my arm followed like something heavy, like I was hauling up an anchor. I closed my eyes and stood still. The pain was overwhelming. I held my breath and tried to keep the pain in check. Suddenly I could feel something odd on my fingertips. Something cold. I opened my eyes. It was the warden's hand. He reached in through the window and lifted my left hand back onto the edge of the slot. He held it there as I watched him. I wanted to pull it away, but I couldn't make it work. Then he slammed the iron window across my fingertips. My arm jerked back and I screamed.

"I thought we had a deal," I hollered from the floor.

He opened the slot. "We still do," he replied. "You just missed the fine print."

Then he stooped down so I could see his eyes.

"There's a price for everything," he said. "I'll get you your date, but don't think it won't cost you. Don't think you're a player. You're not. You got lucky. You don't have brains. You had one moment of luck."

"Jesus. Get me to a hospital. It's killing me." I tried to unfold my swollen right hand so I could run it across my left arm and feel the damage, but it was too infected, too swollen to open. I slowly traced my wrist across my broken arm until I felt where the shattered bone pushed up against the skin. I was scared. "Get me to a doctor," I begged. "Please."

"A bit of advice," he said. "One false word out of you and I'll twist your arm off. People like you should just sit at home, smoke your dope, drink your cheap wine, and stay out of my way. I have real criminals climbing up my asshole in here and I don't need fucking punk kids like you taking up my time."

"Just get me a doctor."

He closed the window, locked it, and walked away.

I sat up with the wall against my back, my arms cradled across my thighs. The pain ran through me in constant waves.

DR. SOBEL OPENED THE DOOR AND LOOKED down on me. "I'm only doing this because I'm a doctor," he said. "I took an oath."

"I'm sorry," I replied. "I didn't mean to set you up."

"Well, you better explain it better than that to your girlfriend."

"Did you talk with her?"

"I gave her the bad news," he said.

"What'd she say?"

"Basically, she never wants to hear from you again. I think 'rot in hell' were her exact words."

Fuck, I thought. I'll make it up to her later.

Dr. Sobel held my left arm, touched it gently, and ran his fingertips over the skin to feel where the bone had splintered. "This is a bad break," he said. "It's going to take a long time to heal."

"I need an x-ray," I said.

"I can't help you," he replied. "I'm leaving, but I'll see to it that they send you to a hospital."

"Where are you going?" I asked.

"I'm not telling you," he said coldly. "I thought you were a friend, but you're not."

Part Three

MEMPHIS

IT WAS 20 DEGREES IN BOSTON, AND I hadn't seen a customer for over an hour. I read the temperature from a bank sign across the street. I was standing, shifting from foot to foot, in the center of a parking lot filled with Christmas trees. It was my job to sell them. It was the only job my parole officer could find for me, so he said. He wouldn't let me find my own job. "How will I know if it's *legitimate?*" he reasoned. "You could be selling dope on the side." He was suspicious of everything I said. But he was full of good ideas. If I wanted to sell hash, I couldn't think of a better place than a Christmas tree lot. "Buy an ounce and get a tree for free." I wish I had thought of it before.

I leaned over the fifty-five-gallon drum where my fire was dying down. The trees were too green to burn or I would have chopped one up with my good hand. I scanned the parking lot for trash, but I had used it all. My bad arm was numb under the cast. I wore an old navy pea coat with the sleeve hacked off and ragged at the left shoulder. I had a leather glove loosely pulled over the swollen fingers on my left hand. The two middle fingers were still taped to a splint. I had cut those fingers out of the glove to make it fit. The heat warmed my face and good arm. I turned sideways, leaned way forward, and lifted my bad arm over the fire like a dog lifting its leg.

When Warden Paris got me my parole date, I gave him the cop's x-ray. It all went as he said it would. I had him send the papers to my lawyer, and when Al gave me the okay, I was marched down to the x-ray developing room. I stood on the overturned trash can, loosened the pipe with my good hand, and pulled out the picture. I smiled when I gave it to the warden.

"You'll never make a sweeter trade in your life," he said, snapping it out of my hand and sliding it into an envelope.

Before I left, I asked if he would sign my cast. "After all," I said, "it represents a special moment between us."

"Sure," Paris replied. He wrote, "Don't be a stranger." Then he squeezed the fingers on my bad hand. "I just want you to know," he said, "I wouldn't be doing this if I didn't think you'd be back here in a very short while."

Now when I looked down at my left arm, which was killing me because the cold metal screws made the bones throb, I saw his name. I felt like a branded cow. What an idiot you are, I thought to myself. The guy breaks your arm, lets you sit in pain for two days before calling a doctor, gives you the worst parole officer in Boston, and you smile at him like he saved your life.

"But you're on the outside," I reminded myself. "The *outside*. Don't fuck it up. Just stick to the straight and narrow path for now, then once things calm down you can dig up the hash, spend your money, and make your own way."

There was one hitch. I had to live in a halfway house until I found a job and had enough evidence of money saved up to move out. Since no one was supposed to know I had forty thousand in drug money, I couldn't use it. And the only job Mr. Mercier, my parole officer, had for me was selling Christmas trees. "You are what I call a can opener," he said, pissed off from the moment he saw me. "You have no home, no job, and no ambition. You just cut your way out of prison. Let me tell you, nobody out here wants you. But you made a deal to get out, and now it's my turn to see to it that when you fuck up, which you will, I'll be there to guide you back in. I know the warden let you slip it to him and he liked it so much he set you loose. Now it's my turn to do him a favor and help send you back. So enjoy these few days on the outside. Think of it as a furlough." He smiled at me.

While he was threatening me, he didn't know I had the $40,000 sewn into the lining of my pea coat. The money gave me a lot of inner peace. I nodded and smiled all the time Mr. Mercier was running me down. The day after my release from West Street I had called Al and asked him to get the cash ready, in large bills. "Very large."

"Are you sure you want this much cash?" he asked, when I went to his office. "I don't think it's a good idea."

But I did. I had given some thought as to where I might keep it and decided my coat was best. It would always be with me if I had to run. I might not have time to get to a safety deposit box. Because one arm of my coat was cut off, no one would want to steal it even if I were mugged.

Now that I had the money I slapped at the sides of my pea coat and smiled. Every time I felt the bundled outline of those five-hundred-dollar bills, it was like checking a life jacket before jumping off a sinking ship.

A car horn beeped and I looked toward the street. It was Mr. Mercier snooping around.

"No wonder you can't sell these trees," he said as he lowered his window a few inches. "You look like a vagrant. You should have a cup in your hand."

"Frozen," I said, and stamped my boots on the curb. I pressed my face close to the crack in his window and the warm air brought a little feeling back into my lips. "I need an indoor job. The metal screws in my arm are killing me. It's unhealthy. I'm calling my lawyer."

"Don't threaten me with your lawyer," he replied and rolled his eyes. "You'll make me mad." He lit a cigarette and offered me one. Before I reached my fingers over the glass to pull it from the pack, I flashed back to when the warden had slammed my hand in the peek window. Mercier might be sadistic enough to zip up the electric window before I got my hand back. I hesitated.

"You want one or what?" he asked.

I reached in and plucked it out of the pack.

"Thanks." I slipped it behind my ear.

"I'll see what else is around. But in the meantime don't fuck this job up. I could have given it to a lot of other guys."

"Just see what else you can find," I said. "This is doing me in."

"I could have got you a nice office job," he said. "But they wouldn't hire a one-handed typist. You're the bottom of the barrel, kid." His electric window closed the gap of warm air between us. He took a long look at me, shook his head, and pulled away.

I wiped my nose across my coat sleeve. "Fuck," I thought as a car pulled in. "A customer."

A GUY NAMED RALPH SHEETS OWNED THE Christmas tree lot. He had ten other lots across the city. He was one of those guys who made his money selling trees at Christmas, fireworks around the Fourth of July, candy around Valentine's Day, flags around Flag Day. At 8:30, he drove up in his Lincoln Town Car and pulled in next to my barrel. He rolled down his window. "How's it going?" he asked.

"Slow," I said. "It's too cold to even buy a Christmas tree." I handed him the few bills from the evening's sales. He counted them, then began to count the trees.

"I didn't rip you off," I said. "If that's what you're thinking."

He looked up into my face as though he were holding it between his gloved hands. "Don't interrupt me while I'm counting," he said and started over. When he finished he winked at me and slipped me a twenty. "Don't come back tomorrow. Nothing personal. It's just that when people want to buy a tree for the holiday they usually bring the kids, make it a big deal. You know what I mean. So when they drive by and see you looking so pathetic, they go somewhere else. I'm glad you're not stealing from me, but you're chasing my business away. You look like you fell out the back of an ambulance. Normally I can sell things that fall off a truck, but the market for med school stiffs is slow."

I shrugged. "I did the best I could," I said. I was worried that he might tell Mr. Mercier that I had robbed him. "I was honest, right?"

"Don't worry about your parole officer," he replied. "I'll tell him you're a good kid."

"Thanks." I waved toward the trees. "They're locked up for the night."

He winked at me. "Good luck," he said, then drove off.

I walked toward the Haymarket subway entrance. I knew Mr. Mercier was going to twist this around and I was going to have to listen to his bullshit. But then he'd have to get me a new job and it might be better than this one.

I took the subway to Copley Square. I went to the cheap Chinese restaurant on Boylston Street that I ate in every night. A sign over the front door simply read "FOOD." There were always people more pathetic looking than me in there, so I didn't stand out. No one had ever asked about my arm, but if they did, I planned to tell them I had a bad skiing accident. I could pass myself off as a student. I was young enough. I just looked perpetually weary and out of style. The students I observed looked pretty lame, as though they didn't have a problem I couldn't solve in an afternoon with a beer in one hand and a girl in the other.

I snatched a newspaper from an empty table and opened the business section to the want ads. I wanted hospital work. There were a lot of jobs listed, but they all required special training. Maybe I could talk Mercier into getting me into a nursing program. I was good at taking care of other people. I couldn't figure out why, because I sucked at taking care of myself.

I finished the noodles and looked at my watch. It was a prison Timex. At one time I had taken the works out and drawn bars over the face, then put it back together. I thought that once I got out I would take it off and crush it under my shoe. But I was still wearing it. I figured I might just open the watch again and erase the bars.

I had a half hour before curfew. I stood up, went to the pay telephone, and dialed Melissa's number. She picked up right away, as if she had been expecting someone to call.

"Melissa?"

"Look, Ray, I asked you not to call."

"I know, but I wasn't sure you meant it. I thought you'd calm down by now."

She sighed heavily, for effect. "Believe me. I'm calm and I still don't want to hear from you."

"But you haven't given me a chance."

"I was giving you a chance when you decided to escape and leave me holding the bag."

"They didn't hold you responsible."

"Oh no. I only got you the money. I only got you the hotel room. They were ready to arrest *me*."

"I explained it all to them. I'm sorry."

"I know," she said, sounding weary. "You're sorry about everything. Look, I didn't want to tell you, but I'm seeing someone else."

"Who?"

"No one you know," she said. "I only go out with him after ten o'clock."

She hung up. I never should have told her I had a ten o'clock curfew. I didn't know anyone else to call. Before prison, I had moved to Boston only because Melissa was going to college there. I hadn't met any other people before I was sentenced. I had been afraid to go outdoors and so I'd stayed locked in her apartment all day smoking hash and drinking cheap wine. Just like the warden said.

After I got out of West Street, when I stepped off the New York to Boston bus Melissa was waiting for me at the station. She drove me straight to her apartment, where all my stuff was packed up in old liquor boxes. I figured I had it coming, but it was still a shock.

"I thought it would be best this way," she said. "We've been through a lot already. There's no reason to have more of the same. Why don't you just take your stuff and leave, and let's call it quits."

I looked into her eyes. There was a certain amount of fear. She didn't fear *me*, but that I would argue with her and make her deviate from the script she had planned. Just as I had dreamed of getting her back, she had dreamed of letting me go. I didn't argue with her. She helped me load my seven boxes into her car, and she drove me to the halfway house.

"Please, don't call me," she said, once we'd put my stuff in my room. "After your last stunt, it's over."

"Okay," I replied. "I'll respect that. Besides, I need to move on."

"Good. That's what both of us need."

I leaned forward to kiss her. She held her hand in front of her face. She looked out at me from between her fingers. "You have no idea how badly you've hurt me," she said. "You're not capable of knowing."

Her pain repelled me. But I had so much of my own, I didn't know whose I was feeling. I stepped back. "I can't even call you?" I asked.

"No," she said, turning angry. "If you do, I'll call your parole officer."

"Don't worry," I said. I was going to say something else about needing a fresh start, but she drove away.

The halfway house was an old Victorian rooming house on Cortes Street next to the turnpike. It was run by two elderly sisters. About thirty years before, it had been a respectable rooming house that only rented out to Christian women. But now the place was so run-down that ex-cons were a better match for the general filth. One sister lived on the top floor and the other on the bottom. We lived in small rooms between them. Each room had a bed, a lamp, a chest of drawers, and a closet filled with wire hangers and broken umbrellas. They never threw anything away. There were no cooking facilities. There was a large date book in the front hallway where we signed in and out. Every night, at ten o'clock, one of Mr. Mercier's employees did a bed check. He'd knock on our doors; we'd open them and show him our parole IDs. If we missed the curfew, it was back to prison unless we had a medical excuse.

I made it back to my room on time. I washed up down the hall. I could smell a combination of dope smoke and air freshener and turned toward a door at the end of the floor. "Don't even think about it," I said to myself and hustled back to my room. I switched on the small transistor radio I had taken from the boat. I didn't care for the music stations but listened to talk radio. The more ridiculous the subject, the more insane the guests, the more I liked the show. It was like having prison company.

Without Melissa, there were only two options left. Drugs and money. The stash was burning a picture into my brain. Shortly before I was sentenced, I had hidden the twenty kilos I had stolen off the boat. I wrapped the package in heavy plastic and duct tape. I didn't want any moisture getting in. Then I put it in a canvas duffle bag. I didn't know where to bury it, so I went down to the Trailways bus station. I looked at the big wall map and picked a town that was close to Boston and heavily wooded. On the ride, I kept looking out the window for a good spot. Finally we passed a pond and some state park land and I got off. I walked into the woods and looked for a landmark.

When I found a tall rock that looked like a horse's head, I stepped back twenty paces. I looked around and listened. I didn't see or hear anyone. I had brought a garden spade, and began to dig. There were lots of tree roots, and it took three hours to dig a hole wide and deep enough to hold the bag. After I packed the dirt down, I covered the spot with dead leaves and a load of rocks. I took one last look and walked away.

IN THE MORNING, MR. MERCIER WAS STANDING over my bed before I could sit up. We were allowed to lock our doors, but he had a master key.

"So you lost the job?" He put his hand flat against my chest and held me down.

"I didn't do anything wrong." I kicked the covers off my legs and twisted out from under his hand.

He looked at me and shook his head. "Don't you own pajamas?"

I still slept in my clothes. "It's too cold," I replied.

"Anyway, I got you another job. You'll be parking cars at the Aku-Aku restaurant on Commonwealth Avenue."

"Thanks. Shifting and steering with one hand will be a thrill."

"You're a smart boy," he said. He looked around the room. There wasn't much to look at. I kept most of my stuff locked up in my backpack under the bed. "By the way, I want to give you a warning." He looked down at me with his hands on his hips. "Don't call and bother your ex-girl. She called my office and gave my secretary a hard time. If she calls again, I'll ask her to file a complaint, and as soon as she signs the form I'll have you pulled in and, baby, you'll be back where you started."

"Okay," I said. "Sorry. It won't happen again. I just got lonely and she flipped out."

"You have to get a life of your own," he said. "You have to learn how to help yourself. She's not going to help you. Your folks aren't around and so it's up to me. Get out of bed. Take a shower. Shave. Eat. Read a paper. Think." He spit out the last words.

"I'm working on it," I said.

"Working on it?" he repeated. "As far as I can tell you don't know what work is. I got guys coming out who are holding two, three jobs. Guys with ambition. Goals. Direction. What do you have?"

"I have some dreams," I said.

He leaned into my face. "Who the fuck do you think you are? Martin Luther King? You have dreams? In your sleep maybe. But not dreams like you know what you want to do with yourself. I can just look at you and tell you don't have those kind of dreams."

I stood up and bent over, trying to stretch my back out. I slept funny with my arm in a cast. The extra weight on my arm left me with a sharp pain down my left side.

"I'm trying to get it together here," I said. "I'm looking at the want ads. Maybe I can find something at a hospital."

"Yeah, right. Like I'm going to place a drug smuggler in a hospital. In the meantime, do good at the Aku-Aku. I drink there and don't want you screwing up my reputation."

When he was gone, I slumped back down on the bed and turned my face into the pillow. My arm was killing me. I slept through the day. I was too depressed to move. That night I stood next to the Aku-Aku valet parking sign and waited. No one wanted to pay extra to have their car parked just to eat at a cheap Polynesian restaurant decorated with a gang of Easter Island statues made out of papier-mâché. After about an hour my arm began to throb. The screws were frozen again. They felt loose. If this kept up my elbow would have a permanent wobble.

There was a pay phone just inside the front door. I dashed in, jammed the receiver between my shoulder and ear, and slipped a dime into the slot. I dialed Melissa's number. I let it ring once, then hung up. "Don't do this," I said to myself as I walked back outside. "Just leave her alone." But I was so tired of being cold and hurt and depressed that I was pretty certain I wasn't going to listen.

About every two minutes a car pulled in to the Aku-Aku parking lot. There was a Christmas concert at Fenway Park and everyone was looking for a cheap parking place. I told the first few they had to look somewhere else.·

Another car pulled in. I shuffled over to the driver's window before he turned off the engine.

"Are you going to the restaurant?", I asked.

"Fenway."

"Five bucks," I said. What the hell, it was half what they charged down the street. He gave it to me and I went back up to the corner. A car full of mothers and kids cruised by. I waved them in. "Five bucks," I said. They paid.

I looked down the street. I didn't see any other prospects. I went to the pay phone. I dialed Melissa's number and let it ring twice before hanging up.

I ran out and parked another car for five bucks. I returned to the pay phone and let it ring three times. I hung up and parked another car. I went to the phone, dialed, and let it ring four times.

"You're playing Russian roulette," I said to myself after I hung up. "You don't even know what you want to say to her and while you're frozen in the headlights she'll blow you away. Get a grip on yourself."

I parked two more cars and went back inside. I stuck my head through the door to see if the manager knew what I was doing. He was busy arranging pu-pu platters at the All-Day Happy Hour steam tables. I glanced over at the bar to see if Mercier was knocking back a mai tai. He wasn't. I returned to the telephone. I let it ring. "I love you. I love you not," I thought. "I love you. I love you not. I love you." She could probably walk across her apartment ten times during five rings. She either wasn't there or wasn't answering. "Come on number six," I said, pulling the trigger to each ring, imagining the rotation of the cylinder. One. Two. Three. Four. Five. Six. Slam.

I stayed inside to warm up. I stood around the

steam tables. I thought I might snatch one of the Sterno cups and take it outside to keep my hands warm.

"You wan' sum foo'?" the Asian busboy asked as he checked the pans.

"Yeah."

He brought me to the kitchen and dipped a ladle into a large vat. He filled a paper coffee cup with hot and sour soup.

"Ou' back," he said, and pointed to the fire exit next to the trash compactor.

"Thanks." I shrugged and left. The soup tasted like spoiled vegetables and burned corn starch. I sipped at it, then wiped my nose on my glove. Beyond the chain-link fence were the train tracks. Beyond them were warehouse buildings. And beyond that I didn't know. I had never been that far.

"You're on the edge," I said to myself and held the warm soup container to my face. "You're halfway between falling off and hanging on."

I thought of myself out on the ocean grasping the end of the rope, bobbing up and down behind the sailboat. The swells elevated me above the masts. For a moment I could see everything from there: the waves running toward the horizon, the roundness of the world, the enormous sky, and the long yellow tow rope wrapped around my hand. Then I drifted down into the trough so deep between the waves the entire boat was obscured. I could see nothing but dark water. My worst fear was that somehow the rope would slip out of my hand and dart away from me faster than I could chase after it. I could see the rope dancing lightly across the swells as I tried to swim up their sides and over the top. It would be futile.

I knew then that Melissa's love could make the difference. I could hold on to her. She wouldn't let me drift away. She'd pull me up, point me in the right direction, and give me a shove. I needed it. I was ready to let someone else tell me how to live. I was doing a piss-poor job on my own.

I set the soup down and walked around the outside of the building and through the parking lot and around to the front door. I removed my glove and fished the dime out of my pocket. I dialed. One ring. Two. Three. Four. Five. Six. Seven. Eight. Nine. I kept firing blanks.

"Hello?"

"Melissa," I said softly.

"I knew it was you," she snapped.

"Look, I know this sounds stupid. I need to talk with you, please. I still love you."

"I don't want to get dragged into a conversation where I already know all the answers. Just forget it."

"I know, but just listen. I've made a lot of mistakes—"

"I'm hanging up," she said.

"I'm coming over. I just want to talk."

"I'll call the cops. I mean it." She hung up.

I ran out to the street and flagged down a cab.

"Forty-four Cedar Street," I said to the driver.

It took less than five minutes to get there. I paid and lurched out of the car. I knew Melissa wouldn't buzz me in to the building. I looked around and then with one kick forced the outside door. I wished I had thought to buy flowers. I walked up the stairs and rapped on her apartment door.

"Go away," she hollered.

"Don't be afraid," I said. "I'm just here to talk." I was panting like a dog.

"I'm calling the police," she cried.

"Don't. I'm already a mess. Just help me. Just listen."

"No! You listen. You keep saying you're a mess, so do something about it. Don't come looking for me to help you. I can't. I don't want to. Now go away."

"Listen," I said, not really knowing what to say to turn her around. "I need your help."

"Listen to this," she said. "I'm pressing three numbers on the telephone. Nine . . . one . . . one."

"Give me a break," I pleaded.

"Hello, Boston Police? My name is Melissa Porter."

"You aren't calling."

"Hello? My ex-boyfriend is harassing me. Yeah . . . Ray Jakes . . . Forty-four Cedar Street."

"Don't," I said. "Really. I'm begging. Please don't."

"Too late," she replied. I heard her stomp away from the door toward the back of the apartment. A door slammed.

I stood there. "Fuck!" I kicked at her door. It gave way. I ran in to her apartment and stopped at the next locked door. "Did you call them?" I yelled.

"Yes," she cried out.

"Shit! Well maybe this is what I wanted anyway. Maybe I'm just looking for an excuse to take off." I said this more to myself than to her. I looked around the living room. There was a photograph of us in a silver picture frame on the coffee table. I grabbed it and shoved it into my jacket pocket.

"I love you," I hollered.

"Just go," she replied.

I ran down the stairs and stepped out onto the street. I could hear a siren, but that wasn't unusual in Boston. Just as I passed Mt. Vernon Street, a cop car came up the hill and took a left on to Cedar. When I reached Beacon Street, I caught a cab.

"Seventeen Cortes," I said. When he pulled up to the halfway house I told him to wait. I climbed the stairs two at a time and unlocked my door. I knew what I wanted. I jerked the backpack out from under my bed and filled it with clothes and my portable radio. I locked the door and dashed down the stairs.

"South Station," I said. "I'm late for a train."

"Where are you headed?" he asked.

"Chicago." I lied.

He dropped me off. I went into the station, then out the back and along the empty loading docks. I sat on a bench in the darkness and collected my thoughts. I wanted to get my hash and I wanted to get out of town. I patted the bulge on the side of my pea coat. "Thank God I have money," I thought. When I had my plan organized, I went back into the station, picked up a train schedule, and marched out the side door. The Hotel Essex faced South Station. Some of the neon lights across the marquee had been intentionally knocked out, and now the hotel advertised "HOT . . . SEX". A line of homeless men were waiting at the alley entrance for a Social Services clerk to place them in unoccupied rooms. I had a wad of five-dollar bills in my pocket and aimed straight for the lobby.

As THE BUS SPED DOWN ROUTE 3 TOWARD Hull, the sun rose behind us. I was tired. I hadn't slept well. I kept listening for the police, but "HOT SEX" is pretty much what I heard all night from the room next door.

I stared out at the trees. I couldn't tell one from another. A few dead leaves hung on like frozen bats impaled on the maze of twigs. I was afraid to blink. I knew I was on the right bus to Hull and I was just waiting for the state park sign to flag where I had buried the hash.

I was filled with anxiety. What if I couldn't find it or the spot had been developed with park buildings? It had been over a year. There might be a parking lot and I'd have to come back with a pickax and rip the whole thing up. What if a dog had dug it up and some lucky guy found it and walked away with my stash, wondering who the asshole was who was stupid enough to bury this much hash under a rock. I started to think about how much money it was worth to me if I had it or had lost it. There were twenty kilos. That made 640 ounces. At $100 an ounce that was $64,000. If I held out and sold it by the gram, I could make big money. But making 20,000 individual sales could be dangerous in a town where I knew only one person. If I sold it only by the kilo, I'd make a lot less. Only $30,000.

Then I saw the state park sign. I yanked the cord, and the driver pulled over at the next bus stop. I hopped out and set my backpack down on a bench and pretended to look for something inside one of the zippered pouches. When the bus was out of sight, I crossed the road and slipped into the woods.

It didn't take long. I found the horse-head rock. I stepped back the twenty paces. I kicked the stones away with my boot, dropped down onto my knees, and dug at the dirt with my good hand. It was frozen, but it came up in chunks after I beat at it with a rock. Then there it was. The hash smelled strong and musty even in the cold, but the plastic wrapping had kept it dry. I worked the package down into my backpack, then stuffed my clothes around it. Then I removed my pea coat and squatted down. I worked quickly to hold off the cold. I took my Swiss army knife and cut open the inner lining. I reached in and touched one of the packets of five-hundred-dollar bills. "This is what you traded one year of your life for," I said to myself. It would have been great to have the hash, the money, and my freedom. I had lost a year, and now that I was jumping parole I was going to lose my identity. Another twenty years down the drain.

For a moment I sat there, wondering who I might become, wondering if it were possible to lose myself and become someone who wasn't driven by his criminal past. I wanted to be clean and well scrubbed like a new object with a fresh memory. I was tired of waking up as the drug smuggler every morning, and if I did this right, I would wake up with a new name, new ID, no history, and new choices.

I pulled one of the bills out of the packet and shoved it down into my jeans pocket. I stood up, put my coat back on, hoisted the backpack over my right shoulder, and stumbled through the woods.

I caught the bus back to Boston and took a cab to South Station. There was an Amtrak train leaving for Washington, D.C., and from there I could transfer to New Orleans, then Memphis. I did my best to stand up straight, not to draw attention to the weight of the backpack as it pulled down my shoulder. My cast already strained my back, and now I felt like I was bent over like Quasimodo. I crossed the street and bought a few things at the drugstore.

When I returned to the station it was still early, so I went into the Boxcar Lounge. It was already filled with the "HOT SEX" crowd. I ordered a beer and took it to the phone booth in the back. I dialed the long distance operator in Memphis. There was only one S. Zimmer. He picked up right away.

"Elvis?" I said. "Is this Elvis?"

"There's no Elvis here," he said coldly.

"I mean Seth. Is this Seth Zimmer?"

"Who's calling?" he asked.

"This is Ray. From West Street, man."

"Doc?" he said brightly.

"Yeah," I said.

"Well, what's happening?"

"I want to come for a visit," I said. "I miss you, buddy."

[226]

"Come on down," he replied. "Heck, I'd love to see you."

"Fine," I replied. "God, Elvis, this is great."

"I've got to tell you one thing," he said. "I'm not Elvis anymore. That prison thing is a long way behind me," he said. "I haven't put on the costume since I returned. I got a job in a bank, and I'm taking classes in accounting."

"That's exactly what I'm after," I replied. "A few more moves and I'll have it all together, be a whole new person myself. I've been thinking of college again. Forestry studies."

"There you go, Doc," he replied. "Now I hear you talking direction. Take control of your life, man. Don't just blow it like all those losers we saw."

I took a sip of beer. "There's more to why I'm calling," I said. "Things aren't going well right now. I thought you could help me out."

"Just say the word," he said. "I owe you, buddy. If it wasn't for you I might have missed my chance to get out of West Street."

"Well, I'll be down tomorrow. My train gets in from New Orleans at around three in the afternoon."

"Great," he said. "We'll have a party. I'll call a few friends. I know some nice ladies."

Yeah. A party. That's what I needed to feel better. I got out of prison and nobody threw me a party. Melissa had greeted me by having all my boxes packed and ready to move out of her life. "That'll be great," I said. "Well, I gotta run. I have a train to catch."

"Tomorrow," he said. "I'll be there."

After I hung up, I pulled the picture frame out of a side pouch on my pack. I looked at the photograph of Melissa and myself in St. Croix, at her parents' house. My eyes were red and shiny. I had just smoked a joint. "This is history," I thought. I turned over the frame and opened the back. I removed the photograph and ripped it into pieces and dropped them on the floor. Man, I felt good. For the first time in a long while I felt great. I didn't need Melissa. Elvis would take care of me. I knew he'd come through.

ONCE THE TRAIN LEFT BOSTON, I DRAGGED my luggage into the bathroom and locked the door. I began to unpack my toiletries and spread them out around the small sink. Because my bad arm was extended so far from my body, I couldn't turn to my right. My left hand acted like the pawl in a ratchet and kept catching on the towel dispenser or the sanitary napkin machine. Every time I needed something just in front of that hand I had to make a one-way circle backwards and sneak up on it from behind.

"You're so fucking cheap," I said to myself. I should have paid for a sleeping car with a private toilet. But this money was all I had. And in Canada the money was worth 20 percent more. I thought of Parker. Cocksucker, I thought. I hope those cactus spines are still in his face.

The only scissors I had were part of my Swiss army knife. I held the knife between my teeth and opened the scissors with my right hand. I set them down, combed my hair forward with my fingers and looked into the mirror.

Someone knocked on the door. I turned to the right and smacked my knuckles on the edge of the towel rack. "Jesus Christ! It's occupied," I shouted.

First, I cut my bangs up above my eyebrows. I trimmed everything around my ears and blindly made about a hundred little snips at the back of my head. When I finished I didn't look much different from the exit photograph they took at West Street, and I knew that was the photo they would use to look for me. I trimmed my bangs up to my hairline. That helped. Then I began to cut everything back so at the end my hair looked like an old feathered bird in some dusty ornithology museum.

Before I started to mix the hair dye I had bought in the drugstore, I carefully read the directions. I had never done this before.

When I was living with my parents in St. Croix, an old friend from Fort Lauderdale called me up. I knew him through Robby, and we had done some shoplifting together. He was fat and wore baggy clothes. I wore a heavy overcoat and dark glasses. We'd enter a store and I'd hang all over the watch counter and ask to see the expensive brands. I'd try them on, take them off, and move them around on the counter and attract a crowd of help while he strolled the store and snatched what he could shove down his pants. He mostly stole clothes his size, so it wasn't such a good deal for me. But he stole an altar chalice out of a church supply shop, which I thought was pretty gutsy. We drank red wine from it, got drunk, and performed fake rituals.

When he called me in St. Croix, he was in trouble.

"Can I hide out at your place for a while?" he asked.

"Sure," I replied. "What'd you screw up?"

"Tell you when I get down," he whispered. "The phone might be bugged."

I doubted it. He was always overly dramatic. When I picked him up at the airport, he looked like a behemoth troll doll with lime green hair standing straight up from his head.

"Jesus. What happened to your hair?" I asked.

"I was in a hurry," he said. "I didn't mix it right. Now I look like a cockatoo."

He was being tracked down for a string of petty robberies. He had driven around town dressed as Santa Claus, raiding Salvation Army donation buckets. It was a pretty low crime. For about two weeks we ate and drank up his Santa money. "Ho ho ho," he'd sing as we tossed back another black Russian and chase it with Heineken. When he was down to a big canvas bank bag of nickels and dimes, I put him back on a plane to go live with his brother in South Carolina. I don't know what happened to him afterwards, but it seemed to me that his rat's nest of green hair could have been spotted by satellite. I didn't want to end up looking like him.

I put on the plastic glove and mixed the hair dye. I squeezed it onto my hair and rubbed it in. I looked at my watch. I had to wait for twenty minutes. Already the smell of the dye was making my eyes water. I coughed.

Someone knocked on the door again.

"It's occupied," I shouted. "Can't you read?"

They stomped off. I looked into the mirror. It was working. My hair was turning a bright yellow and my scalp was turning red. "Oh Christ," I muttered, "I hope I'm not allergic to this shit."

I was. Beneath my blond hair was a skullcap of red bumps that burned as though I had dipped the top of my head in boiling water. But I looked different.

I wanted to feel different too. I dug into my backpack and removed a kilo. I unwrapped the cellophane from one corner and whittled off a couple grams of hash with my knife. I ate it and washed it down with water from the tap.

When I finished I carried my bags down to the club car. Before the bartender asked what I wanted, he looked at my hair. He looked down at my cast, then again at my hair.

"My name is Chuck," I said. "I'll have a Bud."

"Sure, Chuck," he replied, and turned and reached into a cooler. He turned back and set it down before me. "Anything else?"

I looked him straight in the eye. "I'll take a burger."

He popped one into the microwave oven.

I reached into the condiment tray for a packet of mustard.

The buzzer sounded on the microwave. He pulled the burger out with a pair of plastic tongs and slid it onto a paper plate. "How'd you break your arm?" he asked.

"Skiing Aspen," I replied. I could feel the sweat on my scalp. I wanted to run my hand through my hair but didn't dare. I thought it might pull out in clumps. I grabbed my napkins and turned away.

When I sat down, I felt like everyone was looking at me, thinking, "His name's not Chuck. He doesn't ski. His name is Ray and he's a parole jumper. Let's steal his hash and cash and turn him in. Maybe there's a reward."

When I was a kid I wanted to be an actor. I was too shy to tell anyone, so I practiced in private. Several blocks from where I lived was an open field waist-high with straw weeds. I stood out in the middle and waited for a breeze to wave the grass about. When it whipped up, I threw my arms in the air, blocking my face, and screamed, "RUN! MOTHRA! MOTHRA! RUN! RUN!" I dashed off and twisted my face up with anguish. "MOTHRA! MOTHRA! NO! NO! DON'T — AGRHHH!" I fell to the ground but Mothra snatched me up in her giant claw. I was carried away bleeding, with my guts dangling, toward Mothra's jungle nest, while thousands of Japanese gasped in terror.

"LOOK! LOOK!" they shouted. "IIIEEEEE! Mothra has the emperor's son!"

Once while I was lying facedown in the weeds, my arms spread open, screaming out the piercing cries of the Japanese, a kid came up and touched me on the back of the head.

"What!" I shouted and jumped to my feet. My eyes were wild. I was caught between my embarrassment and the fear that Mothra had finally run me through.

"You all right?" he asked. He was my age.

"Yeah, I'm fine. I'm acting." I thought that would explain everything. For a moment he stared at me in disbelief. Then he ran off. I thought he was going to get someone to throw a net over me. I went directly home and never did it again.

I finished my beer and got another. The hash was coming on, and I looked out the train window. I loved that feeling of everything passing behind me. It was like digging a hole and throwing the dirt over to one side. I just wanted to keep digging. Don't look back, I thought. If you dwell on the past you'll be buried alive. But I could feel my mistakes pressing down against me, like when they crushed witches under a pile of rocks. The past carried a lot of weight.

We sped by houses and fields, rivers and highways, entire towns and cities. I'll never see them again, I thought, and it made me feel good. The tracks passed evenly beneath the train. The wheels were locked on to the rails. I listened to the steady clack and rumble of the cars.

"It's okay," I said to myself. "Stay calm. Breath deep. It will all work out."

THE FIRST THING I SAW AT THE MEMPHIS
station was Ebbers bellied up to a freestanding snack
bar. It was a central spot from which he could watch
the revolving doors that opened onto the tracks. But
his attention had shifted away from the doors. Over
his head a fly-specked painting of a roasted pig advertised barbecue. When I spun through the door and
scanned the station, Ebbers was lowering a pork
sandwich into his open mouth. The sauce-soaked
white bread looked like a bloody bandage in his
hand. He stood with one foot off the ground and the
other up on his elevated toe, teasing himself as he
might tease a dog with a bone. Travelers were walking way around him. He took a bite and licked a
dollop of sauce that hung from the crust. But suddenly he stopped chewing and squinted toward me.
He looked confused. On the speakers overhead, the
station master again announced the arrival of my
train. He looked up at the speaker as though I might
slide out of it.

I turned, ducked my head down, and slipped into
the bathroom. Shit, I thought, what's he doing here?

I first thought he must have seen me. But when I
looked into the mirror, I knew he couldn't have
picked me out of a lineup. My hair was fluorescent
yellow and my scalp was blood red. My left arm was

in a cast the size of an elephant tusk. I was filthy and exhausted, and my clothes smelled like burning rags. Serious smokers take trains.

Okay, I thought, Elvis must have sent him to greet me. I don't like him, but he's part of the picture. Elvis might be able to get rid of his Elvis thing but not his fat man. Everybody needs someone to carry their luggage. So did I.

I jerked the backpack up over my shoulder. A pain shot across my back and down my leg. I bent over and walked toward Ebbers. He had finished the sandwich and was licking the red grease from between his knuckles. I thought I might have to write my name in barbecue sauce on his T-shirt before he recognized me, but when I was three feet away and staring him directly in the eye, he woke up.

"Doc," he cried out and opened his arms. "You've changed." He looked me over. "You got a broken arm and you painted your head."

"I was in a movie," I said and stopped short of a hug. "Where's Elvis?"

"Working," he replied. "He got called in, so it's just me to pick you up. Can you believe Elvis is *working*? His parole officer made him get a job." He laughed.

"Can you carry this?" I asked.

He reached for my bag, and I let him pull it from my shoulder and hoist it onto his.

"You got bricks in here?"

"Books. Where are we going?"

"Cheap motel." He smiled. "You know the rules.

Cons can't live with cons. By the way, Elvis wants to know if you're hot?"

"Yes and no," I answered. "We'll talk about it later. Let's just get out of here."

"Either you are or not," he replied, wagging his finger at me. "You can't be a little pregnant or a little wanted."

"It would be best if my parole officer didn't know where to find me."

"Good. We'll go to the less cheap motel. They have color tubes."

"How much cheaper is the other?" I asked.

"Two bucks."

"Is it just as good?"

"It's two bucks worse, which is a lot. No ice and black and white tubes."

We walked out to the parking lot and across it, toward the far corner. It was a hot day and I could smell myself and feel the sweat running under my arms and down the inside of my cast. Ebbers put the bags in the back seat of his red Bronco.

"Nice car," I remarked.

"Elvis gave it to me for my birthday," he said proudly. "I love it." He ran his hand over the hood and grinned. He still had bits of pork between his teeth. He worked at them with his finger.

"Must have cost a lot."

"Hey, that's Elvis. He can get pissed off, but he can't hold a grudge."

I began to wonder just how much money Elvis had. Maybe he could buy the hash from me at a high price. I could get my cash and ID together, fly to Canada, buy a car, and disappear into the mountains. In my mind, northern Canada spread out into an endless carpet of trees. It went on forever. No cops. No criminals. No suspicious friends.

I stepped up into the Bronco and twisted sideways with my arm propped across my knee.

"It's a wicked day," Ebbers remarked, watching me closely. "Why don't you take off your coat?"

"Too much trouble." I looked away from him.

He drove over the Mud Island Bridge, toward West Memphis. When we crossed the Mississippi, I rolled my window down and looked out at the thick water, as shiny as mercury.

"It's cheaper in Arkansas, and less heat," Ebbers went on. "We live on the other side of the river. Close to Graceland."

"Figures," I said.

He grinned. "But we'll move once we get some bucks together."

At the first exit off the bridge, he pulled up to a liquor store. "We got a long afternoon ahead of us while waiting for Elvis. Might as well drink it up. What do you want?"

"Cheap red wine," I said. "And a six of wide-mouth Old English."

He held out his hand.

"Whatever happened to southern hospitality?" I asked.

"You win the war, you pay," he replied.

With some difficulty I reached into my pants

pocket and pulled out a twenty. "One thing," I said, "Do you still call him Elvis?"

"Not to his face. He gets madder'n hell."

Ebbers snapped the twenty out of my hand and closed the door. He skipped over a puddle and up the few steps to the liquor store's double glass doors. He was nimble for a fat man. I watched him through the dull glare of the neon beer signs. He paused next to the beef jerky display and pulled a few toothpicks from a box. He slipped one behind his ear and the other between his lips. He lumbered past the cashier, then turned down a back aisle toward the beer coolers and the wall of cheap wine. He paused, put his hand on his hip, and slowly looked over the selections. He reached for a cold suitcase of Jax.

"Idiot," I said. I scooted across the front seat, turned the ignition, reversed, and slapped the automatic into drive. "You fat, crab-infested, mouse-eating pig." I saw a sign for Loosahatchie: The Land That Time Forgot. That was just what I wanted. I punched the gas and glanced up at the rearview mirror. Ebbers wasn't even out of the store yet.

He'll never call the cops. His first call will be to Elvis. And Elvis won't let him call the cops. He could have his parole revoked if he were connected to me in any way. I turned on the radio. I pressed on the gas. I felt as though I were coming alive, finally in control of something. I wanted to turn the Bronco around and drive straight to Canada.

About five miles down the road, I pulled in at

the River 'n' Road Motel. Air Conditioning. Kitchenettes. Ice. Bank of snack machines. Cheap. It looked forgotten. I parked around back, under an oak tree with a lot of birds.

I checked in to a room with a kitchenette and dialed Elvis's number.

"I figured you'd call." He sounded a little more angry than I thought he should be.

"I thought you were at work," I replied.

"I got a call from Ebbers. Seems he's stranded at a liquor store with only twenty dollars."

"I don't trust him, Seth. You shouldn't have sent him."

"Believe me, Doc, he doesn't like you either."

"The car's fine," I said. "You can come pick it up."

"Look. If you don't trust me, I can't help you."

"I trust *you*."

"He's harmless," he said. "Now where are you?"

"Why don't just *you* show up," I suggested.

"I can't drive. Never had to learn. That's how I met Ebbers. He was my chauffeur. I bought a '57 pink Caddie but needed a driver."

"Okay." I told him where I was.

"Within the hour," he said. "We'll take a cab."

I had to get busy. I needed to hide the dope and find a new place for my money. It was 70 degrees outside and I was burning up under my pea coat. There was so much sweat gathered inside my cast that my arm began to slide around and make sucking noises.

I lifted the covers off one side of the bed. I pushed the mattress back halfway and tapped at the box spring. It was gauze over wooden slats, with a few tired coils wheezing inside. I found my knife and cut open the fabric. I reached inside to feel around. The bottom of the box was lined with thin plywood, perfect. I stashed the kilos of hash inside, then pulled the mattress over to cover the hole.

Every time a car pulled into the parking lot I parted the window curtains and peeked out. The motel was full of nervous action. The rooms seemed to turn over by the hour. That explained the condom machine in the bathroom.

I returned to the bed. I reached into the lining of my jacket and removed the bills. I was thinking that it might be a good idea to remove my cast, wrap my arm with zip-lock bags of bills, then put a new cast on. It would be a good place to hide the money when I crossed into Canada. I didn't want them to find it on me and ask questions and run a search. Even with a new ID. I couldn't be sure something wouldn't pop up. But right now I didn't have a way to get to the drugstore to buy the gauze and plaster. Plus, I wanted to wait until I sold the hash, then add that money to the stash.

I took a piece of aluminum foil from a shelf in the kitchenette and made the bills into a shiny brick. I slipped it into my underwear and pulled out my shirt-tail.

I heard a car. Two doors slammed. I got up and looked through the peephole. Ebbers gave my door the finger, then marched to the back of the motel. Elvis waved him on and paid the cab driver.

I waited until Elvis was about to knock on the door before I swung it open. "Seth," I said and pawed at the air with my bad arm. "It's great to see you buddy."

He looked stunned. I stepped back. He entered the room and closed the door. "What happened, Doc?" he asked. "You look roughed up."

"I'll pull out of it," I said. "But you look great. How are things going?" I pointed to the only chair.

"Thanks," he said, a little too tightly. He was dressed in a beige leisure suit. If I hadn't known he was once an Elvis impersonator, I would never have guessed. He had really moved on. "But this isn't about me," he said directly. "Why'd you take Ebbers's car?"

"I just needed to make sure he wasn't up to something funny," I said. "I didn't see you and I didn't know what he might do. He never liked me in prison so I didn't think—"

"It's all right Doc. You're not in prison now, so don't worry. Just relax. You're a wreck. Now tell me what's happened and then we can think all of this through and get you set up."

"I know I'm tense," I said. "A lot of things just seem to have gone wrong at once. Like, breaking up with my girlfriend and catching a train to Memphis to visit a friend is normal behavior. But since I'm on parole, it's a fucking crime. So it's not like there's an APB out on me. I'm sure the feds aren't searching high and low. They'll just wait for me to make a mistake, pick me up on a speeding ticket. At least, this is how I figure it."

"You should have stayed put up there," Elvis said. He stood up, peeked out the window, and turned toward me. "Look at you. You looked better in prison. Now you look like the guys we made fun of. Maybe you can call your parole officer and work something out."

"To tell you the truth, I don't want to work something out. I just want a new life. I need some new ID and then I've got to disappear. Then who knows? Maybe I'll never do another wrong thing for the rest of my life."

Elvis nodded. "Maybe. Maybe not. You put yourself in a bad spot, but I can help," he said calmly. "I can order you the ID, for a price."

"I have that much," I said. "But I need more."

"Can't help you there," he said. "I've got my job, but Ebbers is on unemployment. We don't have a lot coming in."

"I'm hoping you can help in other ways."

He raised an eyebrow.

"I've got some weight stashed in Boston. If you have the connections . . ."

"What kind?"

"Hash."

"College dope," he said derisively. "We have a university here, but dealing with the college set is a pain."

"What do you mean?"

"Everything to them is a joke. When we did the Elvis seances, they would come in just for kicks. They'd laugh during my routine, then later, after they'd chased away all my prospects, they'd want to be my friend. They either want to destroy everything or buy everything. And unfortunately, they always have more opinions than cash. It's a dangerous imbalance. If they want to be your friend, you know they're broke."

"Can you try?" I asked.

"Yeah."

"What's the heat like here?"

"If you were selling dope or coke, then it would be more of a problem. But hash and reefer are frat drugs. They'll sell their books to get high."

"Then let's do it," I said. I was eager to count money.

"Fine," he said. "No problem." He leaned forward and locked eyes with me. "Things around here are pretty cool, so there is no reason to get freaky. So don't fuck with Ebbers. If you get him pissed off, he's not as easy to operate. You know what I mean?"

"Yeah," I said. "Sorry. I'll try to relax."

"Good. Just remember, everything will be all right."

Ebbers threw his weight against the door. "Let me in," he hollered.

Elvis turned the lock. Ebbers stumbled forward, grabbed at the pole lamp, yanked it loose, and plowed into the bed.

"Keep it down, you clumsy ass," Elvis snapped.

Ebbers pulled himself up and gave me a menacing look. "There's bird shit all over my car."

"Where's my six-pack?" I shot back.

"Fuck you," he said. "If you're arm wasn't broken I'd break it for you."

"Stop it," Elvis said, then turned to me. "Look. Give me a couple days to pull all this together. I'll throw a little party at my place and maybe we can have some laughs and take care of business all at once."

"Fine," I said.

Ebbers glared at me.

"I'm sorry I borrowed your car," I said. "I just don't like to be driven around by a man with a heart condition."

"What do you mean?"

Elvis turned and gave me a puzzled look.

"I took your chest x-ray in West Street," I said. "You have an enlarged heart. I showed it to the doctors, but they said you were a short timer and that by the time it stopped ticking, you'd be outside."

Ebbers paled and looked toward Elvis.

"Is this the truth?" Elvis asked.

"Yes," I said, knowing it wasn't, but getting a kick out of messing with Ebbers. "Do yourself a favor and see a doctor."

"Thanks," Elvis replied.

"I don't feel sick," Ebbers said, his hand over his heart.

"But you are," I said. "Believe me."

A COUPLE DAYS LATER ELVIS CALLED AND said he had a deal arranged. He and Ebbers would pick me up. When they pulled in, Ebbers tapped the horn. I went out and took a seat in the back of the Bronco.

"Here's the deal, Doc," Elvis said, turning toward me as Ebbers pulled away from the motel. "This Wayne guy is a frat boy from Delta House. They have a lock on the campus flow. The word I got is that he's a straightforward guy and that they are eager for the hash because they don't get much through here. So you should get a decent price."

I thought about what he said. "Where are you in all of this?"

"You're on your own, Doc," he replied. I've got my community service at the Boy's Club. You got Ebbers, but he has to stay with the car. But don't sweat it. These guys aren't gun freaks."

That didn't calm me. "We could be talking a lot of money here," I said. "Money and dope make people greedy, and when greedy people don't see any barriers they start wanting things really cheap, and to the *extremely* greedy person, *free* is the best kind of cheap."

"Nobody is going to take you off, Doc. You got to think positive. Just set the price, deliver the goods, get the cash, and split."

"I know how this is supposed to go," I said. "It's how things go wrong is what makes me nervous. If everyone is so honorable, why are you ducking out?"

"Chill," Elvis replied. "I'm helping you. Remember? This is your deal and your money. I'm just doing you a fucking favor."

Elvis turned to Ebbers and pointed down the street. "Drop me off on the corner," he instructed. "And pick me up in four hours."

Ebbers pulled over in front of a barber shop.

"Hey," I said to Elvis. "Did you get the ID yet?"

"It's in the works," he said. "First, you got to figure out what color you want your hair."

"When are we going to get to it?" I asked.

"Look, Doc, give it a rest. We'll take care of it. Now go." He opened the door, stepped down, and closed it, quietly.

"Taking care of business," Ebbers sang, and eased away from the curb.

We drove over to the college and down a side street lined with red oak trees. Ebbers slowed down.

"See that big house set back by the hedge?" he said, and pointed.

It looked like an old plantation home. Above the tall white pillars, "DELTA HOUSE" was painted in large block letters. From an upstairs windowsill the Confederate flag hung, slowly flapping against the weathered siding. On the lawn below were soggy overstuffed chairs and couches. Beer cans littered the lawn along with leftover fall leaves. Three empty kegs and a stack of Charles Chips tubs were lined up on the curb for pickup and delivery. The entire atmosphere begged the police to keep a constant eye on what went in or out. I didn't say anything to Ebbers.

He drove up to the corner and pulled in at a little strip mall. "I'll stay here," he said. He opened the glove compartment and pulled out a biker magazine.

"This is the easy part," I said. "I'll go in and see what he's got in mind. I'll be back in a few minutes."

I walked directly down the street and up to the front door. I glanced into the hedges to the left and right, but I knew if there was going to be trouble, it would be after I delivered, not now. I knocked. The door opened.

"I'm Wayne," said a guy in a red and black plaid hunting shirt. He had a thin blond beard over a narrow jaw. He looked just a little too old and intensely dried up to be a student. He looked more like an entry-level thief.

"Ray," I replied.

"Come on in."

I stepped into a circular anteroom. The ceiling was two stories high. A chandelier hung overhead. Its outstretched arms held a deflated blow-up doll.

"And this is Dave," Wayne said, pointing to an extremely pale kid dressed in gray sweats and a peeling silk top hat.

"Howdy," Dave said. He bowed at the waist, and with his long arms curling up from his sides, he looked like the Cat in the Hat. He didn't seem serious enough to do drug deals.

I followed Wayne and went up a wide set of stairs.

Dave followed us but didn't come into the bedroom. He stood guard outside the closed door. He must have worked deals with Wayne in the past.

"How much do you have and what quality?" he asked.

"A-grade Moroccan," I replied, knowing it was B-grade. Mine was too dry, not enough hash oil from the kif. A-grade was sticky to the fingers and AAA-black was mixed with opiates.

"Let's see it," he said.

I reached into my jacket pocket and pulled out an ounce wrapped in tinfoil. "Cut off a piece," I said.

He was ahead of me. He whipped a jackknife out of his back pocket and sliced a thin layer. It peeled away like hard cheese. The kitchen oil I had rubbed on it kept it together.

"You got a pipe?" Wayne asked.

I had brought mine. I had smoked a lot of hash in it and knew the resin would give it a better flavor and a little more THC.

He filled the pipe and put a match to it. The hash caught and he drew in the smoke. He held it in, then let it out slowly.

"How much?"

"Eighteen hundred a key."

"That's too high," he replied, looking right at me.

"How many do you want?"

"Fifteen," he said.

"Sixteen hundred."

He nodded.

"Are you carrying?" I asked.

"Yeah."

"I've got to take a walk," I said. "Give me an hour."

Wayne lit a match and took a long hit. He exhaled. "I'll be waiting."

I opened the bedroom door. Dave smiled and tipped his hat. No wonder Elvis didn't like the college crowd.

I walked down to the corner. Ebbers was parked just where I had left him. I crossed the street and got into the Bronco.

"Back to the motel," I said. "We have to pick it up. I'll carry it in to Wayne. Park here again so I can get to you fast if something happens."

"I thought the stuff was in Boston."

"I lied."

"What else have you lied about?" We pulled out of the parking lot and headed for the highway.

"Nothing," I replied. "I just didn't want you and Elvis to think I was carrying."

"You didn't trust us," he said.

"It's not a matter of trust. It's just how business is done. Never say more than you have to."

"So, you have more to tell?"

"Not yet," I replied and looked away.

"Everyone's got a secret," he said. "Well I've got a few of my own."

Keep them to yourself, I thought.

We drove over the De Soto Bridge and into West Memphis. I had left a "Do Not Disturb" sign on the motel room door and was hoping the maid could read English. I didn't want anyone messing with the bed until I got the hash out.

When we pulled up to the motel, I hopped out, went inside, and pushed the mattress over to one side. I reached into the hole. It was all where I had left it. I removed fifteen kilos and placed them in two grocery bags. I shoved two bath towels over the top of the hash. I could feel my heart pounding. I was nervous. Before my arrest, I had never thought of the cops when making a deal. I only worried that the money might be late or that the Jamaicans would sell me short weight. Now, I just thought of Wayne whipping out a badge and that imbecile Dave snapping the cuffs on me.

I got back into the Bronco. "Let's go," I said. "After you park down the street I'm going to walk the dope in. I want you to keep an eye on me the whole time. Watch what happens behind my back. If you see cops I want you to quietly drive away. If you see frat boys gathering around the house, I want you to drive up and lay on the horn. Pull the car up on the lawn so I can run out the front door and directly into the passenger seat. You got that?"

"What do you think I am? Stupid?"

"No," I said. "I just don't like anything left to chance when I don't know the people I'm dealing with."

"I'm going to need a drink," he said. He swerved off the road and into the same liquor store parking lot where I had left him behind. "Get out and buy me a quart." He smiled at me.

"Don't fuck with me, Ebbers," I said and reached for the bags.

He got to them first. "Leave them," he said. "I'll wait for you. Trust me."

"Don't pull any tricks," I said sternly. "We don't have time for this shit."

"You don't have a choice. Now get me a quart of Miller and some jerky."

"Just stay put." I opened the door and stepped down. I walked up to the door and pulled it open. I took one step in and then I heard the engine start up. I turned and made for the passenger door. He backed out, but by the time he could shift into drive I had grabbed the door handle. It was locked. He shot forward, then just as suddenly hit the brakes and tried to flick me off. I swung around and slammed against the fender but held on. He lurched forward again, and as I swung back I lost my footing and jerked my hand from the handle. The Bronco fishtailed toward me. I hit the running board, bounced off, and rolled to my left to avoid the wheels. In doing so I rolled over onto my cast. It cracked across the elbow and my arm began to throb.

I sat on the dirt and rocked back and forth at the waist while letting out little bursts of air. Ebbers had stopped at the edge of the parking lot. I saw him look into the rearview mirror. His reverse lights came on and he kicked up gravel as he shot toward me. I closed my eyes as he hit his brakes and skidded up next to my leg. He unlocked the passenger door and shoved it open. The corner swung out and struck me in the forehead. I tipped over and lay against my broken cast with my face pressed into the dirt and gravel.

He ran around the car and bent over me. "I'm sorry, Doc," he said in a penitent voice. "Honest. I was just teasing you. I didn't mean no harm."

I couldn't see his face from where I lay. "Help me up, you fuck-wad," I said, and raised my good arm toward him. "You broke my cast. Probably my arm." I spit the dirt out of my mouth.

He helped me into the front seat. "You don't have to buy me a beer," he said.

"But you better get me one," I said, and spit out more dirt.

He turned and went into the store. I twisted the mirror to look at myself. I had a triangular gash on my forehead. It wasn't deep. It just make me look more demented.

Ebbers returned and handed me a wad of napkins and an open beer.

"Let's get a move on," I ordered, and poured beer on the napkins and began to wipe my face.

He hit the gas and we pulled out of the parking lot.

When we returned to Delta House I had Ebbers cruise around the block. I was looking for cops but didn't see anything. "Now remember what I told you before," I said to him.

"Yes." He pulled into the strip mall and parked.

I got out. "Come around here and put the bags in my good hand."

He did so dutifully, and I crossed the street and headed for the frat house.

Wayne was waiting for me at the front door. We went up to his room. Dave closed the door behind us. I set the bags down and silently felt the relief in my muscles. "Fifteen kilos," I said. "Count it."

He picked one up and set it on a scale. He adjusted the weights. "Looks fine," he said. "Do you take checks?"

I didn't want to show too much anger but I was running out of patience for assholes. "Cash only," I said.

He smiled. "I'm just fuckin' with you," he said. "Be cool."

"I'm not from around here," I replied. "I haven't figured out the humor in this town."

He walked over to a dresser and removed a shoe box from a lower drawer. I took a few steps toward the window so I could take in the view. Ebbers slowly drove by. He stopped at the edge of the lawn, jumped out of the Bronco, and loaded the kegs into the back. I'll kill him, I thought.

Wayne returned and handed the shoe box to me.

I lifted the top and set it down on the bed. Inside were twenty-four bundles of bills, each bundle wrapped with rubber bands. I took the first one out and began to count. A thousand dollars. It was fine. I took the second one out and counted it.

"Can I smoke some more of your hash?" he asked.

"Go ahead," I replied. "This will take me a minute."

I listened to him light up and inhale as I fingered through each bundle. It was all there, twenty-four grand. When I finished I stood up. "Why don't you keep the rest of that ounce," I said. "But I'll need the pipe."

"Cool," he replied. He smacked his lips as he tapped the bowl out in an ashtray and handed it to me. "Funky flavor," he remarked.

Wesson oil, I thought. I slipped the pipe in with the money, then took the box and put it in one of the grocery bags. I glanced out the window. Ebbers was gone.

"Let me know if you want more," I said. "I'll be in town for a couple days."

"Yeah," he said and smiled wanly.

He and Dave walked me down the wide interior stairs of the plantation house. A few frat boys were sitting in the parlor room watching television. They turned to look me over as I walked past. Wayne opened the front door and I stepped out onto the porch. I looked down the stone front path that led to the street. I looked left along the hedge, then right. "Later," I said.

Ebbers was right where I'd left him. I opened the Bronco door and hopped up onto the seat. "Nice and easy," I instructed. "Everything is fine."

He grinned. "I knew you could do it, Doc. Elvis said you were good."

"You're pretty good yourself," I remarked and nodded toward the kegs.

"Every little bit helps," he said. "Can't buy beer with food stamps."

ELVIS LIVED IN A LIGHT PINK HOUSE WITH black trim. The driveway was pink concrete. There were pink flamingos wobbling among the weeds in the overgrown front yard.

"You know," Ebbers said, coming to a stop on the street, "Elvis is doing you a special favor. He swore he wouldn't have a party until he made the house normal. Painted it white with yellow trim and black-topped the driveway."

"He's a nice guy," I said.

"You better believe it," Ebbers replied. "He's the best man I ever met."

We got out of the car and walked across the grass. A life-size portrait of Elvis was painted on the front door. The lens for the peephole was his left pupil. The other eye had been scratched out with the tip of a key. Beneath the portrait, in script, was written *Heartbreak Hotel*.

Ebbers unlocked the door and pushed it open. The interior was like a little Graceland. Wall-to-wall orange shag carpeting. Big overstuffed chairs with lots of gold upholstery. The walls were covered with marbleized mirrors. The drapes were a waterfall of crushed blue velvet. The lamp shades were painted with scenes from Elvis movie posters. I stood there and took it all in.

"Elvis has been meaning to redo the furniture, too," Ebbers said.

"Seems that way." I stepped into the house and then pressed back against the inside of the front door, which was upholstered like the back seat of a car.

"I have to go turn in those kegs and pick Elvis up," he said. "Do me a favor? Don't tell Elvis about your little accident today. He'll be madder than hell with me."

"Okay. You can do me a favor, too. After you pick Elvis up, stop by a drugstore and tell him I need some hair dye. He'll know what kind to get."

"Will do," Ebbers said and paused with his hand extended.

I reached into my pocket and pulled out a ten.

He snatched it out of my hand. "You're catching on."

When he was gone I closed the door again and locked it. I went upstairs to the bathroom and kicked off my shoes. There was a big bathtub and I turned on the hot water. I opened the linen closet. I reached into my pants and pulled out my brick of money and put it in the shoe box with the money Wayne had given me. Then I lifted up a stack of folded pink sheets and slid the box under them. I peeled my clothes off and threw them in a corner. They should be burned, I thought.

I was still soaking in the bathtub when Elvis knocked.

"Come in," I hollered.

He opened the door and closed it behind him. "Ebbers said it all went smoothly."

"Without a hitch. One more good deal and I'll be gone."

"That's great," he said. "I think I have another in the works."

"Then let's do it. I'm pretty anxious to get going."

"First things first," he said. "Let's get your hair done before the party guests arrive."

He wrapped my cast in a towel. "You got to have this looked into," he said. "When does it come off?"

"I'm not sure. They'll have to take an x-ray and see how the bone has healed around the pins."

He put on the rubber gloves and mixed the dye. "I know a doctor," he said. "We'll set up an appointment." He squeezed the dye onto my hair and rubbed it in. "Remember when you saved me in the shower room?" he asked.

"Yeah," I said and peeked up at him. On the ceiling there was a painting of Elvis's face, angelic, on a bank of yellow and light blue clouds.

He saw me spot it.

"You know it used to bother me that I didn't look *exactly* like Elvis. But now it really doesn't matter. Now that I am no longer Elvis, I can rip him as much as everyone else. I never thought it would be this way. I thought I could just leave it all behind and walk away clean. But the fucker has been haunting me. Now a hatred of Elvis has grown inside me. If he were alive I'd kick his ass. What do you think of that, Doc?"

I wasn't sure what I thought. "What do you mean by hatred?" I asked.

"I mean when I see all this Elvis stuff around town, I want to scream. When I see all these Elvis tourists gathering for his death party or birthday I just want to flatten them. I wish someone would burn Graceland down and bulldoze it. Burn his airplanes and all the fucking museum crap. It's sick to worship him like this."

"What about the symbol of working hard and rising from nothing to become something? What's happened to you?" I asked.

"He's fucking dead, Doc, dead. He has become a symbol of hope for losers, for people who don't try to be great but only *wish* to be great. People who sit on their butts all day blaming God knows what-all for not allowing them to be as famous as Elvis. But they're the losers. I gave up my personal self to become Elvis. How sick is that? It's like saying to the world, 'Hey, look at me! I'm a nothing.' "

"That's not entirely true," I said. "You were an entertainer. People loved you. You carried on Elvis's spirit."

"Bullshit," he snapped. "Look at you, Doc. You bought into this whole drug scene. So who are you? Some drug-smuggling pirate? Yo ho ho and a pipe full of hash?" he sang, mocking me. "You bought into someone else's gig. You haven't the faintest idea who you are."

"Hey. I did the drug thing for money," I replied. "Pure and simple."

"And you smuggle drugs because you think you're some big-time operator. Don't you see?"

"I see," I said. "I know I've acted like a fool, but I'm trying to move on," I said, wanting to get him off my case. "But it takes money."

"Me too," he said. "Rolling quarters in the bank isn't great, but it's getting me somewhere."

"Where's that?" I asked. He didn't answer for a while.

"I'm not sure," he sighed, then laughed a little at himself. "The only thing I know is that I finished the first part of my dream. I'm no longer Elvis. I'm no longer headed for immediate death. But I'm not sure where to go from here."

"Well, I'm going to Canada, and maybe you should come with me," I said. "Get a new ID, new start, new everything — leave Elvis and Ebbers behind. What about that?"

"I'll give it some thought," he replied. "I don't know if I'm ready for just taking off. That's a big step. But for now, let's rinse your hair. We got a party to dress for." He sponged my head and neck. He took the detachable shower nozzle and rinsed the dye out of my hair. "It looks a lot better," he remarked. "A little mousey, but it's brown." He scrubbed my back and then my feet. "Stand up," he said. "I have to rinse you off." He reached out for my good hand and pulled me to my feet.

When I stepped out of the tub he dried my hair. Then he used his electric razor to remove the little stubble off my chin and upper lip. For a moment I missed Melissa. I had wanted her to be the one to wash me, clean me up, calm me down. Instead it was Elvis who was taking care of me, and then I realized it wasn't Melissa I had missed, it was being treated with the kindness that had always been missing from my life.

"I hope you come with me," I said. "We'd be great together."

"Don't tease me, Doc," he replied. "Let me sort out some things first."

Then he stepped back and looked me over, sympathetically. "You are all skin and bones, which is good. Most of my clothes are small." He draped a towel over my shoulders and I followed him to his bedroom.

"The first floor is still a haunted house," he said. "But I've made some progress up here." The room was surprisingly spare. Just a pine dresser, a pine bed and white cotton quilt, a chair, and a bedside table with a plain lamp, a clock, and a book. It was all very tidy. He caught me taking it all in before he pulled back the folding doors of the closet. "But I still have some show clothes," he said shyly. "They're about all I have left." He reached in and pulled out a dark blue satin shirt with a collar that dipped down to my nipples. "The sleeves are pretty blousy. It should fit over your cast."

"I've never worn anything like this," I said and turned around so he could slip it on over my arms and shoulders.

"You'll like it. It'll make people notice you."

He reached in again and pulled out a pair of white slacks with a red pleat flaring out of the lower leg. "I've always loved these. They'll look great on you."

He held my good hand as I stepped into them. He gave me a wide belt with an oval buckle embossed with a portrait of Gladys Presley.

"Sit down in the chair," he instructed. I did. He rolled a pair of nylon socks onto my feet, then sorted through the shoe boxes in the closet. He returned with a pair of low, black boots that zipped up the side.

"Stand up," he said. He stepped back from me, then reached forward and smoothed my hair down with his hand. He went back into the closet and choose a hatbox from a high shelf.

"Close your eyes," he ordered. "And keep them closed."

I felt the wig being pulled down over my head. His hands fluttered about, tugging at the scratchy sideburns and straightening the part. He combed the wave up and worked on the back.

"Keep them closed," he repeated. He opened a drawer and removed a container. "One moment." I felt one hand on my shoulder to steady me. "Now keep your eyes still," he said. He plucked at my eyebrows with a pair of tweezers, then penciled in some color. He brushed mascara on my eyelashes. He rubbed makeup on my cheeks and chin. "Open your mouth," he said. I did, and he dabbed at it with lipstick and rubbed it around with his finger. For a moment I thought he might kiss me, that he was in love with me.

"Give me your hand," he said. I did, and he led me back to the bathroom where he positioned me in front of the mirror. "Go ahead and open your eyes."

I peeked out at myself. I did not look like Elvis, definitely *not* Elvis. I looked more like a young Wayne Newton or Roy Orbison. But the hair was huge, and with the tall wave in front and the bushy sideburns it looked like I was wearing a black western saddle on my head. The makeup was clownish, applied in zones like on a paint-by-number face.

I smiled. "Are you trying to make fun of me?"

"Of course not," he said, and held his hand up over his heart. "I just ordered you a Priscilla Presley look-alike for the party and I want you to match up." I caught him looking at me at just the moment when his eyes rolled up into his head and his whole face seemed to moan and turn over, like a ship saying good-bye before it sank.

Suddenly a few tinny bars of "Suspicious Minds" chimed out. "What's that?" I asked looking up at the ceiling.

"The doorbell," Elvis cracked. "What the hell else could it be?"

When I came down the stairs Ebbers grinned and slapped his thigh. "Seth's got himself a new Barbie."

"Ebbers!" Elvis snapped. "Go to the kitchen and get the plates and champagne ready." Ebbers lumbered off. He broke into full laughter once he turned the corner.

When Elvis opened the door there was one Asian woman standing there. She was dressed in a pink miniskirt and a white sleeveless blouse, and she had an enormous beehive wig balanced on her head. She held a cake box straight out in her arms as though it were a ticking bomb.

"Welcome," Elvis said graciously. "Please come in. Ray," he said and turned to me, "meet Priscilla." He removed the box from her hands and marched toward the kitchen.

"Hello, Ray," she said crisply and looked me over from top to bottom. "Do you have a bathroom?"

"Yes," I said and pointed upstairs.

"Give me a ten-minute head start," she whispered and kissed me on the cheek. She steadied the wig with her left hand. With her right, she gently squeezed my balls. "Don't be late."

As she went up I ducked into the kitchen. "What's going on?" I asked.

Elvis had taken the cake out of the box. Drawn in icing was a little man in a black and white striped outfit holding on to a set of prison bars. The little man had a frown on his circular face. "WELCOME HOME RAY" was written in turquoise icing above the man's cap. Beneath the man's feet was written, "FREE AS A BIRD."

I grinned like a loon.

"The cake's for everyone," Elvis explained. "But she's for you." He motioned toward the ceiling.

"Does she know that?" I asked.

"Of course. I paid already. Gave her instructions and even tipped her in advance."

He must have seen that I was confused. He stepped over and put his arm around me. "Hey buddy, don't worry. This is your party time. This is my payback to you. Relax." He turned to Ebbers who had been standing in the doorway with a goofy look on his face. "Lordy, Ebbers. This man has been so abused he doesn't know when he's allowed to have fun."

"Ain't it the truth," Ebbers cracked, and sadly shook his head like an old dog.

Elvis turned back to me. He took a mock swipe at my chin. "I'm sure you'll know what to do once you get back between the sheets." He winked.

I wasn't sure what to say. I just wanted to laugh. At myself. At them. At the entire setup. Here I was, dressed as Elvis Presley and about to be sent off with a hooker dressed as Priscilla. I looked down at the cake and shook my head. There was that frowning prisoner in the striped suit, banging his tin cup against the bars and hollering his innocence. I had always seen myself as something else, something tough and savvy, but maybe I was no different from the little cartoon prisoner or the Elvis rag doll. Maybe prison had changed me more than I realized.

Elvis popped the champagne and poured out three glasses. "To you Doc. To the guy who saved my life." He held up his glass and smiled at me, tilted his head to one side, and pursed his lips. "Thanks."

We touched glasses and drank.

To Canada, I thought.

"Cut the cake," Ebbers said. "I'm hungry."

"I demand the piece with the prisoner's head," Elvis cried out.

"He's all yours," I replied. "Hey. Where's Priscilla?"

"She's upstairs waiting for you. Here. Let me cut her a piece of cake and you can take it up to her. She and you can have my room. Ebbers and I will stay down here and watch TV and have our own party."

Ebbers snickered. "We'll turn up the volume," he said.

I walked up the stairs and into the bathroom. I opened the closet door and reached back under the sheets where I had put the shoe box of Wayne's money and my money from before. This comes with me, I sang to myself. I balanced the cake plate on the box and went into Elvis's bedroom.

Priscilla was lying in bed with the covers up to her nipples. She gave me a shy smile.

"Trade you wigs," I said.

She held out her arms. "You're the King," she said in a sultry low voice that matched my outfit. "Come explore your kingdom."

IN THE MORNING I WALKED PRISCILLA down the stairs. She carried her wig tucked between her arm and side like a hairy football. Her high heels dangled from the fingers of her other hand. Her sunglasses hung down from the neck of her blouse.

Ebbers was still watching television. From the living room I heard the ack-ack war sounds of an airplane dogfight.

I opened the front door. Priscilla's cab was waiting. I wasn't sure if I should recap the evening so I just said, "Thanks. This is the best I've felt since I got out of prison."

"You're sweet," she whispered. "Call me again." She snapped open her purse and gave me her business card. "Just ask for Priscilla and they'll fetch me."

She stooped down and set her shoes on the cement, then stood and stepped into them. Overhead the sky was clear. The air was crisp, fresh, and I breathed it in. I wanted to get going. I felt strong. My mind was clear. My heart was quiet and I wanted to make plans and act on them before the fear of getting caught paralyzed me.

Her cab lurched forward and she waved to me. I waved good-bye.

When I returned to the living room I saw that Ebbers was asleep with his fat cheek pressed against the television screen. The war documentary seemed transformed into a horror movie. Airplanes buzzed around his giant head like a halo of flies.

"So long, trailer trash," I said as I passed by him. He grunted.

I went into the kitchen and poured myself a cup of coffee. To my left the basement door was open and I heard Elvis down there.

"Come on down," he replied when I called. "I'm just getting your ID ready and I need a picture."

I went down the stairs. Judging by the boxes and piles of furniture, framed posters, and stuff, the basement was where all the leftover Elvis decorations were stored. "Is this the vault?" I asked, looking around.

"This is where it all used to happen," he replied. "This is where we had the Elvis seances."

There was a large round table pushed into the far corner. I looked for a big crystal ball and wizard's cap but didn't see one. An Elvis mannequin dressed in white suede was singing into his empty fist.

"Sit down on the stool," Elvis instructed. He stood behind a Polaroid ID machine that was built into a suitcase.

"Where did you get that?"

"This is left over from the fan club days. I made a fortune selling membership IDs. Now smile. I want to take a test shot."

He lined up the focus and snapped the picture. When it developed, he carefully looked it over. "I'll be right back," he said and climbed up the stairs.

He returned with a wet washcloth and tossed it at me. "You still have some mascara around your eyes. Rub your face with this."

Elvis buttoned my top shirt button and combed my short hair over to one side. "Yesterday," he said, "I bought some Tennessee driver's license blanks. This should get you started."

"What about a Social Security number?"

"No problem. I took one from a kid at the Boy's Club."

"Does he have a record?"

"Not yet." He looked up at me and smiled. "You worry too much."

"Have you given any more thought to coming with me?" I kept my voice low.

"Yeah. And I like it. It'll be good for me. It's been hard, in Memphis, for me to move on. Everyone in town knows me as Elvis. No one calls me Seth. Even my Mom calls me Elvis. But I got one problem." He pointed his nose at the ceiling. "Ebbers. He'll flip when I take off."

"There's no way he can come," I said quickly.

"Hey, you'll get no argument from me on that," he shot back. "So we're going to have to get rid of him."

"We can just cut out," I suggested. "It could be simple. We pack up the Bronco and drive up. Is the car in your name?"

"Yes," he replied.

"Then it's not theft."

"I can't just take his car," Elvis said. "It was a gift."

"So, we'll fly up and buy another car. It's not a problem."

"I like that better," Elvis said. "Otherwise I'd feel guilty. Here, sign this. Your new name is Dale Walker." He handed me the blank license.

I signed it and handed it back. "I want to split soon."

"Okay," he said easily. "No sweat. I already have my stuff sold off. I just have to get my cash together and get these IDs finished. I'll have Ebbers take you back to the motel. We can leave this evening. I'm not going to bring anything but the clothes on my back and my money. I don't want pork chop to get suspicious."

"What about the rest of the hash?" I asked.

"We have to deliver it to Westwood. From there we'll drive to Nashville. I'll have Ebbers drop us off at the Hyatt and tell him to go park the car. Once he's out of sight, we get in a cab and go to the airport."

"There can't be many flights to Canada from Nashville," I said. "Did you look into the schedules?"

"No," he replied. "Why don't you do that this morning? And book a hotel for where we land."

"Okay."

"Now, smile," he said. "And look relaxed. Think of Priscilla."

I took a deep breath and let it out slowly. This is it, I said to myself. This is what you've been waiting for. A whole new self. Elvis snapped the picture. I was Dale Walker. In a minute, a laminated Tennessee driver's license rolled out of the machine.

"Here you go, Dale," Elvis said and handed it to me. "Welcome to your future. Now do mine."

He set up the machine and took his position on the stool. I snapped the picture. As we waited for the ID to be processed through the machine I heard Ebbers stirring around in the kitchen.

"Seth," he hollered down the stairs. "You down there?"

"Yeah," Elvis replied. "I'll be right up. I'm just finishing Ray's ID."

"Hurry," he replied. "I'm hungry. I want some grits, biscuits, and gravy."

"Sure," Elvis hollered. Then he turned to me and whispered. "Let's keep him happy today."

I GOT OUT OF THE CAR IN FRONT OF MY MO-tel room. Elvis rolled down the passenger window.

"I'll call you," he said. "Be ready to leave around five."

Leaving that late would never get us a direct flight to Canada. But I thought we might get something to Chicago or New York and take the first morning flight out. I went inside and called the airlines. There was a flight out of Nashville to Chicago at 9:00 P.M. We couldn't make Canada until the morning, so I booked a hotel at the airport.

With that finished, I strolled down to the motel office and settled my bill. While I was there I bought a packet of thread and needles from a vending machine. Back in my room I unwrapped the money I had earlier wrapped in aluminum foil. I was afraid the foil might set off the metal detector at the airport, so I wrapped the bundles in newspaper and tied them up with thread. I slipped them into the lining of my pea coat and sewed it back up. I put the coat on and looked in the mirror. There was no visible bulge. No one could tell it was on me unless they patted me down.

I went through everything I had brought with me from Boston and threw most of it away, including the picture frame. I started to think of Melissa but caught myself in time to keep from getting sentimental. You are Dale Walker, I said to myself, you never knew Melissa. The only thing you know is ahead of you. It filled me with hope to have a future that wasn't already wasted because of my past.

I pushed the mattress off the bed and removed the remaining hash. I counted out the kilos and wrapped them up in a plastic laundry bag. There was nothing more to be done. I turned on the television and waited.

Elvis and Ebbers pulled up at five. I got into the Bronco and pulled the door shut, then set the bag of hash on the seat next to me.

"Howdy," Elvis said, as he turned to look at me. "Are you ready to roll?" He winked when he said, "roll."

"You bet," I replied.

Ebbers pulled out of the lot and we made for State Highway 40, north.

After a few minutes I asked, "How does this deal go down?"

"When we get to Westwood," Elvis said, "We call Bill. He'll give us a meeting site. We'll drop you off. You do the deal and we swing back and pick you up."

"Aren't you staying with me?"

"Nope," he said curtly. "You're making the money, so you take the risk."

"Do you know these people?" I asked, already worried about being left alone in the parking lot with some doped-up psycho hicks.

"Hey," Elvis said, "Don't worry. If anything goes bad, I got my DEA badge and we can move in and make an arrest."

He pulled open his jacket for me to see the badge fastened to his shirt. "It's real," he said. "It's the same one Nixon gave Elvis. I bought it at an auction."

"Yeah. Elvis the narc," Ebbers remarked and shook his head from side to side.

"I'm not in the mood for cop talk," I said.

"Relax," Elvis said. "Everything went well with the frat boys and all will go well here."

I took a breath and sat back in my seat. Just get me out of here, I thought.

In an hour we reached Westwood. Ebbers pulled into a gas station. Elvis handed me a slip of paper with a phone number. "Ask for Bill," he said.

I called and Bill answered. "Meet me at the Piggly Wiggly on Mercer Ave.," he said. "I'll be in a white van with roof racks."

"I'll be at the front door. My left arm is in a cast."

"Ten minutes," he said.

It only took a few minutes to find the giant pink

pig sign. Ebbers was drawn to it like a magnet. He and Elvis dropped me off at the entrance. "We'll be back in fifteen minutes," Elvis said.

In a few minutes, a white van pulled up. The driver rolled his window down. "Come around to the passenger door," Bill instructed.

I walked around, opened the door and stepped up into the cab. "Let's take a drive," I said. Out of the corner of my eye I noticed another guy in the back of the van.

"That's Chuck," Bill said. "Give the hash to him."

I unzipped my bag. Bill pulled off onto a residential street and let the van idle while Chuck weighed one of the bricks on a scale.

"Okay," Chuck said.

Bill pulled a roll of hundreds out of his windbreaker and passed them back to Chuck. "Count it out," he said.

Chuck did. It was all there. Another $6,000. Chuck handed it to me and I shoved it into my pants pocket.

In a minute I was again standing in front of the Piggly Wiggly. I spotted the Bronco in the back of the lot. When I got into the car Elvis said, "Let's go to Nashville and get wild."

"My treat," I said, thinking the treat would be to give Ebbers the slip. "You guys have been great. I'll really miss you."

Elvis said, "I admire your guts, Doc. As much as I love money, I could never sell dope. But I'd let other people sell it for me."

"Every person has his own talent," I said. "I can't dress up in sequins and go out on stage."

"Well, I'm not doing that anymore. I'm doing something else."

"That's right," I remarked, thinking that we were just keeping this conversation going for Ebbers's benefit.

Elvis leaned forward and opened the glove compartment. Then he turned and pointed a pistol at the center of my face. He cocked it. "I didn't want to do this until you had sold all the hash. But as I said, selling the dope is too risky for me, I'd rather just take your cash."

Ebbers whipped around and stared at me. He clucked his tongue.

"Keep your eyes on the road," Elvis snapped.

Ebbers turned back. "I just wanted to get a good look at his face," he sputtered. "I've been waiting a long time to see what he looks like with my foot up his ass."

Elvis laughed a little. "Well, did you see what-all you wanted?"

"Not enough," Ebbers said. I caught his eyes flashing at me in the rearview mirror. "I still got a surprise for him. I thought about it all last night."

"You wouldn't be thinking of *Deliverance?*" Elvis asked.

"Naw, he's not plump enough. I got something else in mind." He slowed and turned down a country road.

By now, the sun had set. The horizon light was

fading. I figured if they kept driving until it was dark enough, I could jump out and run into the woods. I slowly shifted my hand and felt the package of money inside my pea coat. Then I glanced at the door lock.

"Move and you're dead, Doc!" Elvis reached forward and locked the door.

"You won't kill me," I said. "It would cause you too much trouble."

"You're so right," Elvis said. "We're just going to take all your money and leave you your life, your freedom, and a few good memories."

Ebbers pulled over onto the dirt shoulder. "I think I'm lost," he said to Elvis.

"Idiot," Elvis snapped. "Go around and open his door." Then he looked directly at me with the gun held in both hands. He didn't look at all like Elvis, but more like some squinty-eyed gas station robber. All the kindness was gone. The transformation was so sudden I thought he might shoot me.

"You're not a cop, are you?" I asked.

"No, but I'm doing a cop's job by fucking over drug users like you."

"Bullshit," I said. "You're just a fucking con artist."

"Hey, you were dumb enough to fall for it, so you deserve it."

Ebbers opened my door.

Elvis spoke slowly and clearly. "I want you to get out of the car and stand with your arms up over your head. And no funny stuff. I won't shoot to kill but I will shoot you in the leg if you try something."

I stepped out and raised my arms as best I could. Elvis pressed my face against a window. The inside light of the car was enough to see everything clearly. Ebbers unzipped my bag and dumped it out on the seat. He sorted through my stuff — my clothes, my radio, my knife — and flipped through the pages of a book. He turned the bag inside out and slapped at it.

"The money must be on him," he said to Elvis.

"You know, Ebbers," I said. "Elvis always told me it was his dream to leave you behind. Get rid of you and the whole Elvis thing and stick with me."

"Dream on, Doc," he replied. "Elvis is always talking that crap just before he sticks it to you."

"You know what my real dream is," Elvis said, mocking me. "Suckers like you are what I dream of every day of my life." He laughed. "If I had one Ray Jakes a month I'd be set for life. Dimwits like you make my dreams come true." He held the cold tip of the pistol against my ear and twisted it back and forth.

"Got it," Ebbers said, as his hand passed over, then squeezed down on the lump inside my coat, "Now take off the jacket."

He flipped me around so my back was against the car. He unbuttoned the coat and held it open so I could slide out of it. "Keep the gun on his face," he said as he spread the jacket out across the front seat. "He isn't going to like this."

I turned my head to watch as he ripped the seam I had sewn together.

"Hit the jackpot!" he whooped, as he pulled out

the packets. He peeled the newspaper off of one. "Holy shit," he said thumbing the edge of the bills. "These are five hundreds." He held them out for Elvis to see.

Elvis was amused. "Been holding out on us, Doc? Now let's see what you have in your pockets."

Ebbers folded the coat over and tossed it on the back seat. Then he stepped toward me and reached into my pants pockets. "We got another winner!" he cried out and struggled with the wad of cash until he yanked it free.

He patted me down on the inside of my legs. "You got anything in your underwear?"

"No," I replied.

"Well, let's see." He plunged his hand down into my pants. He grabbed my balls and squeezed hard. I dropped down to my knees.

"Aww," he moaned, letting go. "Nothing in here but a roll of pennies."

"Come on," Elvis said impatiently. "We don't have time to fuck around." He took a few steps away from me. "Go on. Get out of here, Doc, before I call the feds. I might get a reward for turning you in."

"I'll tell them what you've done to me," I said coldly. "I'll go down with you, motherfucker. I'm not kidding."

"No one will believe you. There's no evidence. No nothing. Now beat it. We're doing you a favor by not calling the cops."

Ebbers rummaged around the back hatch of the Bronco and came out carrying something. "Don't run off before I give you my present, Doc," he said. He turned to Elvis. "Hold the gun on him."

He walked toward me while shaking a can of spray paint in his hand. "This will help you hitch a ride outta here," he said. He yanked the sleeve on my shirt up over my elbow. He grabbed the lower end of my cast and began to spray up around my shoulder. The color was blaze orange. It came out of the can like a flame. He laughed as he sprayed up and down the plaster. He sprayed a big X across my chest, turned me around and sprayed another on my back. Then he dropped down and sprayed my shoes. When he finished he stepped back and shielded his eyes from the glare. "Jesus, that's bright."

He walked back to Elvis and removed a walkie-talkie from the glove compartment. "See what I have here?" he said, squinting. "Nine . . . one . . . one. Three little numbers and you are on the run."

Elvis raised the pistol up over his head. "Gentlemen," he hollered. "Start your engines."

"Do you want me to run?" I asked.

"You are so stupid, man," Elvis said. "You are more stupid than Ebbers, and he's really a complete bonehead." He pointed the pistol over my head. "Go."

I stepped back. "You know I'm not going to disappear. I know where you live and work."

"Yeah. Good luck trying to find that bank," Elvis said and grinned. "You really must think I'm as big a loser as you are. Me? Work at a bank? Guys like you are my bank."

"Fuck you," I said. I turned and started to walk away.

"Hey, Doc," Ebbers hollered. "Go heal thyself."

I picked up a rock, turned, and whipped it at him. I didn't get much on the throw and the rock sailed way left.

"So long," Elvis said. He squeezed off a round. The report cracked overhead. I hunched my shoulders and ducked down. "And don't come looking for me at the house, Ray. I'll shoot you on sight."

When I was about thirty yards down the road, I turned around. Ebbers started up the engine. The brake lights dimmed and they pulled away. In a few minutes, they veered right and were gone.

I had a thousand dollars in each shoe. I'd get to the next town, catch a bus to Memphis, and somehow get my money back if I had to kill them both to do it. I'd kill them just because I had fallen for that friendship thing again. I couldn't believe I had thought an Elvis impersonator was going to bail me out. How many times did I have to tell myself that people were trouble. Nothing but trouble. Money was the only thing that hadn't fucked me over. And they had taken my money. It was the only thing I had left, and I was going back for it.

I walked along the side of the road for about an hour before a cop car passed me. My arm lit up like a neon arrow pointing directly at the X on my chest. The car slowed down then stopped up ahead. As soon as I saw the white reverse lights, I cut down the bank.

The driver's side spotlight swept across the field as the other cop got out of the car and gave chase.

"Stop!" he shouted.

I reached a wood fence. I jumped it and ducked down as I caught my breath.

Robby and I and the rest of the X-15s used to play flashlight tag in our neighborhood. If you got caught in someone's light, you were dead. We didn't play in teams. It was every man for himself until the end, when all the dead guys teamed up like a pack of dogs to flush out the remaining guy. One night I was the last one and I heard them coming. I rolled out from under the bush where I had been hiding and cut hard across a backyard. I was almost to the other side when a wire clothesline garroted me across the neck. I let out a yelp as my head yanked backward. I landed on my back and gasped for air. My throat was pinched together like a kinked hose.

The guys ran up to me and shined their lights down into my eyes. I couldn't breathe. Robby squatted down and rubbed the sides of my throat until it eased open. "Next time," he advised, "get caught early and run with the pack."

Now I heard the cop's legs thrashing through the weeds. "Come on out," he hollered.

I looked left, then right. Overhead the spotlight captured the trees, the peak of an old barn, a splitting silo. I crouched down and dashed past an old tractor. I had to make it to the other side of the barn, away from the sweeping light. Even when it didn't shine on me directly, I was lit up like a firefly. I tripped over a rusty tiller and rolled forward. I bounced up and cut across a dirt road to the front of the barn. I kicked off my bright shoes and tossed them to my left. I could feel the crisp money in my socks. It was enough to get me out of town. I pulled at my shirt and ripped the buttons off as I yanked it over my head. I tried to peel off the cast but it wouldn't break apart. I gripped it between my knees and was trying to wiggle my arm out when the cop turned the corner and shone his light on me. I stumbled back and hit the barn wall. He ran at me. There was nothing more I could do. I slid down onto my side and closed my eyes. In an instant he had one hand on my neck and his knee in the middle of my back. He snapped his cuffs around my good wrist, then jerked my bad arm back. I winced. "I didn't do anything wrong," I cried out, then fell face-down and tasted dirt.